SUNNY SUNDAYS AT PRIMROSE HALL

JILL STEEPLES

Boldwood

First published in Great Britain in 2024 by Boldwood Books Ltd.

Copyright © Jill Steeples, 2024

Cover Design by Head Design Ltd

Cover Illustration: Shutterstock

A CIP catalogue record for this book is available from the British Library.

Paperback ISBN 978-1-78513-353-4

Large Print ISBN 978-1-78513-349-7

Hardback ISBN 978-1-78513-348-0

Ebook ISBN 978-1-78513-346-6

Kindle ISBN 978-1-78513-347-3

Audio CD ISBN 978-1-78513-354-1

MP3 CD ISBN 978-1-78513-351-0

Digital audio download ISBN 978-1-78513-345-9

Boldwood Books Ltd
23 Bowerdean Street
London SW6 3TN
www.boldwoodbooks.com

To my family
With Love

1

'Drive carefully! And let us know when you get there,' Pia called. She stood alongside Jackson and Tom in front of the magnificence of Primrose Hall, as the early-morning sunshine broke through the clouds and cast a golden glow over the stonework. Pia wrapped her arms around her chest and watched as Ronnie carefully manoeuvred the camper van around the gravel driveway.

Rex, who was sitting in the passenger seat, had the side window wound down and leant out, a big grin on his face.

'Well, we're not sure where we're going yet, but we'll definitely let you know when we get there! Wish me luck!' His eyes widened and his mouth twisted in mock horror, but Pia knew he was only joshing, the exaggerated grimace for comedy effect only. The pair of them, much more happily divorced than they'd ever been married, were heading off on an adventure to the Continent. Ronnie, always a free spirit, had a bad case of wanderlust and insisted that she wanted to go off on her travels, in her camper van, for one last time. Once Ronnie had managed to persuade Rex to accompany her, after recently rekindling their romance, there was absolutely no stopping her.

'Rather him than me,' said Jackson beneath his breath.

'Oh, don't!' Pia nudged Jackson in the side with her elbow. 'I'm going to miss them. Especially Ronnie, and our putting-the-world-to-rights sessions around the kitchen table every morning. I hope they don't prefer wherever it is they're going and decide to stay away.'

'There's absolutely no chance of that. I know from experience that Ronnie always turns up, like a bad penny.'

'Stop it!' Pia chided him.

'Besides, she has Dad to keep her in check. And she's given me strict instructions not to start making any plans for the wedding until they get home again so she won't want to stay away too long. We need to make the most of the peace and quiet while we can.'

Jackson wrapped an arm around Pia's shoulder, squeezing her in an embrace. Tom stood alongside and Bertie, the Dalmatian, wound his way in between their legs, always eager to be at the centre of any proceedings. Little Teddy, the newest member of the family, ran up and down, yapping excitedly. With a toot of the horn, Ronnie gave a wave and the camper trundled off down the driveway, with Rex still leaning out the window, calling their farewells. They all waited and watched as the van disappeared into the distance, and only shifted from their spot when the departing campers were finally out of sight.

'I hate goodbyes,' said Pia with a sigh, blinking away the tears in her eyes. 'They always make me feel so sad.' She turned to Tom, noticing that he'd been rather subdued too. Perhaps he felt the same way about farewells. 'Come on, let's go and have some coffee and cake to cheer us up.'

Back inside, as they gathered in the country farmhouse kitchen, Jackson made the coffees while Pia cut slices of carrot cake and laid them out on a colourful hand-painted plate, placing it in the middle of the long oak table. Tom accepted his coffee gratefully, and took a seat.

'I'm glad I came down to see them off. I know they'll only be away for a few months, but it feels strange waving Dad off when I've only just got to know him. It was almost as though, in that moment, I came to realise how much it's meant to me, having him in my life. I'll miss not having him around.'

Pia nodded in sympathy. So she hadn't been the only one experiencing a wave of unexpected emotion this morning. Although Jackson was clearly immune to the highly charged atmosphere as he gave an unmistakable roll of his eyes and shook his head.

'Honestly, what are you two like? They'll be back before you know it and it will be as if they've never been away. Knowing that pair, they'll probably have a huge falling out before they've even crossed the Channel. I wouldn't be surprised if they turn around and come straight back home tonight.'

'You don't mean that!' Pia chided Jackson. 'I think it's lovely that your mum and dad are getting on so fabulously these days, making up for all that lost time they spent apart. It's very romantic.'

Jackson raised an eyebrow and twisted his lips in an undisguised display of doubt.

'Hmmm, well, they're hardly love's young dream, and I'm still not convinced it will last, but I guess they have both mellowed over the years and if it keeps them happy and out of mischief then who am I to judge?'

'Exactly!' said Pia, triumphantly.

'If you hadn't told me otherwise, it would be easy to believe that they'd been happily married for a lifetime. They seem very well suited, and clearly adore each other,' said Tom, who was still getting to grips with the family dynamics at Primrose Hall.

It was only last year that Tom had turned up in Rex's life, breaking the news that he was his long-lost son. It had been a huge shock to Rex, realising that the short-lived fling he'd had with Diane, Tom's mother, decades earlier had resulted in a child that he'd never known about. When the initial shock had subsided, it was replaced with a sense of wonder and joy, and father and son had been enjoying getting to know each other as adults, making up for all the years they'd been apart.

It had been a big adjustment for everyone. At first, Ronnie had felt threatened by Tom's arrival, worried that she might be sidelined in Rex's affections, but that hadn't proved to be the case, and she and Tom had hit it off as soon as they met, bonding over a glass of red wine and a slice of Parkin on a cold November night. Now they were always delighted to see each other, picking up their conversation easily from the last time they'd met.

Jackson and Tom's relationship hadn't been quite so smooth in the making. Jackson by nature was reserved and self-contained, only opening up and trusting a few people within his inner circle. He felt no natural affinity to Tom just because they shared a father and Jackson only agreed to meet Tom in the first place to appease Rex. Since then, there had been a misunderstanding over Pia, which resulted in a scrap between the brothers in the kitchen at Primrose Hall, but thankfully since that low point they had found some common ground. They played squash together every fortnight and Jackson always extended an invitation to Tom to Sunday lunch at the hall and any other family celebrations.

'Well, don't be a stranger while your dad's away,' Pia told Tom now. 'You're always welcome here, you know that.'

'Thanks, Pia. That's kind of you.' Tom cast a glance towards Jackson, relieved to see him nod his agreement as well.

'I've been meaning to ask, how are you fixed workwise these days?' Jackson pulled out a chair at the table.

'I'm still doing some days down at the builders' merchants and helping out at the estate agents on an ad-hoc basis with the viewings, which I enjoy. I find it really interesting. I get to meet a wide range of people and it gives me the chance to have a nose around all sorts of properties. You should see some of them! I should probably start to think about getting a proper job again, but I can't say the idea appeals much.'

Tom had given up a successful career in pharmaceutical sales last year, after discovering the truth about his father. Knowing that his late mother, who he'd adored, had lied to him for the entirety of his life had made him question everything he knew about himself. He had to contemplate who he really was, where had he come from? As well as throwing in his job, his relationship with his long-term girlfriend, Anna, was another casualty and he'd walked away from their home together, to start afresh. Finding Rex, his biological father, and a brother, Jackson, who he hadn't known existed either, had been the starting point in coming to terms with this new version of himself. He'd never met anyone before that looked like him, who shared his colouring and his mannerisms, so to see himself reflected in the faces of Rex and Jackson had been a revelation.

'Well, if you're after any more work then I'm looking for someone to oversee the open days at the stables. They'll be starting up again at the end of the month and we'll be running them fortnightly this year.'

Tom's eyes widened in interest as Jackson spoke.

'Mainly, it will involve setting up, making sure each of the units are clean and ready for the traders. Then dealing with any problems that may crop up, and closing up at the end of the day. It's not too onerous a job, but it needs someone on site all day.'

'I'd definitely be up for that.' Pia noticed the way Tom's face lit up, his surprise at Jackson's offer evident.

'Pia's been doing a great job of organising and running everything up until now. There's a great system in place, but with us increasing the timetable to fortnightly, it's time to pass the reins on to someone else. Pia needs to take the occasional day off, even if she might say otherwise.'

Jackson shared a fond glance with Pia across the table. They were busier than ever, with a full calendar of summer events lined up at the hall, so they'd recently discussed how they could manage the work schedule going forward. Pia would be sad to relinquish control of the craft days at the stables. They had been one of her first responsibilities when she'd arrived at the hall and she was proud of how successful and popular those Sundays had become. Not that she had any intention of letting go completely.

'The traders are a great bunch of people,' Pia told Tom. 'There's a real community vibe over there and they all help each other out. I'll introduce you to them and show you around so you'll know exactly who's who and what's what.'

'Great. I can't wait to get stuck in.' Tom's acceptance came as a huge relief to Pia. She'd promised Rex that she would do her utmost to ensure the brothers would still be on talking terms when Rex and Ronnie returned from their travels. 'I'll feel like a proper part of the Primrose Hall family.' Tom grinned, and Pia could only think that had to be a good thing.

2

Sophie gave one last glance around the room that had been her home for the last few months. It was a perfectly adequate space with a double bed, a small wardrobe and a rickety chair, which she had never quite trusted enough to sit on, but had served as the ideal spot to throw her clothes over at the end of the day. The room, with its faded floral sprig wallpaper and matching curtains, its uninspiring view over some dilapidated garages, represented so much more than a place to lay her head. It had been a lifeline when she needed it most.

'Are you all packed?'

'I think so,' she said, turning to face Greta with a smile.

She would be eternally grateful to her friend. They'd met at the Saturday morning yoga class in the village hall, only exchanging pleasantries over a few weeks until one particular session when ninety minutes of slow and purposeful movements and measured breathing had done nothing to help Sophie's peace of mind. After the class, Sophie had dashed out of the hall, rushed to her car and closed the door behind her before giving in to the tears that had been brewing inside her all morning. She'd dropped her head on her forearms, resting on the steering wheel, and had been totally oblivious to the rapping on the driver's window. It took her several moments before she looked up, mopping her tears away on her sleeve before noticing the blonde lady, who she recognised from the class, peering in at her. Sophie opened the door slightly, plastering on a smile and adopting a jaunty tone.

'Don't worry, I'm fine,' she'd spluttered through her tears, totally unconvincingly.

'Are you sure?' The woman's voice had been filled with concern as she delved into the pocket of her hoodie and pulled out a tissue, handing it to Sophie. 'Look, do you want me to give you a lift home? I'm not sure you should be driving when you're like this.'

'No, there's no need,' she'd blurted, rather too quickly. 'But thank you.'

Sophie's breath had snagged as she'd tried to get in control of her sobs. It was very kind of the lady to be so concerned, but really Sophie wished she could be left alone. She really didn't want to inflict her unhappiness onto anyone else.

'There's a lovely cafe in Primrose Woods. I don't know if you've ever been there? It's only five minutes down the road. We could go and grab a drink if you fancy it?'

Sophie was about to refuse when something stopped her. An instinct. What else was she going to do? Sit here becoming ever more miserable by the moment? She certainly didn't want to go home. The longer she could put off that eventuality, the better, so, on a whim, she'd gratefully accepted the woman's offer and climbed out of her car, locking it up, before getting into the passenger seat of the other car. As they drove the short distance to the country park, Sophie discovered that her name was Greta and she lived on the new estate with her husband and teenage children. She chatted away gaily, not asking any questions of Sophie, for which she was entirely grateful, and hearing about Greta's family life was exactly the distraction Sophie needed right then.

They found a window seat in the Treetops Cafe, which gave a panoramic view of the surrounding breathtaking landscape, and while they'd waited for their order to arrive, Sophie had been happy to sit and soak up the atmosphere, finding solace in the protective embrace of the tall trees.

'I suppose this defeats the object of today's class,' Greta had said, with a wry smile, when the order arrived and she looked down to survey her creamy cappuccino and bacon roll. The aroma was mouth-watering, but Sophie's iced bun looked equally as appetising, and she wasn't going to forgo her pick-me-up coffee for a cup of herbal tea. She shrugged.

'I've never been one of those people who loses their appetite when they're upset. It's the opposite for me. I just want to eat everything in sight,' Sophie had said, tucking in eagerly to her bun. 'I suppose it's a comfort thing.'

'I get that, and I agree, now is no time to deprive yourself. I sometimes think that it's the simple pleasures in life, a cup of tea, a walk in the woods, or a chat with a friend that can lift your spirits and help you get through the tough times. Although...' Greta's gaze scrutinised Sophie's expression. 'I'm guessing whatever it is that's troubling you can't be easily fixed with a sticky bun.'

'No.' Sophie exhaled a big sigh. 'Unfortunately not.'

'I'm a great listener if you want to talk about it, but equally,' she held up her palms to Sophie, 'I understand if you never want it mentioned again.'

Sophie smiled, more grateful to Greta than she would know, for taking the time to be concerned, showing a kindness that Sophie hadn't expected from a relative stranger. The problem was she hadn't spoken to anyone about Kyle, there was no one she could confide in and she'd been hugging her unhappiness all to herself for months now.

'It's Kyle,' she said, and it was as if saying his name aloud gave her permission to talk about her situation for the first time. 'My boyfriend. We've been together for eight years now and when we first got together, it was great. I thought I'd found my soulmate. We met at work. It's his family's business, an engineering company, and I joined to help out in the office. I quickly got promoted to office manager and I suppose our relationship grew from working so closely together. We were happy. We found a place and moved in together and everything was great. For a while.'

Greta had nodded, without making comment, allowing Sophie to continue after a moment of reflection.

'Then, well, things changed. He's always enjoyed a drink. We both did. It was part of our routine. After a busy day at the office, we would call in at the pub and he'd have a beer and I'd have a glass of wine and we looked forward to those times, the opportunity to chat and debrief after the stresses of the day.' Sophie fell quiet, her gaze wandering out of the window into the woods beyond, her thoughts drifting away with her. 'Trouble is, it got to the point where one or two drinks would turn into three or four. I would move on to the soft drinks because I was the designated driver, but Kyle would continue to knock back the pints. I guess that was when it all started to go so wrong.'

'I'm really sorry to hear that.'

'Yeah.' Sophie's gaze had flashed over to Greta's, gauging her reaction, and then she shrugged. 'It's not great.'

'What will you do?'

'I don't know. I ask myself that every day, but I never come up with any answers. Really, I should leave, but it's not as simple as that.'

'Why not?'

'Well...' Greta's question had stopped Sophie in her tracks. She'd made it sound as though it was straightforward. 'It means not only walking away from him, but his family, our house, my job, our future. Everything.' She took a breath. 'I wouldn't know what to do or where to go.'

'Can you see any type of future with... Kyle? Do you want to make it work?' Greta probed gently. Sophie shook her head.

'Not any more. I've tried so hard to make it work, but I realise now he's never going to change. He doesn't see that he has a problem, and I just can't cope with his drinking any more. It's only getting worse.'

Greta nodded.

'He's not violent, is he?' she'd asked, concerned, leaning across the table.

'Not physically. But he can get very aggressive. Mouthy and confrontational. It frightens me. I spend my time tiptoeing around him, not wanting to upset him. He's not the Kyle I used to know, the one I fell in love with.' Sophie's eyes had filled with tears as she spoke, and Greta had noticed the fear in her expression.

'That's no way to live your life. It seems to me that you know you have to get away, for your own safety and mental well-being. It's just taking those first steps. Putting a plan in place and doing it. Once you're set in your mind about what you need to do, then it will become easier.'

Sophie had nodded. It seemed anything but easy. She knew she had to get away from Kyle, but she'd been ignoring the reality of that fact, with all her energy spent getting through the days as best she could, putting up some kind of pretence of normality. It had felt cathartic to talk to Greta and helped to put her thoughts in order. At work she hadn't felt able to tell any of her colleagues the truth about her life with the boss's son, although she suspected there might be plenty of rumours and gossip flying about the office.

'Is there anywhere you could go? Do you have family around here?'

'Not really. My mum's got MS, she's in a local nursing home so I need to stay in the area. I visit her every day, but she's got enough on her plate. I don't want her worrying about me, it will only make her situation worse. I've got an older brother too, but he lives down on the south coast with his family so I don't get to see him too often, only when he comes up to visit Mum. There's usually so much to fill him in on, about Mum and her care, that it doesn't leave much time for anything else. If I was just thinking of myself, I would walk away and leave everything behind. Put a rucksack on my back and head abroad, but I could never do that to Mum.'

'Look, let me take your number.' Suddenly Greta had appeared very businesslike. 'I can't make any promises, but I might be able to help. I would just need to make a couple of phone calls first.'

Sophie had appreciated the opportunity to offload her worries onto Greta, to have a listening ear, away from her everyday life, in the beautiful surroundings of the cafe in the woods. She'd dried her eyes and gained a clearer perspective on her situation, realising more than ever that she had to find a way to get away from Kyle. When she'd offered her thanks and said her goodbyes to Greta on that Saturday morning, she hadn't expected to hear from her again until the next yoga class, so when she received a text from Greta the same evening, saying 'Call me as soon as you can!' Sophie had been curious and intrigued. Not for a moment had she expected Greta to offer her the spare room in the house that she shared with her husband and teenage children. Sophie's first reaction, after thanking Greta profusely for the offer, was to decline, not wanting to take advantage of her new friend's generosity, but when Greta had insisted, reassuring Sophie that there'd been a family conflab and everyone was in agreement that Sophie should stay, she was taken aback and deeply touched by the humanity shown from people she barely knew.

Now, taking one final look at the room that had been her sanctuary for the last six months, she experienced an overwhelming swell of emotion, and she bit on her lip to hold back the tears gathering in her eyes. What would she have done if Greta hadn't stepped in to offer her a place to stay? Would she still be living a miserable life with Kyle, tiptoeing around his moods, dreading going to work each day, but dreading going home at the end of the day even more?

Greta had held out a hand to Sophie and pulled her ashore and Sophie would be forever grateful to her friend for the kindness and support she'd shown her.

She took a deep breath and closed the bedroom door behind her. Now, she wouldn't need to look back. She could look forward to a brand-new start as she prepared to move into a tiny two-up, two-down cottage overlooking the village green in Wishwell.

'Good luck,' said Greta, pulling Sophie towards her in a hug. 'Not that you'll need it, of course. It's great knowing that you'll be just around the corner. Remember, you're always welcome here for a cuppa, especially if you promise to bring a batch of those chocolate brownies.'

They'd been a thank you gift from Sophie when she'd first moved into the house and they'd been such a hit with the whole family that they'd insisted on her baking them for every celebratory occasion since.

'Definitely. You won't be able to get rid of me that easily. We're friends for life now, eh?' she said, laughing. 'You know, perhaps now's the time to pick up where we left off at those yoga classes. After all, it was where we first met.'

'Hmmm.' Greta pondered on that idea. When they'd got into the winter months, they'd stopped going to the weekly classes. They'd pledged to start them up again in the new year, but they had never quite made it happen. 'We could, or else we could forgo the yoga and go straight to the coffee and cake sessions afterwards at the Treetops Cafe. What do you reckon?'

Sophie laughed as she bumped her bags down the stairs.

'That's why you're my friend, you know? You always come up with the best ideas, and they haven't seen me wrong yet!'

3

'Mummy, what are you doing?'

Katy was settled at the dining room table, with all her drawing and crafting materials around her, ready for a session making the greetings cards, bookmarks and stationery that formed the basis of her small and growing business. This was the part she liked best. Coming up with ideas, creating designs, and then seeing her vision turned into finished products. She found it relaxing, to be able to switch off from her role as mum and wife, and concentrate on something else entirely. Although today she wasn't finding the peace and quiet she was hoping for.

'I'm working. I have lots of greetings cards that I want to make so that I can sell them to my customers.'

'Can I help, Mummy? I'll get my crayons.' Little Rosie padded off to the wicker storage unit that housed a myriad of toys and yanked open a drawer, delving inside to find her coloured pencils.

'No!' Katy said, rather too forcibly. 'Remember you're going to soft play with Daddy.' She glanced at her watch. What exactly was Brad doing? Knowing she wouldn't get anything done all the time they were still at home, she pushed back her chair and went in search of her husband.

'Brad? Are you ready?' she called up the stairs, while she found coats and shoes for Rosie and Pip, who was transfixed to the television in the living room, within sight of Katy.

'I'll be five minutes!'

Katy sighed, frustration bubbling up inside. Why was it when she had organised rare precious time to get on with her own work that Brad was always dragging his heels, leaving everything to the last minute? She knew he had a busy job, that there were always emails to reply to or pressing research work he needed to get on with, but her time was just as important as his. It wasn't fair on her or the children that they all had to wait around until he was ready.

With the children wrapped up in their coats, Katy called again, trying to keep her voice even.

'Brad, come on. The kids are ready and waiting.'

Moments later, he came bounding downstairs with his normal wave of exuberant energy.

'Are we ready?' A big smile on his face, his enthusiasm radiating from his broad masculine physique. 'Are we going to have fun?'

'Yes!' the children squealed, their high-pitched screams like a drill through Katy's head. She pressed her lips together and winced. At least it would be Brad who would have to deal with their high jinks, their over-excitement and the inevitable exhausted and fractious slump that would come later.

'I could really do with getting on with some work afterwards,' he said, as an aside to Katy as he bundled the children into the back of the car. 'Are you okay if we come back before lunch?'

'Brad! You promised. How often do I get a chance to have some time to myself? I won't get anything done once you bring them home. I'll have to pack all my gear away.' Brad would disappear upstairs to his office and Katy would be left to deal with two overwrought children. 'You said you'd take them out for lunch and then into town. I've got my first stint at the stables coming up soon and I really need the time to get everything organised.'

'Fine. It just means I'll have to work tonight. Sorry, Katy, but there's a lot of preparation I still need to do for next week's conference.' He kissed her on the forehead before climbing into the car. She plastered on a smile and waved to Rosie and Pip, who were grinning from the back seats.

Of course, she realised the importance of Brad's job. He was a senior lecturer at the university, a demanding and time-consuming role, and it was that which paid the bills. Her fledgling design company had started out as a hobby but it was so much more than that now. It was her escape, her passion, something of her own that she could put her energy into, where she could express herself creatively. On those rare occasions when she had the opportunity to work on her projects, she would completely forget about everything else going on in her life. For that short space of time, she wasn't mum to Rosie and Pip, or wife to Brad, she could simply be herself, Katy.

When the car was out of sight, she returned to the table and set to work, feeling a load leave her shoulders. Her task for today was to turn her recently drawn illustrations of woodland creatures, rabbits, deer, foxes and ducks in bright eye-catching designs into individual and packs of cards. She was also putting together colouring cards for children, which she knew might be popular if Rosie's reaction had been anything to go by. It was two weeks until the first of the craft fairs this year at Primrose Hall and Katy was excited to get back to the stables to meet up again with the other traders. Last year they'd formed a lovely little community and those Sundays selling their hand-crafted wares to the visitors had been such enjoyable and positive days with a group of people she now considered to be her friends. There'd been so much laughter, chatter and support and she'd missed those sessions over the winter period. In the meantime, she'd been as busy as her limited time had allowed, adding to her range of products, and she couldn't wait to put them on sale to gauge the reaction from her customers. She only hoped Brad had remembered that the craft fairs would be fortnightly from now on, which meant he would need to step up for childcare duty. She sighed and took a sip from her mug of coffee. Well, she had told him often enough and if he hadn't remembered then he would get a sharp reminder very soon.

4

'Ooh, look at this!' Pia was sitting at the kitchen table, poring over her mobile phone. 'It sounds as though Ronnie and Rex are having a whale of a time. They've had a few days on the coast and they're off to Rouen tomorrow for a bit of sightseeing. Then they're going to drive all the way down to the south to find a campsite. The photos look amazing.'

Pia scrolled through the stream of pictures that Ronnie had sent over, feeling a pang of longing for them both.

'Do you want to see?' Pia held the phone over to Jackson, who took a cursory glance. 'I'm so pleased they're enjoying themselves, but it's very quiet around here without the pair of them dropping in and out of the kitchen at all hours of the day, don't you think?'

'I know, it's great, isn't it?' said Jackson, with undisguised glee.

Ronnie lived in her well-loved motorhome, a van that had transported her to many destinations around the UK and Europe, but had been happily parked up in the grounds of Primrose Hall for the last couple of years, ever since her son Jackson had moved into the newly refurbished hall. She'd been offered her own living quarters inside the grand house, but Ronnie had insisted she would prefer to stay in the van, which was decked out, in her distinctive style, in colourful fabrics and cushions, with all her knick-knacks around her. It gave her a sense of freedom and independence to know that she could head off in the van if ever she needed to. It was something she'd often done in her younger years, especially when Jackson was growing up, leaving her son to live with her sister Marie, while Ronnie had gone off to follow her dreams, but in recent times she'd given up on her wanderlust tendencies.

That was until Rex popped up again in their lives. He'd turned up in the village after several years living on the Continent and had found a place to stay with some old friends, eager to build bridges with the son whose childhood he had largely missed out on. He hadn't known that his ex, Ronnie, was in residence in the grounds of the hall, and getting to know each other again had been fraught with tension, with all their past grievances being brought to the surface. It had only taken a few weeks, though, before Ronnie was charmed all over again by Rex's cheeky chappie persona and while Jackson had been very wary about his parents rekindling any kind of relationship, not relishing the idea of revisiting the drama he remembered from his childhood, they had done exactly that, in spite of him. Towards the end of last year, Rex had accepted Jackson's invitation to move into the hall and Pia, for one, loved living alongside Jackson's family, probably more so than Jackson did, if you were to believe all his mumbles and grumbles.

'I miss them.' Pia let out a heartfelt sigh, putting the phone down on the table. She suspected Jackson did too, but she knew he would never admit to such a thing. 'I hope they don't stay away too long.'

'Don't worry, they'll be home before we know it and it will be as if they'd never been away. You know, we could surprise them.' Jackson reached across the table and took hold of Pia's hand. 'We could take some time off and go and get married somewhere. Just the two of us. It would be romantic, don't you think?'

Pia flashed him a glance to check that he was joking, but saw from his expression that he was absolutely serious.

'No! You can't mean that? Just think how disappointed your mum would be if we presented it as a done deal.' Pia glanced down at the diamond sparkling on her left hand. It was a few months since Jackson had proposed unexpectedly and she still hadn't got used to the sight of the ring on her finger.

'But it shouldn't be about anyone else. It should be about us. What we want?'

'Oh, Jackson!' She leant out of her chair and flung her arms around his neck. 'I know that. And it's exactly what I want, sharing our special day with all our family and friends. Don't you?'

Jackson shrugged noncommittally.

'To be honest, as long as you're there on the day, I'll be happy.' He gazed across at her, his dark brown eyes sparkling with intent. 'You do realise Ronnie will want to take over. She'll be absolutely unbearable.'

'No, she won't. She's just happy for us. And why shouldn't she be? It's not every day that her only son gets married and it's to be expected that she would want to play a central part in the preparations for the wedding. Here at the hall. You can't deny her that small pleasure.'

They'd already hosted a couple of weddings in the renovated oak barn at the hall, one for Pia's brother, Connor, and his wife Ruby, and another for Pia's friend Abbey and her husband Sam. They had been joyful, intimate occasions made all the more special by the beauty of their surroundings. Why would Pia want to get married anywhere else?

Jackson sat back in his chair and puffed out his cheeks.

'Fine. As long as you're happy with the arrangements then that's all that matters. We should definitely get the date in the diary, though, so we can start to make plans, or else the year will run away from us.'

'No sooner said than done!' Pia jumped up from her seat and dashed into the office, returning moments later with her laptop. She opened it up and pulled up the calendar. They'd already decided upon a winter wedding, as it was Pia's favourite time of the year, and the hall was at its most imposing and welcoming when it was set aglow with a myriad of lights against the dark sky. The Christmas carols evening held in the grounds of the hall had proved to be very popular, drawing in crowds from not only the local area, but further afield too, and it was the last event on the social calendar, a celebration and culmination of all the hard work in the year. Jackson peered over her shoulder to look at the screen.

'You know, it makes sense to do it then.' He waved a pencil over the calendar. 'It's the weekend after the Christmas carols, the place will look at its best and what better way to round off the year?' He paused, tilting his chin to the ceiling as he did when he was mulling over an idea.

'Does that work for you?'

Pia's eyes lit up. The wedding was something they'd spoken about for weeks now, but to get a firm date on the calendar would make it seem so much more real and it would be something wonderful to look forward to at the end of a busy year.

'I think it would be the perfect time to do it. We'll all be feeling suitably festive and Ronnie will be around to help out with all the arrangements.' Pia raised her eyebrows at Jackson, a grin on her face.

In the absence of her own parents, who had both sadly died in recent years, Pia loved having Ronnie's and Rex's presence in her life. She considered them her new family, along with Mateo, who was the head gardener and had joined the hall around the same time as Pia. They'd quickly bonded over their shared delight at snagging a job, as well as a new home, in the most beautiful of surroundings. They'd also provided moral support to each other, nattering over a morning cup of coffee, as they got to grips with their new roles and as they tried to fathom the demands of their boss, Jackson.

The set-up at Primrose Hall was totally different to the family life Pia had enjoyed with her mum, dad and Connor growing up at Meadow Cottages, which had been traditional and secure, and wholly comforting, but that was a different place and time. Now, she'd fully embraced her new dysfunctional family in all their glory. She adored Ronnie's spontaneity and enthusiasm, and Rex's laid-back jovial manner, and now that Tom had arrived in their lives too, they were a proper tight unit.

'Hmmm, that's what I'm worried about,' said Jackson now, with a crooked smile. 'Maybe for all our sakes, we should keep the date to ourselves for a couple of months at least. I don't want Ronnie making an early special trip home just on the pretext of sourcing some table decorations.'

Pia laughed.

'So that's a date then?' she said, typing the event onto the calendar, in capital letters and followed by several exclamation marks.

'Absolutely. Set in stone. It's already been too long and I cannot wait to make you Mrs Moody and Lady of the Manor.' He placed his hand over hers. 'How does that sound?'

Mrs Moody? Lady of the Manor? It sounded absolutely ridiculous, but utterly enticing at the same time. Pia was under no illusions. She knew being Jackson's wife wouldn't be an easy undertaking. He was mercurial, spontaneous and bold, but that was everything she admired about him. Who knew what adventures were ahead of them, but what she did know was that she couldn't wait to find out. It would likely be her most difficult role to date, but she had never felt more excited about a proposition and more ready for the challenge.

5

Sophie couldn't believe her luck. She felt certain there was someone up there, keeping an eye out for her. How else could she explain finding such a perfect picture-postcard cottage in the heart of the charming village of Wishwell overlooking the village green? It was an ex-farm worker's cottage and she'd heard about it through word-of-mouth at the local community shop. She'd popped in there, a few weeks previously, on the way home from her new job as office manager at an import and export company. She wanted to pick up some locally sourced products to put into a hamper for Greta and her family as a thank you for taking her in at a time when she was at her most vulnerable. She picked up some honey, sweet chilli jam, piccalilli, home-made cookies, local beers, cheese crackers and elderflower cordial, and was just queuing up to pay for her items when she tuned into the conversation between the woman working behind the till and a male customer. The middle-aged man was explaining how the cottage on the green had recently been vacated and how they would be re-letting it, as soon as they found the right tenant for the property. Sophie, not one to normally push herself forward, had been unable to stop herself and interrupted their discussion with an apology.

'I'm sorry, but I couldn't help overhearing. Did you mention that there is a cottage to let in the village? I'm looking for somewhere myself.'

The man had looked her up and down and said something about there already being someone else they had in mind, a local person, but if Sophie wanted to send her details to the email address he provided, then they would get back to her. Sophie felt certain it was a brush-off. Not for a moment did she believe anything would come of it, but when she was sent an application form with a section specifically asking about why she wanted to live in the village, she jotted down all the details of her recent break-up, her new job in the neighbouring village and her mum living in a nearby nursing home. Too much information possibly, but she reasoned that it couldn't hurt and she was later to find out that it had been her ties to the local area that had swayed the decision in her favour.

Now, as she dropped the couple of boxes that she'd brought in from the car into her new living room, she couldn't stop the big smile from spreading across her face. Moving into Greta's home had been a spontaneous and urgent decision, born out of necessity, whereas coming here had been part of her main plan for getting her life back on track. She'd managed to get away from Kyle, she'd found a new job and now, the final piece of the puzzle, she had a place of her own that she could call home.

There was a brick open fireplace on one wall and a sofa that had clearly seen better days on the other. Not that it mattered, Sophie would drape a couple of colourful blankets over it and once she'd unpacked her personal belongings and displayed them on the alcoves to either side of the fireplace, it would definitely look more cosy. At the far end of the room was an archway that led to a galley kitchen which had everything she would need and there were two further rooms at the back of the house, a small loo and a boot room which would make an ideal hobby area. She'd wanted a designated space where she could start making her silver jewellery again. When she'd lived with Kyle, there had been a spare bedroom which she would often disappear to, a retreat where she could immerse herself in making silver bangles, earrings and necklaces, and forget about everything else going on in her life. When she was sitting at her desk, the Anglepoise lamp at her side, her tools in front of her, her whole focus was on the project between her hands and she found it totally distracting and relaxing.

The first of this year's Sunday craft fairs at the stables at Primrose Hall was in a couple of weeks' time so, once she'd unpacked, she would sort through her existing stock and put together some more items for sale. She'd been lucky to pick up a stall at the stables just before Christmas. Pia Temple had called her to say that a spot had unexpectedly become available and she'd invited Sophie to take up the pitch. Sophie had deliberated for a moment. She was living at Greta's at the time, all her jewellery and equipment were packed away in a storage box, and she wasn't in the best frame of mind, emotionally. Her initial instinct had been to decline, but she knew there was a waiting list and if she didn't accept the offer, then she might not get the opportunity again for a long time. Hesitantly, she'd agreed and had to scrabble around to unearth all her stock, which fortunately was quite plentiful.

She'd been so apprehensive about the day, worried that there would be no interest in her distinctive brand of jewellery, and that she would feel out of her depth amongst the other more established traders, but she needn't have worried. Pia had greeted her warmly, even when she'd turned up almost an hour early, and had plied her with hot drinks and biscuits when she'd had a major wobble and had threatened to go home. All the other stallholders had been equally welcoming and, once the visitors started arriving, Sophie had quickly forgotten about her concerns. She was surprised to sell so many items, but with her pieces pitched at affordable prices, they had proved to be very popular with customers buying them for Christmas presents. Pia had bought a small selection too.

As she remembered that day, a kernel of excitement built up inside of her for all the possibilities ahead. There was no bad-tempered boyfriend to worry about, no one waiting on a cooked meal when she got home from work, which meant her time would be entirely her own. While she would be forever grateful to Greta, she had felt as though she'd been intruding on their family life. It was a relief to have her own place after so many months in the wilderness. Now she could do what she wanted whenever she wanted to, and it was something she would never take for granted again. She had so many plans for her small business and here in this cosy, but perfectly formed cottage, she could forge ahead with those ideas. As well as securing a regular spot at the stables, she hoped to build an online store, and take commissions for bespoke personalised items.

This was the start of a new chapter in her life and she couldn't wait to throw herself wholeheartedly into the adventure ahead.

6

Tom splashed aftershave over his jawline, checking his profile in the mirror, first one way and then the other. He ran a hand through his thick brown hair, giving an encouraging nod to his reflection. Why the heck was he feeling so nervous? He'd been an area sales manager for years, his job involving extensive travelling around the country, talking to a wide range of people. He could go into any situation and strike up a conversation with anyone. He had a proven track record as a problem solver and since leaving his job and taking up a number of part-time roles, he'd adapted easily to a variety of opportunities. This one, though, seemed to have a whole heap of pressure attached to it.

While he was grateful to his brother for offering him the position at the stables, Tom was a little apprehensive about how it might work out in practice. He knew how exacting Jackson could be, how he had very firm ideas about the way the hall and its associated businesses were run, and he just hoped that he didn't fall foul of his brother's demanding standards. They were still finding their way with each other, discovering what they had in common, trying to establish the brotherly bond that they'd missed out on while growing up. Since he'd found out about his true parentage, and got to know his dad, Rex, and his family, he'd found a connection that he hadn't experienced as a child.

His dad, Ronnie and Pia had welcomed him warmly and he'd struck up easy relationships with them all, and Tom was enjoying nurturing and building on those, but his connection with his brother hadn't been so straightforward. Tom couldn't quite put his finger on it, because Jackson was always perfectly polite and friendly towards him, but he suspected that it wasn't born out of a natural affinity, but rather out of a sense of duty and responsibility. Tom wondered if Jackson would even bother with him if his dad wasn't around. Still, it probably wasn't worth dwelling on. It was still early days for them and they had plenty of time to get to know each better, even if it might take them months or years even to create the brotherly closeness that Tom craved. He just had to ensure there were no major disagreements in the meantime. That was why he was so relieved to see Pia when he turned up for his first shift at the stables on that sunny Sunday. She greeted him as she always did with a big hug and a peck on the cheek.

'Hey, Tom, it's so great to have you onboard. We know that the stables are going to be in great hands with you at the helm.'

'I'm thrilled to be here and looking forward to getting involved. Where's Jackson this morning then?'

'Out on his bike. It's his usual Sunday-morning jaunt. He likes to take a ride out around the country lanes. He loves the freedom of the open road. The chance to be alone with his thoughts, just him up against the elements in the great outdoors.' Pia shrugged. She couldn't understand the appeal herself, but that was probably because she was worried sick all the time Jackson was out on his bike. It was a huge beast of a machine, whose throaty roar could be heard from miles away, and Pia could never fully relax until she knew Jackson was safely home in one piece. After all, it had been a motorcycle accident when Jackson was a teenager, involving a friend of his, that had been the catalyst for him leaving the village. It was only natural that her mind would drift to all those worst-case scenarios. 'He'll be back later, though, and will probably pop over if you need to speak to him,' said Pia, rallying herself.

'Not especially, although it's always good to catch up with my little bro!' he said, laughing.

'Come on,' said Pia, slipping her arm through Tom's. 'Let's go and see who's arrived. I didn't realise I would be quite so excited about the craft fairs starting up again.'

Pia and Tom had got together earlier in the week to talk through what Tom would be doing. She'd shown him around the buildings, where the extra furniture was kept, and most importantly where the tea and coffee supplies were in the small kitchen. She'd handed over the folder containing details of all the traders with their contact details and today she would introduce him to each of them in turn.

In some ways, she would be sad to relinquish responsibility for the craft days. She'd been there from the very first one when they didn't know how popular they might prove to be and if it would just be a one-off event, or if they might consider running them every month. That first Sunday had proved such a hit with the customers and the traders that they'd pencilled in further dates in the diary by the end of the afternoon. Word spread locally and beyond and soon it was a regular feature on the Primrose Hall social calendar, and so popular that they'd taken the decision to run them even more frequently this year.

'Let me show you the book exchange.' Pia directed Tom to one of the stables that had been converted into a mini-library, with shelves of books organised into different genres; crime, romance, historical, non-fiction and children's. 'This started out as a temporary feature when the library at the village hall was closed down. The library was a real lifeline to me when my parents were ill. I used to wander down there for a brief respite and pick up some books for us all. I always felt lifted by just spending some time away from the house, flicking through the pages of the books which held all sorts of promises. That's why I wanted to provide a local facility for those people affected by the village hall closure. People can come here and bring any books that they no longer need and swap them for something we have on the shelves. It's proved to be very popular. When we started out, we had one small bookcase of paperbacks, but as word spread, our stocks grew and grew, and just look at it now. You can see how much it's grown. So much so that I open up on a Wednesday afternoon as well. That's when the kids come in with their parents on their way home from school. I love seeing the children's excited faces and hearing them talk about the characters as though they are their friends. They always go away clutching another pile of books, it's great. So do spread the word and tell people that we're open on a Wednesday after-noon as well.'

Pia introduced Tom to the traders as they arrived, and he tried to make mental reminders of their faces so he could match each of them to their names. He was sure, given a couple of weeks, everything would fall into place.

'You'll remember Sophie, won't you?' Pia prompted him.

They'd arrived at the stable unit at the far end of the block and a woman with warm brown hair tied up in a messy bun turned to greet them. She was wearing loose denim dungarees over a white shirt. Her face lit up in a smile.

'Hello!'

It caused Tom only the briefest moment of panic, before he realised exactly who the attractive woman was.

'Hello, Sophie, it's good to see you again. Although I'm afraid you'll have to deal with me on these Sundays now, rather than Pia.'

He'd met Sophie once before, on Christmas Day. She was a last-minute guest at the dinner table at Primrose Hall and they'd sat next to each other, enjoying the wonderful hospitality of Jackson and Pia. He would go so far to say, if asked, that her company had made the day, which was the first time he'd spent Christmas with his biological family, even more special than he could have anticipated. They'd laughed so much, although how much that was down to the free-flowing wine and the silly games of charades, he didn't know.

'Really?' Now, Sophie turned her attention to Pia, a quizzical look on her face.

'Yes, it's true. I'm passing on the reins to Tom, who I know will do a fantastic job, but it is quite a wrench. This project was my baby, but I'm just pleased that it's up and running, and will continue to thrive.'

Pia must have noticed the disappointed expression on Sophie's face because she quickly added, 'Don't worry, you won't be able to get rid of me that easily. I'll be popping down all the time and you've got my number if you need to contact me. In fact, we're well overdue a catch-up, aren't we? I'll pop back over the lunchtime lull and you can tell me all your news.'

Sophie looked marginally appeased. She certainly remembered Tom from Christmas Day. What an unexpectedly joyful day it had been and Tom had been easy and enjoyable company. She recalled feeling full of turkey, trimmings and a big dollop of goodwill, and more than a bit merry at the end of the day. Despite her misgivings, she'd been pleased that she'd acted spontaneously in accepting the invitation in Pia's early-morning text asking her to join them for lunch. Greta and her family had travelled up north on Christmas Eve to visit relatives so the alternative for Sophie was a ready meal for one in front of the telly.

Now she felt a pang of disappointment hearing that Pia wouldn't be her first port of contact at the stables. It was Pia who had held her hand and given her a rallying pep talk when Sophie arrived for that first time. She'd had a bit of a wobble, hijacked by nerves, and had been close to walking away, so she would always be grateful to Pia for encouraging her to stay and supporting her that day.

'Here's my details, Sophie.' Tom handed over his business card. 'Any problems at all, just give me a call.' He flashed her a smile and Sophie was reminded of how similar he was to his brother, Jackson. They shared the same bone structure and strong Roman nose, but Tom's features were softer around the edges than Jackson's, making him appear friendlier and more approachable. The short time that Sophie had spent with him on Christmas Day had only confirmed that impression, so maybe it wouldn't be such a hardship having him around instead of Pia, especially as she knew she and Pia would keep in touch anyway. From the first moment they met, the two women, who were both in their late twenties, had hit it off immediately, striking up a genuine friendship, and they had kept in contact since through texts and emails. There was no way they would lose touch now.

If there was one thing Sophie had learnt in recent months, it was how much she valued her female friendships, which had seen her through some of the most difficult times of her life. As for men, well, one in particular had caused her enough heartbreak and stress to last her a lifetime. She could certainly do without that kind of hassle ever again so if she was destined to be single for the foreseeable future then she was more than happy with that state of affairs.

7

The whole idea behind getting Tom to oversee the running of the craft fairs at the stables was so Pia could have at least one day off in her working week. Not that she'd instigated the plan. That was all down to Jackson. If it were up to her then she would be more than happy to continue because the craft Sundays had always been so much fun. It didn't seem like work to her at all, but Jackson had been insistent.

'You can't be working seven days a week, Pia. Your workload has increased hugely anyway because of the number of events we're now running and while I understand that it's difficult to let go of something that you feel so passionately about, something has to give and this seems like the obvious solution.'

She hadn't argued with him, because ultimately she knew that it made sense, especially as Jackson would want to get away some weekends, either for a visit to London for dinner and a show, or else to travel to a classic car show around the country. She enjoyed those special times spent together away from the hall, and knowing the stables would be in safe hands would make it all the better for relaxing. Although, as much as she enjoyed getting away on short breaks, she relished getting home all the more, to see to the animals and to be at the place where she was at her happiest.

Today, though, when it was handover day to Tom, she had the perfect excuse for hanging around at the stables just in case she might be needed. She'd sloped off for a short while after she'd introduced Tom to everyone, to share breakfast with Jackson, having heard his bike make its noisy arrival down the main driveway. He'd come back with the Sunday papers and dropped them on the kitchen table, before reaching into the cupboard to pull out the frying pan to make a start on the cooked breakfast which was a staple part of their Sundays these days.

'It's so lovely to see everyone again,' Pia told Jackson. 'They all seem really pleased to be back, and Tom is wandering around chatting to everyone as though he's always been part of the team. I hope we get a reasonable turnout today.' They'd done some advertising on local websites and had emailed everyone who had signed up to the newsletter, but Pia felt the same sense of nervousness as she had the very first time they'd opened up the stables.

'I'm sure we will. It might take a few weeks for the word to spread again, but I don't think there's any cause for concern. You know how popular those days were last year and I can only think that it will get even busier this year.'

After they'd finished their fry-up, Pia picked up the dirty plates and took them across to the dishwasher.

'I might just pop over again to see how Tom's doing.' Jackson raised his eyebrows at Pia's suggestion.

'You really don't need to. Tom's more than capable.'

'I know, but it is his first time. I'll just check that there aren't any problems. Besides, I haven't had a chance to chat to everyone yet, and I really would like to catch up with them all. I feel as though I'm missing out!'

'Fine. You go ahead,' said Jackson with an indulgent smile, knowing full well that there would be no stopping Pia even if he'd wanted to. The new regime might take some getting used to.

'I'll take the dogs round the gardens, and I'll probably pop over a bit later.'

'Great!' Pia said. 'Tom was asking if he might see you.'

As she stepped outside, closing the kitchen door behind her, Pia was encouraged to see signs of activity over at the stables. People had already begun to arrive and were milling around, while more cars were coming along the main driveway. The old vintage coffee van was in place and already a small queue had formed and Pia felt a sense of relief that it looked like they had a good day in store.

'Hey, how's it going?'

After a leisurely mooch around the stalls, her attention taken by all the pretty items on sale, and a chat with the various traders, Pia had ended up at Sophie's unit.

'Good, there's been a steady flow of customers. I've sold a couple of pieces, which is great. I'm just really pleased to be here. I've had some business cards made up so I've been handing them out when I can. Who knows, maybe the time will come when I'll be able to give up the day job. That's the grand plan, anyway!' Sophie's laughter rang out, her hazel eyes sparkling, and Pia was reminded how much Sophie had changed since the first time they'd met. Then Sophie had been reticent, fearful even, her whole being filled with sadness. Now, there was a positivity and lightness that radiated from her that was heartening to see.

'Talking of the day job. How is it going?' Pia asked.

'Yeah, great. The people seem really friendly and the work's quite varied so time goes quickly. It pays the bills, which is the main thing, and it feels really good to be back in control of my life again. Especially now I've moved into my new place in Wishwell. The cottage is small but perfectly formed and just right for me. It feels as though everything is falling into place at last.'

'I'm really pleased for you, Sophie, and Wishwell is a lovely spot to live. I have another friend, Abbey, who lives there, with her husband Sam, and their springer spaniel, Lady. You're bound to bump into them.'

'Is that Abbey from Rushgrove Lodge?'

'That's right. Do you know her then?'

'I've met her. My mum lives at the home so I've spoken to her a few times. She's always been really friendly and helpful. It's nice to know that she lives in the same village. I'll look out for her there. Anyway, how's life with you?' Sophie asked.

'Good,' said Pia beaming, instinctively looking at the sparkling ring on her left hand. 'We've actually set the date for the wedding now.'

'Have you? That's so exciting. When is it going to be?'

'Not for a little while yet – 21 December, after we've completed all the social events lined up for the year. It will be perfect because it'll be the anniversary of our engagement.'

'A winter wedding! How lovely. That will be so romantic and something to look forward to, that's for sure. Are you having it here?'

'We are. Jackson was talking about eloping, but I didn't fancy that. I want all my friends and family around us when we take our vows and that includes you, of course!'

'Really?'

'Yes! We'd love you to be there. There'll be about fifty or sixty people in total, I think, so it should still be nice and intimate. So keep that date free, won't you?'

'You bet I will.' Sophie was delighted and surprised that Pia would even invite her to the wedding because although they got on really well, they hadn't, in reality, known each other that long. Not that it mattered. With some people you hit it off straight away and that's how it had been for her and Pia.

Just at that moment, Tom joined them.

'I thought it might be a good idea to arrange a semi-regular get-together for the traders at one of the local pubs. I was thinking the Three Feathers in Wishwell. The first one will be this coming Friday at about 7 p.m. There's no obligation to attend, but if you'd like to then you'd be most welcome. What I've quickly learned from being here this morning is that there's really not the opportunity to chat amongst ourselves as invariably there are constant interruptions. Not that I'm complaining, of course. It's what we're here for. We want to give our full attention to our visitors and customers while they're here, but it would also be good to have the opportunity for a proper catch-up, then if there are any issues or queries we can chat them over in a relaxed environment.'

'That's a really good idea,' said Pia. 'I'm not sure why I didn't think of it myself.' She laughed.

'Well, you're obviously welcome to come and join us too, if you'd like to.'

'Thanks, Tom. Jackson and I are out to dinner this Friday, but I'd definitely be interested in any future get-togethers, so keep me posted, won't you?'

'I will.' Now Tom turned his attention to Sophie, gracing her with a wide smile. 'Come along, if you fancy it, Sophie. I think Katy and Roger said they would try and make it, and I'll see if I can gather a few more recruits.'

'Great. I should be able to come. I've recently moved to Wishwell so it's literally within staggering distance for me.' Not to mention the fact that her social diary was depressingly empty at the moment. 'I'll look forward to it.'

Tom laughed.

'I think the last time we shared a drink you led me astray and we got merrily tipsy together, do you remember? So I can see that you're probably going to be a bad influence, or maybe a good influence, in that respect.'

'Hey, I can take no blame for that. It was all down to Jackson and Pia's wonderful hospitality and the free-flowing champagne, but you know I think we should definitely raise a toast to them on Friday in light of their good news.'

Tom's brow furrowed as he looked from Pia to Sophie.

'Oh, I thought Jackson would have told you,' butted in Pia. 'We've set a date for the wedding – 21 December! Save-the-date cards will be coming your way very soon so make sure you put it on the calendar. We can't wait to share our big day with all the special people in our lives.' Pia grabbed hold of Tom's hand and squeezed it tight.

'Well, that's definitely cause for celebration then,' said Tom laughing. 'On Friday night, we'll raise a glass to you both and your future happiness, won't we, Sophie?'

In the absence of any other plans, Sophie was only too happy to agree and was already looking forward to spending some more time with Tom.

8

It was the thing that Sophie enjoyed the most about her new lifestyle. The delicious sensation that her time was her own to do whatever she wanted, whenever she wanted, without having to report to anyone else. She was making the most of it while she could. Most evenings after work she would return to her little cottage, light a candle on the hearth, make herself a mug of tea and decide what she would have for dinner. She loved pottering about her small kitchen, rustling up a quick pasta dish or frying a fillet of fish to have with some salad, or sometimes, a simple cheese and pickle sandwich would hit the spot perfectly. After dinner, if she wasn't too tired, she would head out to the back room to work on some of her designs. With her headphones in, listening to the radio or a podcast, her full concentration would be on her latest project. She was currently working on a range that was inspired by the elements, using a gentle hammered effect to create the illusion of movement within the pieces.

She was pleased to have sold a couple of pendants, a ring and two sets of earrings on Sunday at the craft fair. She'd known it wouldn't be as busy as the first time she attended, which had been just a few weeks before Christmas and when she'd sold pretty much all of her stock. This time round it had been a more leisurely and relaxed affair with visitors browsing and chatting interestedly. It wasn't Sophie's style to go in for a hard sell. She was simply happy to display her wares and to build connections that she hoped might prove fruitful in the future.

She'd managed, in the quiet spells during the day, to have a look around the other traders' stalls, and was amazed all over again by the breadth of talent on display. Josh, a friendly guy in his late thirties, sporting closely cut red hair and a matching full beard, had a beautiful range of hand-crafted wooden products including coasters, chopping boards and personalised cheese boards. Maddie was a crocheter and knitter, selling cute children's jumpers and beanies, and beautiful patch-work blankets. Sophie definitely had her eye on one of those for the armchair in the living room, once she had enough spare money to buy one. Cecily made beauty products like soaps, bath salts and bombs, which filled the stables with a sweet fragrant scent that was a reminder of hot summer days. Mike was a photographer who took the most amazing shots of wildlife including magnificent red kites in flight, hares boxing in an open field, and beautiful wide-eyed deer on alert in the countryside. He framed his photos in simple black frames, allowing the strong images to speak for themselves. As well as those traders Sophie had already had the chance to speak to, there were a few more that she hadn't yet met so she was looking forward to putting that right at their meet-up in the pub.

Unsurprisingly, Sophie felt a few jitters of nerves on that Friday evening as she got ready to go out. After a speedy dinner of a salmon fillet on some salad leaves, one of her favourites, she changed out of her work clothes, freshened up and pulled on some jeans, a black lace-trimmed vest with a floaty pink blouse over the top. She carefully applied some eyeliner, smudging it with her finger for a smoky look, brushed her lashes with some mascara and added a sweep of lip gloss. Running her fingers through her tawny-coloured hair, she gave one last glance in the mirror and took a deep breath, pushing aside those intrusive thoughts that were telling her she didn't have to go, that she could stay at home with a glass of wine. One thing she'd learned since breaking up with Kyle was that she needed to push herself out of her comfort zone. Being introverted by nature, going to events on her own wasn't something she found easy, but this evening Sophie had no excuses. The pub was literally a stone's throw away from her house and if she found it too excruciating then she could always make her excuses and leave.

Even so, she was so relieved when she walked through the doors of the Three Feathers and immediately spotted Katy standing at the bar.

'Hey, Katy, it's good to see you,' she said, the relief evident in her tone.

'Sophie!' Katy's face lit up. 'We've nabbed a table in the back bar. Unfortunately, I can't stay too long. Brad is meeting a colleague who's over from Australia so I've got to get back to look after the kids, but I just wanted to come and say hello to everyone.' Katy picked up the tray of drinks she'd been served. 'See you in a minute,' she said, wandering off.

Sophie ordered a white wine spritzer for some Dutch courage, and made her way through to the other bar, where a group of the traders were sitting around an old oak table. Tom spotted Sophie and gestured for her to come over, shuffling up along the bench to make room for her beside him. Josh, Mike and Maddie were there along with Aysha, who Sophie knew by sight but hadn't spoken to before. She sold a range of candles, incense sticks, essential oils and reed diffusers.

'How long have you been at the stables?' Sophie asked her.

'Since the very beginning. I was lucky enough to get a spot when they first opened up and I haven't missed a session since. It's been good for me because I've seen a lift in my online sales as well and I've also attended some other craft fairs that I've heard about through meeting people at the stables. You're fairly new, aren't you?'

'Yes, last week was only my second time at the stables.'

Aysha nodded, her brown eyes shining warmly.

'You were fortunate to get a place. I think Pia said there was quite a waiting list now.'

'I know. I feel very grateful that I was able to sneak in when I did. I'm really just starting out on my business so I'm still finding my way, which products are the most popular, how to price my items, the best way to package them, that sort of thing. There's a lot to learn, and I think the stables is the ideal place to test the market. I know it might take some time but I'm hoping that I can grow the business so that one day it can become a full-time career. That's the dream, anyway.' Sophie gave a wry chuckle. 'It has to beat working nine-to-five behind a computer screen in an office.'

'Well, if there's anything I can help with, then just let me know. You should come along to the business breakfast club hub. We meet at the Treetops Cafe on the first Wednesday of the month and it's a great networking opportunity for small and medium-sized businesses. If you have any specific issues, then there are experts in different areas such as finance, marketing and sales who you can talk to. I've always found them to be really welcoming and supportive, and it's a great way to spread the word about your company. You also get to hear about any local grants that might be available. If you let me have your number, I can send over the details if you like?'

Sophie found everyone around the table just as friendly and helpful, and she spent time chatting with Maddie, who told her about her life living aboard a narrowboat on the canal. As well as the crocheted and knitted garments that she made, she gave tarot readings, which Sophie found fascinating, although she didn't fancy having the cards read for her. She had no desire to find out what the future held in store. She would much rather discover that as it unfolded. Besides, she was in control of her own destiny now so she wasn't leaving anything to fate. She knew exactly what lay ahead; independence, security and her own peace of mind.

'I wish I could stay, but I have to go.' Katy jumped up, looking at her watch. 'Next time, I'll make sure I get a babysitter lined up for the whole evening, but I'll see you all next Sunday.'

After Katy left, most of the others trailed away too, citing other engagements, with a promise that they too would make sure to come along for the whole evening next time. It left Sophie alone with Tom and a sense of deflation that now she was relaxed, and enjoying the wine and the conviviality, the evening had been brought to a premature end.

'Well, I don't know about you,' Tom said, gracing Sophie with an engaging smile, which reminded her so much of his brother, 'but I've got no intention of going home.' He placed his hand around his empty beer glass. 'I'm going to have another drink. Are you going to join me?'

It seemed like the most natural thing in the world to say yes and when Tom returned with the drinks from the bar, they picked up the conversation easily where they'd left off.

'They seem like a lovely crowd,' Sophie offered.

'Aren't they? And they've been very generous in welcoming me aboard. I know Pia has a great relationship with them all so I hope they don't feel short-changed having to deal with me instead.'

'Never!' Although Sophie wasn't about to admit that initially she'd felt a pang of disappointment when finding out Pia would no longer be in charge.

Tom laughed, but it wasn't the first time she'd sensed an insecurity beneath his friendly, outgoing exterior. She liked that about him. As though he didn't take himself too seriously. It made him seem approachable and maybe a tad vulnerable too.

'Is this the first time you've worked with your brother? I used to work for a family firm, my ex's, so I know how intense it can get.'

'Yes. I was surprised when he asked me, to be honest with you. But very pleased to be a small part of the Primrose Hall team. You know I've only actually known Jackson for a few months?'

Sophie's eyes grew wide.

'No? How come?'

'Well...' Tom gave a wry smile. 'It's a long story, but basically I found out last year that the man who I'd always thought was my father, wasn't. Which, as you can imagine, came as a bit of a shock.'

'Yeah...' Sophie was probably guilty of staring too much, scanning Tom's features for answers. This newly discovered information made her look at him in a different light, revealing as it did another part of his personality.

'Although it certainly explained a few things,' Tom went on. 'Like why my dad never showed much interest in me when I was growing up and why we pretty much lost touch after he left my mum.'

'That must have been tough.'

'It was. What I found most difficult was discovering that my mum had been part of that lie. She obviously knew the truth about who my real dad was, but for whatever reason, decided not to tell me. Now, because she's no longer with us, I can't ask her all those questions I have.'

Sophie took a sharp intake of breath, feeling a pang of hurt on his behalf.

'I'm sorry.'

Tom looked up, his dark brown eyes latching onto hers, the half-smile on his lips matching the shimmer in his gaze.

'Thanks. It was a big upheaval and caused me a lot of soul-searching, but don't get me wrong, it's been mainly a very positive process. It's like I know who I am now. I found my real dad, Rex, and discovered that I had a brother that I never knew even existed. I now have a family and people who actually look like me.' He shrugged, turning his palms up to the sky, as though he could still hardly believe it himself. 'They've all been really friendly and welcomed me into the fold.'

'That's amazing. Honestly, I would never have realised. When I joined you all for Christmas lunch at the hall, it struck me what a lovely, tight-knit family you were. I'd just imagined, seeing you all sitting round the table, that it was a tradition you'd carried out for years and years.'

'Nope, not at all. It was my first time spending Christmas with my dad and my brother, so it was pretty special. I have to say I'm very grateful to Pia and Ronnie for smoothing the way, they've really been instrumental in including me in family events, which has been great. And now working for "the firm", hopefully that will be just as rewarding. Although...' Tom's mouth twisted in a grimace. 'Are you telling me it's not the best idea then, working with your family?'

He tilted his head to one side, inviting Sophie to elaborate.

'Oh, I'm sure working with Jackson and Pia will be absolutely fine. I used to work for my ex-boyfriend's family firm, that was all, which was great initially, but then it became awkward when things started to go wrong. Living and working together brings its own problems when there are lots of other factors involved too. I'm just relieved that I've been able to move on from that situation.'

'I'm sorry to hear about that. Was that fairly recently then?'

'Last year. A friend of mine offered me a place to stay when I was at my lowest ebb and I jumped at the opportunity. I turned my back on my old life; that was my job, my home and Kyle, my ex-boyfriend.' Sophie's gaze drifted out of the pub window for a moment. It seemed like a lifetime ago and in the same breath she could recall it as though it was yesterday. 'It was traumatic at the time, but it was absolutely the right thing for me. Now, I'm much more settled. I love my little cottage, I have a new job and I'm enjoying making my jewellery in my spare time.'

Saying the words aloud to Tom, who was listening interestedly, made her realise just how far she'd come in recent months.

'Sounds like you've been through some pretty big changes too then?' There was an understanding smile from Tom.

'Yes. It's been a difficult couple of years.' Sophie gave an imperceptible shudder when thoughts of Kyle and everything that had happened filtered into her mind. 'Nothing like you've had to contend with, though,' she said.

'I don't know. All those big lifestyle changes can take their toll. Like me, you've moved home, changed job and broken up with your partner all in the space of... a relatively short time. It takes some adjusting to.'

Sophie nodded in confirmation.

'That's true. You've been through a break-up as well, then?' Sophie questioned, latching onto his words, wondering how one person could have so much bad luck.

'Yes. When I found out about my dad, it put me in a bad place. It affected me deeply and I sank into a depression. I had this compulsion to get rid of everything that I knew and loved. Where I lived, where I worked, my relationship. It wasn't Anna's fault. She tried to support me through that period, but I was pretty foul to be around at the time. Looking back now, I think it was probably right for us to split up. We'd been together for years, and I guess we'd got into something of a rut. That whole episode made me take a closer look at my life and decide what I wanted from my future.' Tom picked up his beer and took a mouthful, lost in contemplation for a moment. 'I suppose I wanted to get a bit of control back over my life, if that makes sense?'

It made perfect sense to Sophie.

'Now, you can see,' he said, with what she'd come to realise was his customary humility, 'that I've got this whole life shebang worked out. I'm single, living alone in a poky one-bedroomed flat and have said goodbye to a hugely successful career, trading it for a variety of part-time jobs. Hey,' he laughed. 'Things can only get better.'

9

The poor girl. Tom took another swallow of his beer, shaking his head, wondering what on earth had possessed him. Tonight should have been a light-hearted, convivial affair but instead he'd been left alone with Sophie, who he couldn't deny was very pleasant company, and for some reason, he had decided to tell her his life story. It was hardly the most upbeat tale, but in fairness to her she'd been nothing but an attentive and interested listener. She was too polite to be anything else, Tom suspected, and was probably just waiting for the right moment, planning her escape. He gathered himself, and plastered on a smile, looking into her eyes, which he'd noticed before were a fetching grey-green colour.

'Sorry, I've been boring you. Don't let me keep you if you need to get away.' He turned his arm over to look at his watch. 'I should probably make tracks soon anyway.'

'Oh...' Sophie copied his gesture, glancing at her own watch, and Tom had to wonder if that was a flicker of disappointment he saw spread over her features. 'I was hoping to make a night of it, but perhaps next time people will stay for longer. I'm new to the village so it's nice to get out. This is a lovely pub to have on my doorstep.' She looked around her, taking in the old oak beams, the bar with its wide range of optics and ornate beer pumps, the flowers in the hearth of the fireplace, as she listened to the sounds of chatter and laughter ringing out around her. 'You haven't been boring at all,' she said, genuinely.

'Good, I'm pleased to hear that,' said Tom, his laughter filled with relief. 'In that case, are you hungry? I might grab some food. I didn't have a chance to eat before I came out tonight.'

'I've already eaten,' said Sophie, 'but I can always be tempted by a pudding. I've got such a sweet tooth.'

They spent some minutes poring over the menus and Tom was pleased that any earlier awkwardness seemed to be only imagined on his part, although he was glad that he'd managed to steer the conversation away from his personal life. He hadn't really opened up to anyone about what had happened, only to his new family, Rex, Ronnie, Jackson and Pia, but he'd found talking to Sophie easy and cathartic, like speaking to an old friend.

With their food order placed – Tom plumped for fish and chips, while Sophie opted for a slice of honeycomb cheesecake – they picked up their conversation where they'd left off, chatting about the stables, the local area and what they both liked to do in their free time.

'You know what we haven't done yet?' Tom picked up his glass, looking at Sophie expectantly.

'What?'

'We haven't made a toast to Pia and Jackson's good news.'

'You're right. And we said we would.' Sophie lifted her glass, clinking it against Tom's. 'To Jackson and Pia, wishing them a very long and happy marriage together.'

'I'll drink to that,' said Tom, with that same wide smile as his brother. 'I think they make a great couple, don't you? They seem to complement each other very well. Jackson is impulsive, go-getting and single-minded. I suppose you'd have to be to achieve what he's done in his career and up at the hall. And Pia, well, she's an absolute sweetheart. She's caring, kind and has a quiet competence. She definitely smooths out Jackson's rough edges too.'

'Yes, well, I've only met Jackson once, on Christmas Day, and he was very friendly and welcoming to me. As for Pia, she took me under her wing on that day I turned up at the stables. To be honest with you, I wasn't in the best state of mind. It was my first time and I was so worried that no one would like my jewellery. I had real imposter syndrome, and I was on the verge of walking out before I'd even set up my stall, but Pia talked me round. She was so kind to me. She made me a cup of tea, gave me a hug and a rallying talk. She even bought some of my pieces, and she assured me she didn't do it because she felt sorry for me.'

Sophie's laughter tinkled out around them.

'From what I've seen of your products, they look great, and are affordable too. I don't think you should have any worries on that front. I must say I'm blown away by the talent of all you guys at the stables.'

'Me too. I feel so lucky to be a part of such a creative group. It's a brilliant community. And of course it's such a beautiful and amazing venue too. I must admit in those quiet lulls at the stables, I spend my time just gazing out of the window, drinking in the scenery.'

'Yep. You can see why Pia wants to have the wedding there. I'm sure Jackson would be happy to go off somewhere, just the two of them, and tie the knot, but I think Pia's put her foot down over this one. She wants to have all her family and friends around her when she takes her vows and I can't say I blame her.'

'Me neither,' said Sophie wistfully, her thoughts lost for a moment, as she imagined the bride and groom in all their finery against the backdrop of the magnificent Primrose Hall. 'I'm really happy for them.'

'Have you been married?' Tom asked. The question popped into his head and trotted off his tongue before he had chance to consider whether it was appropriate or not.

'No.' She shook her head. 'I was with Kyle for about eight years and with us living and working together, in some ways it felt like a marriage, but now I'm very happy being single. I feel as though I've got my life back. That I've rediscovered the person I was supposed to be. Does that make sense?'

'It does. I feel exactly the same way. I'm enjoying being on my own, not having to consider anyone else. Like tonight. I can come out and not have to worry about getting home to someone. It's the freedom I'm appreciating the most.'

Tom couldn't help noticing the similarities between himself and

Sophie. Perhaps that's why they'd bonded so easily. Being at similar points in their lives, having recently come out of long-term relationships, they'd found a connection and understanding that went beyond their working connection. He liked Sophie, he found her easy company and their conversation flowed naturally. It was as though he could talk to her about anything. Although, after offloading all his problems onto her earlier in the evening, he probably needed to remember that he shouldn't overload her with all his inner thoughts and feelings. She was a nice girl, but he didn't want to take advantage of her sweet nature.

The pub was beginning to empty out, with customers saying their goodbyes and leaving for the evening, while the bar staff were collecting the finished glasses from the tables. Sophie shuffled in her seat and stretched her arms out in front of her.

'I suppose I ought to make a move, but thank you for tonight. I've had a great time. It's been nice to get out and forget about everything else.'

'Well, thank you for coming and staying the course.' Tom gave a low chuckle. 'Next time there'll be a few more of us so you won't get stuck with me all night, I promise.'

Sophie laughed, and their gazes locked for the briefest moment.

'Honestly, it's been great, and no hardship whatsoever. I've enjoyed myself.'

They stood up and wandered out the front door into the cool night air.

'Do you want a lift home?'

'Thanks, Tom, but you can literally see my cottage from here, so I'll be fine.'

'Great.' There was a moment of awkwardness where Tom wondered if he should hug Sophie. It certainly seemed the most natural thing to do, but he didn't want to overstep the mark or make Sophie feel uncomfortable, so he decided against it. 'See you next Sunday.'

Tom watched as Sophie walked away in the direction of her cottage and smiled, relieved to know that he would only have to wait a little more than a week until he saw her again.

10

'Look,' said Pia excitedly, sorting through the post just delivered by Dave, their friendly postman. He arrived in his van every morning, between ten and eleven, and sometimes would stop for a cup of tea, but today he'd had to rush off to make some time-sensitive deliveries.

'There's a postcard here from your mum and dad.'

She held up the card to Jackson, which showed a gloriously beautiful beach, bathed in sunshine, on the Côte d'Azur. 'Let me read it to you.'

Dear Jackson and Pia

We've made it to the South of France! We've found a lovely camp-site overlooking the sea where we've parked up and will stay awhile. We're spending our days walking along the coast and discovering the local countryside. We're sampling lots of the local delicacies including plenty of wine and cheese, of course! Wish you were here! Much love, Ronnie and Rex xxx

'Isn't that lovely?' said Pia, reading it for a second time. 'People don't often send postcards these days, do they? It reminds me of when I was a kid. It always seemed so exciting to receive those colourful cards from far-flung places, and I used to gaze at them, wondering if I would ever get to see such exotic places. My mum used to put them up on the mantelpiece and they would stay there for months on end.' Pia looked around her. 'I shall pop this up on the fridge, and it will remind us of them both.'

'As if we need any reminding,' said Jackson with a wry chuckle. 'Ronnie gives us daily updates as it is, so it's not as though we could ever forget about them.' Pia cast him a sharp glance. 'Not that we'd ever want to, of course,' Jackson added as an afterthought. 'Come here.'

He pulled Pia into his embrace, his expression full of warmth and kindness, as his brown eyes scanned her face.

'You're such a sweetheart. Sometimes I wonder what I've done to deserve someone as special as you. I love how you've fallen in love with my family nearly as much as you have done with me.'

'That's true,' said Pia, with a sigh. She missed her own mum and dad hugely, but in the short space of time she'd got to know, first Ronnie, and then Rex, she'd become very fond of them both. Ronnie was gregarious, funny and emotional, and Pia loved the colour and energy she brought to the hall. Rex didn't take himself too seriously and seemed to have a permanent smile on his face. From what Pia had gleaned, Rex had been something of a hedonistic wild child in his younger days, when his love of booze and his freedom ruled his life to the detriment of his family, his relationships and his work. Now, older and wiser, he was sober, with a desire to put right the wrongs of the past, and make it up to Jackson, and now Ronnie and Tom too.

Jackson's lips pressed gently against Pia's and butterflies stirred in the base of her stomach. His arms around her gave her a sense of safety and belonging that she would never take for granted. She pulled back to look into his face.

'You know I really can't wait to tell your mum that we've set the date. I know she's going to be so excited... when we finally get round to telling her.'

'Far too excited. We'll probably hear her screams in France from here,' said Jackson, laughing. Pia raised her eyebrows, running a hand around the hard contours of Jackson's face. She looked into his eyes imploringly, a soft smile resting on her lips. She didn't need to say a word, the look said it all.

'Fine!' He chastised her with an indulgent shake of his head. 'Tell her now, if you really want to, but do insist that she doesn't need to rush back home. There's still plenty of time until the wedding and tell her we have everything under control.'

'Do you mean it?' asked Pia, unable to contain her own excitement now. 'It's been killing me keeping the news to ourselves, although I suppose I have already told Abbey, Connor, Tom and...' Her voice trailed away. She'd pretty much told everyone to save the date, apart from Ronnie and Rex, although she knew nothing would stop them both from being there, whatever the date. She kissed Jackson on the lips, gently extracting herself from his hold.

'Have you given any thought to who you might have as your best man?'

'Not sure yet. There's a couple of contenders. Maybe Ash. Or possibly Mike. I'm not sure Ash would relish the opportunity, though. I need to have a think about it.'

Jackson had known Ash since he was a kid and although their paths in life had taken very different directions, Jackson made a point of keeping in touch with his old pal, meeting up with him regularly in the local pub. Pia had met him a couple of times, and although he was always polite, Pia found him shy and not terribly forthcoming. She found it hard to imagine him taking centre stage at their wedding. Mike was Jackson's ex-business partner, and she could certainly see him taking on the role – he was articulate, confident and charming, but the decision was entirely down to Jackson, and she would support him in whatever choice he made.

'Right,' she said, reluctantly glancing at her watch. 'I should get into the office and make a start on my to-do list. First job is confirming your hotels for the upcoming London trips.' As well as his commitments at the hall, Jackson was in demand as a motivational and after-dinner speaker for events in the city, and he also sat on the board of several charities. It meant he had to stay away at least a couple of times a month and although she always missed him when he was away, she relished the time alone to read, catch up on some podcasts or binge-watch the latest reality shows. 'I also want to check where we are on the entries for the car show, and after that I'll need to start on the promotional materials for the literary festival.' She pressed her forearm to her brow in a dramatic gesture. 'There's never a dull moment around here, is there? Oh, did I tell you I've managed to get G. G. Williamson for our main headline spot?'

Jackson, who wasn't up on his authors, gave a questioning glance.

'Yes, you know G. G. Williamson! He writes that series of funny mystery stories that they've recently televised. We watched one of them and said we needed to watch the rest. Well, it turns out George, G. G. Williamson, lives in Little Leyton, so only down the road. I couldn't believe it when he agreed to take a session at the festival. He's such a big name.'

'That's quite a coup then. Sounds as though this year's event is going to be even more successful than last year's.'

'I really hope so. We've already had lots of interest and lots of signs-ups, but I think once we announce that we have George attending, the remaining tickets will sell in a heartbeat.'

The classic car show was the next big event on the Primrose Hall events calendar and the one closest to Jackson's heart. It was a chance for him to indulge his passion for vintage cars and motorcycles, and to reconnect with all the friends and colleagues he'd met through his love for old vehicles. Pia had been surprised to discover at last year's show just how many people Jackson knew in the classic car community and how happy and engaged he was talking to other petrol heads. It had been a joy to see him so clearly in his element.

In the same way, the literary festival was Pia's very own personal project. She'd come up with the idea last year, on something of a whim, not knowing the first thing about running a writing weekend. She'd never attended one herself, but she'd always longed to and so this had been her opportunity to stage an event that would be filled with workshops, readings and author interviews. She'd been uncertain of herself, afraid that she would fall flat on her face when all she'd wanted to do was put on a successful event to prove to herself, and perhaps more importantly, Jackson, that she was capable of doing so. Thankfully, the weekend had been such a success for readers, writers and children alike that even before it was over Pia was already drawing up mental plans to make it an annual event. Now she was looking forward to this year's festival later in the year, still with an element of apprehension and nerves, but mostly with a growing excitement inside.

'Oh, I meant to say, I'm probably going up to Yorkshire next Saturday. There's a car auction and I've got my eye on another bike to add to the collection. It's a Norton Commando 1975, a pretty rare find. I could put in an online bid, but there's a few items going through that I wouldn't mind taking a look at. I thought I could make a day of it, take Ash with me and see what prices they're making at the moment.'

'That sounds like fun,' she said with forced brightness. Jackson liked nothing better than to spend his free time mooching around looking at old engines. Pia tried to show an interest, but she hardly knew one end of a car or a motorbike from another, and her conversation around the subject was exhausted once she'd asked what colour any particular machine might be. Going on a boys' day out with Ash would be ideal for Jackson and it would give Pia the chance to have the hall to herself for a day. She would walk the dogs as she usually did, fit in some reading time and visit her brother Connor and his wife Ruby at their new home. They'd recently decorated the nursery in preparation for the arrival of their baby in a couple of months' time, and she'd been dying to see how it looked. She would also pop in to see her friends Abbey and Sam as well, who were expecting their own baby any day now.

'Will you go up on the bike?' she asked, as casually as she could muster.

'Yeah, we'll take a leisurely ride, along the country roads. It should be a good day.'

'Great,' said Pia, with a forced smile. What else could she say? Jackson knew how she worried about him when he went out on his bike, but it was something he'd done ever since he was a lad, so it wasn't as though she was ever going to stop him now. He was a grown man, an accomplished and safe rider, but even so she knew she would probably spend the whole day worrying and she wouldn't be satisfied until she heard the familiar sound of his motorbike returning along the drive to Primrose Hall.

11

Sophie dashed into the big superstore on the retail park on her way home from work. She picked up a box of eggs and a loaf of white bread, planning to have scrambled eggs on toast for her dinner, but was also tempted by a bottle of white wine and a sharing bag of chocolate buttons, not that she had any intention of sharing them with anyone.

Just as she was putting her items through the self-serve checkout and popping them into her tote bag, she heard someone calling her name. She didn't need to look around to see who it was, the familiar tone sent her heart plummeting to the bottom of her stomach.

'Hi, Kyle,' she said, turning around to greet her ex, despite the overwhelming desire to turn and run in the opposite direction.

'Hey, Sophie, you look well. How are you?'

'Good, thank you.' It felt strange looking into his face, so familiar, and yet so unsettling here in the supermarket where she would least expect to bump into him. She collected her bag and moved out of the way, allowing the person behind her to use the till, and Kyle fell in step with her, walking out towards the car park. The scrutiny of his gaze on her profile made her uncomfortable, causing her skin to prickle. She had no idea what to say to this man whose life she had shared for so long. She was tempted to ask about his mum and dad, and his brother, just to break the awkward silence between them, but she didn't want to get embroiled in a conversation, to bring up the past and give him the wrong idea that she might be interested in what he was doing now. In that moment, all she really wanted was to get away, to get home to the peaceful sanctuary of her lovely little cottage.

'Why did you do it, Sophie?'

'What?' She swallowed hard, biting on the inside of her cheek. This was no place to have this kind of conversation. Besides, he would definitely know the reasons why. It was all in the past now. What was the point in bringing up old wounds?

'You left so suddenly without giving me any warning. Walking away from me is one thing, but you walked away from our home, your job, my family without so much as an explanation. It was shit, Sophie, not only having to deal with my own bloody hurt, but having to contend with all the questions from my folks. You could have given them some notice at work. We had to get a temp in.'

Sophie's gaze drifted around the car park, unwilling to face Kyle's questioning expression. Part of her wanted to laugh in derision. Was that his main issue with her leaving? The inconvenience she'd caused to the staffing plan? She suppressed a sigh. She couldn't allow her emotions to get the better of her. Not when she'd come so far. Nor would she let him make her believe that she had acted unreasonably in walking away from the situation. She had done nothing wrong. She'd walked away to save her own peace of mind and sanity.

'I had to leave. Things hadn't been right between us for months. You must have realised that. It could hardly have come as a big surprise to you.'

'It did, Sophie. It bloody destroyed me. I tried contacting you, but you blocked me on every single means of communication. Where did you go? It was almost as though you vanished off the face of the earth. You clearly didn't want me to find you.'

'I thought it was the best way. Look, I'm going to have to get going.' She glanced at her watch, as though she had somewhere else she needed to be. 'Give my regards to your parents, won't you?'

'C'mon, Sophie, don't be like this.' Kyle reached an arm out to her, his gaze imploring her to stay, as she made to walk away. She recoiled from his touch. 'We could go for a drink or something, we need to talk about this properly.'

Sophie's eyes widened and her eyebrows shot up involuntarily.

'I didn't mean like that, Sophs. Give me a break. I've cut right down on my drinking. Just speak to Mum and Dad, they'd tell you. I meant something like a coffee.'

'No, Kyle. I'm sorry. There's nothing to talk about.' She took a deep breath, steadying her emotions. 'I've moved on. Made a new life for myself. You need to do the same.'

He blew out his cheeks, shaking his head, frustration threatening to get the better of him, but Sophie could tell that he was making a conscious effort to remain in control of his emotions, to not fly off the handle as he had done so many other times in the past.

'Have you met someone else, is that it?' he said evenly.

'No!' She shook her head emphatically, annoyed at his assumption. 'There's no one else. I'm at a point in my life where I want to be on my own. I don't wish you any ill will, Kyle, but...' There was no easy or kind way to say what he must surely already know. 'It's over. Now I really must go.' Her patience was running out and she would rather be anywhere than here having this pointless conversation with Kyle.

'Can't we stay in touch, Sophie? Let me have your number at least. I've still got some of your stuff at home. I can drop it off round at yours, just let me know where you are.'

'It's fine. Keep it,' she said, with a shrug of her shoulders, determined this time to get away. She marched towards her car, not looking back, relieved at least that Kyle wasn't following her. She had nothing to feel bad about, but she couldn't help feeling a pang of regret and sadness for everything that they'd lost, the fact that he was still obviously upset. She'd loved him once and her heart wasn't completely made of stone.

During the car journey home, she managed to hold it together, ignoring the thoughts taunting her mind – could she have handled the situation differently? Perhaps she shouldn't have even entertained a conversation with him and simply walked away, but Kyle hadn't really given her the opportunity. Had talking to him simply stirred up old grievances, especially when she'd been at a point when she was moving on in her life, feeling a freedom and an excitement for the future that she hadn't felt in years?

Arriving back at the cottage, she couldn't get through the front door fast enough. With the adrenaline still buzzing around her body and tears threatening to fall, it took all her emotional strength not to succumb to the feelings. Instead, she threw down her coat and bag on the sofa, and went into the kitchen, filling the kettle and switching it on at the wall. Then she took a moment, closing her eyes as she rested against the work-top, taking a few deep breaths to settle her nerves. It was fine. She had it all under her control, or at least she thought she had, until a loud rapping on the door made her jump out of her skin. She startled, looking across at the front door as though someone might come charging through it at any moment.

It couldn't be Kyle, surely? He wouldn't know where to find her and she was certain he hadn't followed her from the supermarket because she'd made sure to check her rear-view mirror on her way out of the car park, wanting to avoid that possibility. There it was again, louder this time, the sound sending a frisson of fear along her body so that she held herself stock-still, certain that whoever it was outside would hear her breathing. She was just giving herself a stern talking to about not being so ridiculous when a familiar voice came wafting through the letter box.

'Come on, Sophie. Open up! I know you're in there!'

Relief flooded through Sophie's body on hearing Greta's familiar voice, and she went rushing across to open the door to her friend.

'Oh, thank goodness it's you!'

That's when the emotion that she'd been suppressing ever since she'd run into Kyle came rushing out in a torrent of release so that she greeted Greta in a flood of tears.

'Who on earth were you expecting it to be?' said Greta, her face a picture of concern.

'Oh, ignore me. I'm just being stupid,' said Sophie, able to laugh now as she wrapped her friend in a hug. 'You arriving has just made every-thing better. Let me make you a cuppa, I've just boiled the kettle.'

Over tea and biscuits, Sophie told Greta about her run-in with Kyle, the way it had made her feel and all the old emotions it had brought to the surface.

'I honestly don't know why I'm crying,' she said, sniffing and mopping up her tears with a sheet of kitchen roll. 'I suppose it was so unexpected, bumping into him like that. It took me completely by surprise and my instinct was to run, but of course I couldn't. And I had all these thoughts rushing through my head of things I could say, and I had to properly bite on my tongue to stop myself from doing so. That would have been a huge mistake. It was just so unsettling. It made me really jittery.' She held out a quivering hand.

'I can imagine,' said Greta, her own hands cupped around her mug of coffee. 'You haven't seen him or spoken to him in all that time and then suddenly, it's like coming face to face with your past.'

'Exactly!' Sophie nodded. 'In a way, it's probably a good thing. Living around here, I was bound to run into him at some point and now it's done and over with.' She held up her hands in a gesture of finality. She shook her head, a shudder running through her body. 'He was so indignant that I'd left him, as though he couldn't understand why I'd done it. As though I was somehow the person in the wrong. He had me thinking *was it me?* Was it not as bad as I thought it was? Should I have stayed and tried harder to work it out with him?'

'Hey. Don't go doubting yourself now. When I think back to how you were when I first met you, so unhappy and lost, and seeing you now, well, it's like looking at a different person. You're so much more confident, happier, settled with so many great plans.' Greta leant across the sofa where they were sitting and squeezed Sophie's wrist. 'Don't let this meeting with Kyle derail you.'

'Yeah, you're right,' said Sophie, grateful for Greta's reassurance. She took a sip from her mug of tea. 'He told me he's cut right down on the booze so that has to be a good thing, at least.'

'And do you believe him?'

Greta was well aware of all the problems Sophie had faced in her relationship.

'I'm not sure. He'd promised to give up on so many occasions before and it never came to anything, or else he would do it for a couple of days and then quickly go back to his old ways. I really hope, for his sake, and his family's, that he has given up drinking. It changed the person he was and not for the better either.'

'Do you think it would have made any difference to the way you felt about him if he had got sober?'

Sophie pondered on that before shaking her head.

'No. I've thought about that a lot, but it got to the point where I couldn't see a way back for us. I saw a side of Kyle that I really didn't like and I would never want to put myself in that situation again. Bumping into him again made me realise that I'd made exactly the right decision in leaving. I have no regrets. This is my home now...' she paused to look around her, '...and I can't tell you how good it feels to have somewhere special of my own.'

'That's the thing, Sophie. You've come so far in the short space of time since I've met you. You've got a new job, found this gorgeous cottage and it's obvious to anyone who knows you how much happier you are these days. I'm so proud of everything you've achieved.'

'Thanks, Greta,' Sophie said, grinning. 'I couldn't have done it without you.'

'Seeing Kyle must have been upsetting, taking you back to a time that was difficult and unhappy for you, but he can't hurt you in the same way any more. You're a different person.'

Sophie exhaled a huge sigh of relief. Just talking it through with Greta had made her feel better. To get all that pent-up emotion out of her system had been cathartic. Her gaze travelled around the cosy living room of the cottage and her overriding feeling was one of gratitude and relief. Greta was right. She had come so far in such a short space of time and she could look to the future with a sense of hope and excitement, something she'd never been able to do all the time she was with Kyle.

'Did I tell you about the stables? It was the first one the other Sunday.'

'Of course, yes, how did it go?'

'It was great. Not as busy, obviously, as the first time I was there, but there was still a really good turnout and it's expected only to get busier for the rest of the season. The people there, the other traders, are really friendly and helpful, and there's just a lovely vibe about the whole place.

I sold a few items and got to hand out some business cards so it was all good.'

'Great, well, I will come along next time. When is it?'

'This Sunday. Did you ever meet Pia?' Greta shook her head. 'She's Jackson's fiancée and is in charge of all the events at Primrose Hall. She ran the open days at the stables last year, but she's handed them over to Tom. He's Jackson's brother, but I've met him a couple of times now and he seems really nice too.'

Sophie's eyes lit up as she spoke and her earlier upset was quickly forgotten. All she needed to do was to consign Kyle very squarely to the past and concentrate firmly on the future.

12

'Well, we couldn't have picked a worse day for it.'

Katy had laid out all of her items on the table and display stand in her unit at the stables. There were personalised notepads, greetings cards, stationery sets and framed prints, all adorned with her quirky drawings of animals, including squirrels, foxes and hens. As she took a step backwards to give one final check of the display, she couldn't help feeling proud at the sight of all her work gathered in one place. Sometimes she wondered if she was wasting her time, if her items didn't have the artistic and commercial merit she hoped they had, but when she viewed them all together like that, it struck her just how much she had achieved.

'Do you know, it might work in our favour,' Tom said, peering out of the full-height glazed door to watch the rain in its relentlessness as it pounded the paths outside. 'All those people who were going to visit the woods today but have been put off by the bad weather might hopefully come and see us instead. Fingers crossed.'

Katy didn't really mind what the weather was doing out there. For her, coming to the stables was a much-needed escape from her domestic responsibilities at home. Obviously, selling her products was the main aim, but she enjoyed mixing with the other traders and meeting her customers, just as much. Here she could be herself, Katy Richardson, not mum to Rosie and Pip, or wife to Brad, but, as daft as it might sound, a person in her own right. As much as she adored her family, she some- times felt as though she might drown from the drudgery that came with being stuck at home with the children for most of the week, with the main topic of conversation being *Peppa Pig*. At the moment, the stables were her only outlet. She'd considered going back to work on a part-time basis but she quickly discovered, with the cost of childcare, it wouldn't be worthwhile so she and Brad had made the decision for Katy to stay at home until the children went to school. Everyone reassured her that these demanding years would pass in a trice and she would look back on them fondly, and she was certain that she would. It didn't stop her from relishing those opportunities when she could snatch a break from the family, though.

'Looks like the coffee van is open for business,' said Mike, who had the unit next to Katy's. 'I might do a drinks run before the rush.' He glanced at his watch. 'Who wants one?'

There was a collective show of hands and Tom offered to go with Mike to help with the order, which included a few requests for bacon and sausage butties as well. There was a buzz of excitement and anticipation wafting around the old oak beams of the stables as the traders put the finishing touches to their displays.

'Hey, Sophie, I think these are for you. I hope that's right.' A little while later, the guys were back, with a tray of drinks. Tom handed her a cappuccino and a bacon roll in a paper bag, the enticing aromas wafting in the air.

Sophie peered inside, her face lighting up.

'Perfect. Thank you. How are you?' she asked, looking up into his eyes, surprised by her own strong reaction to seeing Tom.

'Yeah, great. It's good to see you again,' he said, matching her own thoughts. 'How have you been?'

'Busy, as hopefully you can see.' She laughed, indicating the jewellery stands behind her, which displayed the new pieces she'd been work- ing on.

'It's looking great,' he said, nodding, and she couldn't help noticing the genuine tone to his voice.

It was one of the things she really appreciated about being a part of the community at the stables. Everyone was so supportive of each other, showing a real interest in the breadth and artistic talent of their peers. It was reassuring to be able to swap stories and ideas, or even to just have a grumble at the frustrations of working alone, creatively, on a tricky item, and then knowing the satisfaction of overcoming those obstacles to complete whatever they were working on; a piece of jewellery, a print, or wooden bowl. Sophie felt as though she was among friends who understood her.

'Let me run an idea past you,' said Tom. 'A couple of the others have been asked by visitors how they got started, and the processes behind making the products. I was talking to Josh about running some workshops where people can have a go themselves at the different skills used here. We're fortunate that we have all this expertise and talent, it seems a shame not to share it with others who might be interested.'

'Sure. Although I'm not sure if I'd be qualified to teach anyone,' Sophie said. 'Everything I've learned has been through books and YouTube videos. I don't know all the correct terminology or the right way of doing things. I've just muddled my way through.'

'Well, that's exactly what I think might be interesting to visitors. I'm not suggesting these sessions will be a masterclass in silversmithing, or wood turning, or drawing, but more a chance for visitors and customers to see how the products are brought to life from their original designs. We would probably need to sit down as a team and think about the best way of presenting any sessions. It might be that we do it on the Sundays and use the barn to run hourly or two-hourly periods so that people can then have a wander around the units afterwards, hopefully in the mood for shopping.'

'Sounds great.' Sophie liked Tom's enthusiasm and vision. It was something he shared with his brother and it was definitely a quality she found attractive. If left to her own devices, she would probably not put herself forward for anything like that, but Tom made everything sound possible and, more importantly, enjoyable. Besides, she was all about stepping out of her comfort zone these days.

'I'll run it past Pia, see what she thinks and then we can set the wheels

in motion. Ah, talk of the devil. Her ears must have been burning.'
Sophie followed Tom's gaze out of the window and she saw Pia coming
across, holding a folder on top of her head to provide some shelter from
the driving rain.

'Yuk, it's dreadful out there.' Pia shook herself down, littering rain-
drops around her. 'How is everyone?' she said with a big smile. 'I thought
I'd pop over with these posters for the classic car show. I'll stick up a
couple on the beams, but there are also some flyers here that I'll leave on
the table for anyone who's interested. So just a reminder that if you get
the opportunity to mention it then please do.'

'It should be a lot of fun. I'm looking forward to it,' said Sophie.

'Well, it will mean that you get a whole raft of visitors so it should be
good for spreading the word and hopefully finding some new customers.
Make sure you all have your business cards at the ready,' Pia said,
grinning.

'And we can arrange it so that we cover each other's units so that we
all get the chance to have a look around the show,' said Tom. 'Do you
have a moment?' he asked, turning towards Pia. 'There was something I
wanted to chat to you about.'

Sophie gave some last-minute tweaks to her display. Not that she
needed to, just that it calmed her nerves to rearrange her items, until she
gave herself a stern talking to and stepped away, resolving not to touch
them again. She picked up one of Pia's flyers instead, while she had one
ear on Tom and Pia's conversation as they spoke about the possible workshops. Judging by Pia's warm and enthusiastic reception, it looked as
though she thought it was a great idea too.

'Hang on a minute!' Pia's attention was taken by the beeping of her
phone and she snatched it out of her jeans pocket. 'Oh, my God!' Her
hand flew to her head. 'I'm sorry, but I'm going to have to go. Great idea,
though, Tom. Go ahead and make it happen,' she said, entirely distracted
now, as she tapped something into her phone.

'Is everything okay?' Tom ventured.

'Oh, yes, it's just that my goddaughter is on her way. I have to go.'

'Yep, you go. No problem,' said Tom. 'Where's she coming from?'

Pia, with one foot already out of the door, turned round, a big smile on her face.

'Abbey! My friend. She's in labour, at the hospital, and she wants me there. It's so exciting. She's going to have a baby!' she added, in case anyone might be in any doubt as to what she actually meant. 'Wish us luck!'

'Is she?' squealed Katy from the other end of the stable building. She was a good friend of Abbey's too and the news had her dashing along the walkway.

'Yes, tell your mum, won't you?' Pia said with a big grin. 'And I'll let you know as soon as there's any news.'

'Good luck! All the best to your friend!' A chorus of greetings rang out from the traders as Pia dashed out the door and ran across to the hall, totally unconcerned this time by the pounding rain.

13

After stumbling through the back door to the hall in her haste, telling Ivy, the housekeeper, what was happening, and firing off a quick text to Jackson, who was out on his bike again, Pia jumped in her car and started on the journey to the hospital, a fifteen-minute journey away. She deliberately drove slowly and carefully, aware that her mind was a kaleidoscope of butterflies as her emotions ran riot around her body.

Abbey was Pia's oldest and closest friend from school and they'd seen each other through so many good and bad times over the years; Abbey losing her mum, Pia giving up her place at uni to look after her poorly parents, taking on the role of carer for several years, followed by the sad loss of them both. Then Abbey being stuck in a miserable relationship for far too long before finding out that her fiancé, who she was soon to marry, had been cheating behind her back. Pia shook her head as she drove, hardly believing everything they'd been through together. Within weeks of breaking up with her ex, Abbey had met Sam and they quickly fell in love and moved in together, and Pia, forced to move out of the family home following the death of her mother, had found a job and a happiness at Primrose Hall that she could never have anticipated. Life had improved immeasurably for them both since those earlier dark days.

Now with Abbey and Sam's baby about to make her entrance into the world, this had to be the most exciting and special event they would share together, a new stage in their lives, and Pia simply couldn't wait.

She'd been delighted when Abbey had asked her to be godmother to her unborn daughter, and then only recently, with the big day approaching, Abbey had confided how nervous she was about giving birth, and asked if Pia wouldn't mind being there, if they needed her, along with Sam. Pia had agreed immediately, without hesitation, not really believing they would call on her, but now they had and she was battling so many conflicting emotions. She would do anything for Abbey, but she could never admit to her friend that the prospect of attending the birth filled her with trepidation. She had no idea what to expect or how she would react being in that situation. She'd never been very good at the sight of blood, but she couldn't let her fears get the better of her. She would be there in the capacity of deputy hand-holder and support-giver. With her hands gripping onto the steering wheel, she smiled. This had all the makings of a very good day. Even the driving rain had stopped and the sun had broken through the clouds.

Pulling into the car park, she managed to snag a place near to the payment machine and hurried across to the maternity wing, her entire body filled with excitement and nerves. Getting past the receptionist and through the various security doors took far too long, but finally Pia found the delivery room. She knocked tentatively on the door and was relieved to hear Sam's familiar voice beckoning her inside.

'Pia!' Abbey's face lit up at seeing her and Sam's relief was almost palpable, although Abbey's smile was quickly replaced by an anguished flinch across her features as a wave of pain clearly overcame her.

'We've been waiting for you to arrive before we properly got going,' said Sam, with a grin. 'I think we can get this party started now, don't you reckon, Abbey?'

'What do you think I've been doing all this time?' she grumbled to Sam. 'The pains started in the early hours of the morning, and we held off coming into hospital as long as we could, but when my waters broke we were told to come in.' Abbey wiped the hair back from her face and gritted her teeth as another pain racked her body.

'I'm so pleased to see you,' sighed Abbey, with a weary smile when she caught her breath. 'Honestly, I was about to murder Sam. Tell me, what has he got to be so cheerful about? When it's his fault that I'm going through all this pain! Come here,' she said, reaching out a hand to Pia and clutching her fingers so tightly that there could be no escape, not that Pia had any intention of going anywhere. Sam though looked as though he could do with some fresh air and, when Pia suggested that he go and fetch some coffees, he jumped at the chance to escape the emotional intensity within that hospital room.

'Thanks so much for being here, Pia,' said Abbey once Sam had left. 'I'm not sure I could get through this without you.'

It was Pia's privilege and those long hours spent in the delivery room with Abbey and Sam, sharing those intensely private and intimate moments, would be imprinted in her memories forever. When little Willow Elizabeth Finnegan finally made her entrance into the world with a hearty cry and a head of black hair, all the struggle, pain and hard work was forgotten in an instant, replaced with tears of joy and an over-whelming love and happiness that permeated the entire room.

With another round of hugs and kisses, Pia wiped away her tears and said her goodbyes, wanting to give the new parents this special time alone together to get to know their daughter. She promised to pop in just as soon as they got home. Bill, Abbey's father, was on his way to meet his new grandchild along with Lizzie, his partner and good friend to Abbey and Sam.

Walking outside the doors of the hospital, Pia took a deep breath, almost unable to believe that the world was still turning as normal. She'd almost expected the traffic to have stopped, for there to be a fanfare, a moment of recognition of the amazing event she'd just witnessed. People went about their business as usual, and Pia felt that she wanted to tell everyone that she came across what had just happened in her world, how it had moved her and how everything that she knew had been shifted inexorably. She suspected she had a permanent grin on her face, judging by some of the strange looks she was receiving, but she didn't care, she wanted to spread the joy she was feeling. In something of a daze, she headed toward the car park, pulling out her mobile phone to check her messages, jumping back to avoid an ambulance, with its blue lights flashing and its siren wailing, watching as it turned into the accident and emergency department. A reminder that not everyone was having such a good day.

In the car, she quickly sent a flurry of texts and she looked at the text received from Jackson much earlier in the day.

Hey, that's exciting! Send Abbey and Sam my love and good luck. I should be home about 5.00 ish. Much love, J xx

Seeing Jackson's name in her inbox always made her heart lift, but especially so today. She pressed on the button to call him, but it went straight to voicemail so she dashed off a text.

Little Willow Elizabeth arrived at 4.06 p.m. weighing 3.5kg! She's beautiful *heart emoji* Both mum and baby are doing brilliantly, and Sam is a very proud dad! Can't wait to see you. Love xxx

Pia glanced at her watch, noticing that it was almost 6 p.m. The day had disappeared and she'd given barely any thought to what had been going on outside the walls of the hospital. The stables would be closed by now and she wondered how busy it had been. She would speak to Tom later for an update. Jackson would be home by now and she was looking forward to catching up over a glass of wine and some supper. The thought made her realise just how hungry she was and her appetite stirred even more knowing that Jackson would be in the kitchen, having poured himself a beer, and would be making a start on the dinner. There were a couple of steaks in the fridge and some salmon fillets. What would he plump for, she wondered, although either of those choices would be fine by her. She was just grateful knowing that she was going home to Jackson who would be in his element, in his pinny, pottering about the kitchen, cooking up something delicious. *Home!* A smile spread across her lips. Would she ever get used to the fact that Primrose Hall, the gorgeous manor house, was actually her home now? She couldn't imagine a time when she would. It still took her breath away every time she drove through the gates to the hall and along the long driveway, seeing the magnificence of the house coming into view.

Parking the car in her usual spot, Pia went running round to the kitchen door, barely able to wait to see Jackson again to tell him all the news, but disappointment caught in her chest as soon as she fell through the door. The kitchen was an oasis of peace and calm. There was no evidence of Jackson having been there recently or any warm cooking smells to welcome her home. Bertie and Teddy were waiting with their usual effusive greeting, their tails wagging furiously as they danced around her legs in their demands for attention. Half-heartedly she bent down to give them each a friendly rub, but she couldn't ignore the swirl of irritation that ran around her body. Where was Jackson? Perhaps he'd headed straight for the office to make some calls or to deal with an urgent email, but it seemed unlikely on a Sunday.

'Where's your daddy?' she asked the dogs, and she was rewarded with some cute head tilts as they padded along after her towards the office, but as she suspected there was no sign of Jackson there either. She peered out of the window over at the garage block, wondering if he was tinkering with his bike, but all the doors were closed tight.

'Oh, Jackson!' she sighed. There was so much she wanted to tell him, so many photos she wanted to show him, but most of all her arms felt empty where she wanted to hug him. It had been such an emotionally intense day and she really needed a cuddle from Jackson. *Where the hell was he?*

She pulled out her phone and called him, but like before, it went straight to his answering service. An odd sensation trickled along her spine, irritation mingled with fear. She was just considering what she might do next when she heard a movement from the kitchen.

'Thank goodness!' she said aloud, her heart lifting in relief as she went dashing back along the corridor to see him, the dogs following her every move, picking up on her excited anticipation.

'There you are!' No sooner had the words left her mouth than she realised her mistake when she ran straight into Mateo.

'Oh!' She couldn't hide her disappointment. 'I thought you were Jackson. Have you seen him at all?'

'No, he has not been back.' Mateo shook his head. 'I not see him this afternoon.'

Pia forced a smile for Mateo's benefit, but inside her stomach folded. She'd been brimming with excitement and couldn't wait to see Jackson so that she could share with him the wonder of everything she had witnessed and experienced earlier. People had babies every day, yet it was something Pia had never really given much thought to before, and now she couldn't get out of her head just what a miracle it was to bring a new life into the world.

'I wonder where he is then?' she said, mainly for her own benefit.

'I don't know.' Mateo shrugged, lifting his hands to the air, as if it was one of life's eternal mysteries, which at that particular moment it seemed to be. 'You must ring him.'

'I have done. Several times now, but he's not picking up.' She sighed heavily, going across to pick up the kettle and filling it with water at the sink. She pulled out two mugs and popped a teabag in each before turning sharply to face Mateo.

'Do you think he's all right?' Pia was unable to hide her fear now and she looked to Mateo for reassurance. 'He should have been home ages ago and he's out on that stupid bike of his. The rain was torrential earlier, the roads are probably treacherous.'

'It is okay. It no rain no more. Jackson will be home soon.'

'Yeah, you're right. I always worry when he's out on that bike.' She shrugged away a cold shiver that ran down her spine. 'He went to a motorcycle rally. He's obviously got caught up with one of his pals and they'll be chatting about bikes and all things engine-related. They'll be making plans for the car show next week, I bet. He's really pumped for it and as much as I try to show an interest in all the old vehicles, I must admit my eyes glaze over when he goes into all the detail. I don't know a crankshaft from a carburettor and all I can express an opinion on is the colour of a car. Jackson knows that he can't have a sensible conversation with me on the subject.'

Pia gave a rueful chuckle as she poured milk into the mugs and then handed one to Mateo. They sat down together at the kitchen table and Pia's gaze drifted outside, hoping to catch a glimpse of Jackson's bike returning down the drive. The light was beginning to fade outside, but the beauty of the grounds was still visible through the window. The ornamental trees in shades of magenta and blue were eye-catching and the flowerbeds were filled with lupins, roses and ravishing peonies that smelled every bit as good as they looked. Mateo took great pride in his work and made sure the gardens looked their best whatever the time of year. Next weekend the grounds would be brimming with visitors, intent on enjoying the spectacle of the car show, but Pia knew that some people came just to wander around the gardens and soak up the atmosphere and scenery of Primrose Hall.

'Did I tell you my friend Abbey had her baby today? I was with her at the hospital and it was probably the most amazing experience of my life.'

'It is always a miracle. A new baby.'

'Oh, it really is, Mateo. I had no idea,' she said, laughing.

Mateo listened intently as Pia gave a full-blown account of the birth, although she did spare him the gorier details. Instead she focused on the tide of emotions that had filled the hospital room and the happiness and relief when little Willow finally made her appearance. Pia showed Mateo the photos she'd captured of the baby wrapped in a blanket, of Abbey flushed with happiness and pride, cradling Willow, and the first one of all the new family together.

'It is wonderful,' Mateo agreed, after he had made encouraging sounds at all the images on Pia's phone. He pushed back his chair and took his empty mug over to the sink. 'I am very happy for you and your friends. Now I must go and have a shower. Please do not worry. Mr Jackson, he will be home soon.'

'I hope so,' said Pia quietly, a fear taking hold of her again, as she watched Mateo head to his living quarters. She hoped she hadn't bored him to pieces about her friends' good news. It had been a welcome distraction talking to Mateo, but she couldn't rid herself of the cold sense of dread that was creeping around her body.

It seemed like hours, but was probably much less than that, when finally her phone lit up with Jackson's name. She almost wept with relief as she snatched it up from the table.

'There you are!' she said, her voice high with excitement at finally tracking him down. 'I was beginning to get worried.'

'Hello, am I speaking to Pia Temple, please?' an unfamiliar voice asked her.

'Yes?' she said hesitantly as a flurry of thoughts ran through Pia's head. Why wasn't Jackson on the end of the phone? And who was this person exactly? 'Where's Jackson?' she blurted.

'Hello, Pia. My name is Amit Singh. I'm a doctor in the A&E department at Royal Parkway Hospital.' Pia heard the words but they jumbled together in a mess as she tried to make sense of what they could possibly mean. 'Jackson has been involved in a road traffic accident and has come off his bike. He was brought in by ambulance.'

'Oh, God!'

'We've managed to stabilise him, but he's undergoing a number of tests at the moment. It looks as though he's suffered some significant injuries, but we won't know the full extent until we've finished our investigations. He's asking to see you.'

It was as though Pia's world had stopped spinning in that moment. How could this have possibly happened? Fear and apprehension ran riot around her body. She played over the doctor's words in her head. What did they even mean? Although if Jackson was asking to see her then that had to be a good thing. *He was alive!* That was the main thing. Anything else they could cope with.

'Oh, God! Yes, of course. He will be all right, though?'

Avoiding answering her question, the doctor continued. 'I understand this is a big shock so it's probably sensible if there's someone there who can drive you in. Would that be possible?'

'What? Yes, of course.' She looked around her, trying to get her thoughts in order. Mateo could take her in the van. 'I'll be there straight away.'

Putting down the phone, her heart thumping in her chest, she gave a heartfelt call.

'Mateo!'

Then she grabbed her bag and made plans to return to the hospital that had earlier been the setting of so much happiness and joy. Now, with a sense of dread in the pit of her stomach, she steeled herself for what might be waiting for her this time when she reached the A&E department.

14

It certainly hadn't been planned that way, but Sophie couldn't help smiling at finding herself alone again with Tom in the snug bar of the Three Feathers. A small group of the crafters from the stables had decided, after packing away their wares, that they would pop into the pub in Wishwell, on their way home, for a quick drink to celebrate another successful Sunday's trading. There had been a steady flow of visitors during the day and Sophie was pleased with the number of items she had sold. A happy atmosphere had permeated amongst the traders as they chatted about next week's additional opening of the stables to coincide with the car show.

In the short space of time that she'd come to know the other crafters, Sophie had been heartened by how they'd immediately welcomed her into the fold and how she now looked forward to seeing them and catching up with all their news. Pia had been right when she'd described the group as one big happy family.

When they'd first arrived at the pub, they'd nabbed a table in the walled beer garden and had enjoyed soaking up the last of the warmth of the day, but as people started to make moves to leave, Katy had suggested moving inside as the temperature dipped with the light fading away.

Indoors, Sophie looked up at the chalkboard showing today's specials.

She'd had a quick bowl of cereal for breakfast and then a ham and cheese panini from the vintage refreshments van at the stables. Now, as the aromas of home-cooking met her nostrils in the warm and cosy bar, she realised how hungry she was.

'Do you know, I might have a roast dinner,' she said, more for her own benefit than for anyone else's, tempted as she was by the description of the beef with all the trimmings. *Topside of Beef. Fluffy roast potatoes. Seasonal vegetables and thick rich gravy.* Her mouth watered at the thought.

Katy nodded keenly.

'Honestly, they look and smell delicious. I saw a couple of plates go past and the puddings were huge. I would be tempted myself, but hopefully Brad has got the dinner on at home and I know the kids will be waiting to see me. See you next week!'

With a wave, Katy breezed out the front door and Sophie was left with Tom, whose attention was also distracted by the menu board. Not that Sophie had been hinting in any way. She hoped he didn't feel obliged to choose something just because she'd mooted the idea. The Three Feathers was the kind of place where you could sit down and eat a meal by yourself without feeling self-conscious, and on the few occasions she'd previously visited, the landlord Malc and his wife Jan had always made a point of saying hello and asking how she'd been settling into the village. She'd also got to know some of the other bar staff, who were equally as friendly and welcoming. She would be more than happy to sit there and eat her dinner alone.

'I'm going to join you,' said Tom, his face lighting up.

'Well, that would be nice, but don't feel as though you have to.'

'No, absolutely not. I'm starving. That's if you don't mind me joining you for dinner, of course?' His eyes flashed a questioning look across at her.

'Not at all. It's always nicer to share a meal with a friend, and a roast, for me, is a proper treat. I love them, but it's not really something you cook for yourself, is it?'

'Exactly! If I'm lucky, I sometimes get invited to the hall for Sunday lunch. Pia and Jackson are great hosts and Jackson is a fabulous cook.'

'I can imagine, especially if it's anything like Christmas lunch was.'

With their meals ordered and their drinks refreshed, Tom sat down on the cushioned pew beside Sophie and turned to her, his gaze perusing her face.

'So how have you been?'

Sophie's eyes caught on Tom's, and she saw and heard the genuine interest in his question. They had been chatting on and off throughout the day, exchanging pleasantries, laughing, but now she could tell that he was asking something deeper, that he really wanted to know how she'd been actually doing.

'Good,' she nodded. 'Work's great, a lot less stressful than my previous job. I get on well with everyone, it pays the bills and I like the way that I can walk away at the end of the day and forget about it. Maybe that's not really the attitude, but to be honest, I'm much happier when I'm working on my own projects at home. Like the jewellery. I've also started crocheting in my spare time.' She gave a rueful laugh. 'Not that I have much of that, but I was talking to Maddie the other week, admiring her blankets, and she gave me a quick lesson in how to get started. She showed me how to cast on and how to form the basic stitches, and while I didn't have a clue at first, she also pointed me in the direction of some online tutorials so I've been spending my evenings getting to grips with that.'

She paused, hearing her voice wittering on about crochet stitches. What must Tom think? It was hardly the most scintillating conversation. Probably the sort of chatter he might expect if he took his granny out for tea. Although Tom was far too polite to show any hint of boredom. Instead, it was as though he was hanging on to her every word as she spoke, holding her gaze and smiling interestedly. That was something she'd discovered about him on that very first occasion she'd met him over Christmas lunch at the hall. Although at the time she'd put her ease and candour down to the very quaffable free-flowing wine and the fact that she thought she was never likely to run to into the good-looking stranger again. She'd since discovered that he was always that easy to talk to, so much so that it was easy to forget that really they didn't know each other as well as their easy relationship might suggest. What was it about him, she wondered, that made her feel so comfortable in his company? She gave herself an imperceptible shrug to shake away that thought and instead switched her focus onto him.

'What about your job... jobs?' she added with a smile. 'Are you still enjoying what you're doing at the moment?'

Tom shrugged. 'Yeah, I guess but I have been giving *my future career...*' – he loaded those words with some light-hearted intent – '...some serious thought. Like you, I enjoy the work and it's not too demanding or stressful, and that was just what I needed when everything blew up last year, but now I'm wondering if I shouldn't consider a better long-term career. What I'm doing at the moment, it's not what you would call a proper job. I'm definitely Jack-of-all-trades and... well, you know the rest.' His chocolate-brown eyes shone with humility. 'You know, I look at Jackson and Pia, and the wonderful set-up they have up at the hall and it makes me look at what I've achieved in my life and realise it's sadly lacking...'

'Don't say that! You can't compare yourself with Jackson even if he is your brother.' Certainly the physical similarities between the pair were hard to deny. They shared a tall and broad physique, and had the same sweep of thick hair, but it was their mannerisms that singled them out as being related. It was something about the way in which they held their head, the jut of their jawline and the way they scrunched up their eyes when deep in thought that highlighted the familial connection.

'No, I realise that and I try not to, but it has made me consider what I want for my future. I'm living alone in a small one-bedroomed bachelor pad and I'm not certain I'd still want to be doing that in five years or even one year's time. I'd not want to go back to my old career, that's for sure, but I probably need to find something that offers a more stable future. My savings won't last forever and I'd probably want to buy another house at some point, as well.'

Sophie nodded, remembering that Tom had told her how, when he'd walked away from his relationship with his ex, he'd signed over his share of the house to her, which had been a lovely and honourable thing to do, although Sophie suspected it was driven from guilt on Tom's part. Now, he picked up his beer glass and took a glug of ale before continuing.

'From what Dad and Ronnie have told me, Jackson is a changed man ever since Pia entered his life and to see them so happy, working together, with their family and animals around them has given me a different perspective on what's important in life. I think I'm in a better place now, having found my family and come to terms with what happened with my mum and dad, to put down some roots of my own. If that makes sense?'

'It does. Definitely.'

It wasn't the first time that she'd noticed the similarities between their lives. Maybe it was fate that had brought them together as friends to help support each other out of those difficult times. Sophie knew all about starting over. After the trauma and upset of extracting herself from a situation that had made her desperately unhappy, she was now in a good place, energised and positive about the changes she'd made for herself.

'Well, I hope you won't be leaving the stables anytime soon. You're doing a great job at managing the open days. I'm sure I speak for all the traders when I say we'd be lost without you.' She wouldn't admit that in such a short space of time she'd come to look forward to those times when she knew she would be seeing him again.

Tom looked up from his beer, his gaze snagging on Sophie's, and a smile spread across his lips.

'Thanks, Sophie, that means a lot. And rest assured, I'll keep my Sundays free to make sure I can still get along to the stables, whatever else I might be doing.'

With their meals delivered to the table, they concentrated on the delicious feast in front of them. With tender beef, roast potatoes, carrots, spring greens, and cauliflower cheese piled high on their plates, along with the biggest Yorkshire puddings Sophie had ever set eyes on, all covered with a delicious rich gravy, she didn't take any time in getting stuck in.

'This is great, just what I needed,' she said, looking up and across at Tom, who bit back a smile and leant across the table with his napkin to wipe away some gravy that Sophie could feel clinging to her chin. 'Ooh, sorry,' she said, laughing, 'what am I like?'

'Don't apologise on my account. I'll probably be doing the same any moment now, and it's always good to see someone enjoying their food.'

There it was again, that sense of familiarity. She didn't need to put on any airs and graces with Tom and didn't feel any sense of self-consciousness tucking into her dinner with gusto. It was as though Tom had accepted Sophie for who she was right from the start and she didn't need to pretend to be someone she wasn't, which she found entirely refreshing.

Finishing their meals, they both sat back in their seats, fully sated, declaring that they couldn't possibly eat another thing. That was until the friendly young waitress arrived to clear their plates and offered to show them the pudding menus. After some prevarication, Tom said, 'Well, it will do us no harm to look. See what we might be missing.'

That was the deed done. After they'd perused the menu, Tom had opted for a sticky toffee pudding and Sophie, only to keep Tom company, had chosen the crème brûlée.

'I won't need to eat for an entire week,' said Sophie when she had managed to clear her plate. 'Not that I regret a single mouthful for a moment.'

'Me neither,' said Tom, with a smile. 'This has been great. I've really enjoyed myself,' he said, as though it was something of a revelation to him.

Sophie glanced at her watch as she became aware of the tiredness slowly seeping around her body. It had been a long day and this had been the perfect way to finish it, but she needed to make a move to go home. She still had some chores to do to get ready for work tomorrow so she would get back to the cottage, sort out her clothes for the next day, read a chapter of her book and then head to bed. Although if she would be able to easily fall asleep, she didn't know. She suspected she might be far too overstimulated to drop off, knowing her mind would be replaying every single moment and interaction of the day. Now, she stretched her arms high above her head and made her excuses to Tom as she popped to the loo, stopping, on the way, to have a chat with Rhi, who was working behind the bar. She'd only recently got to know Rhi. Pia had introduced her one day up at the stables, and ever since Rhi had always made a point of talking to Sophie whenever they bumped into each other. It was another reason why Sophie felt so comfortable coming to the Three Feathers, everyone really was that friendly.

On her way back to the table, with a smile on her face, Sophie stopped, hearing her name called. She didn't give it a moment's thought, suspecting it would be Malc or one of the locals asking after her. She turned round, still smiling, her heart dropping when she realised it wasn't a friendly regular after all, but the last person she wanted to run into.

'Ah, so this is where you've been hiding?'

'Kyle!' Somehow she managed to plaster on a tight smile in an attempt to conceal her devastation at seeing him in what had been, up to that moment, a safe haven. Now her old reality and all the bad feelings associated with it came rushing in around her. 'Do you live around here then?' he asked.

A shiver ran up her spine. She was under no obligation to tell Kyle where she was living now, so why did she feel so guilty about keeping it from him? It was easy to fall back into old patterns of behaviour, but she shook herself down and told herself that she wouldn't allow Kyle to spoil what had been a lovely day so far.

'Not really, no,' she lied. 'I was just meeting a friend. I ought to get back.'

She turned her back on him, not believing her bad luck. She hadn't run into him for months, and had barely given him a second thought, and now in the space of a few weeks she'd bumped into him twice. She walked with determination back to the table and to the safety of Tom's company, knowing she would feel reassured just by seeing his friendly face, but she noticed that he was distracted, poring over his phone, which was probably just as well. She was in no mood for making awkward introductions.

'I suppose we ought to make a move,' she said brightly to Tom.

She just hoped that... But any hope that Kyle might not have followed her was dashed just as she returned to the table and she felt Kyle's presence hovering over her shoulder. At that moment, Tom looked up, his gaze momentarily sweeping from Sophie to Kyle, before quickly returning to his phone. What was suddenly so important to him that he couldn't pick up on the situation currently unfolding in front of him?

'Ah, I get it now,' said Kyle, whose attention was fixed firmly on Sophie. 'This is why you've been blocking my calls. You have a new boyfriend. Well, aren't you going to introduce me?'

Sophie knew Kyle well enough to realise that the expansive grin on his face was entirely unnatural. Her stomach churned and a heat rose in her cheeks. She was mortified, noticing how their interaction was creating a few curious stares from some of the other customers.

'Kyle, don't do this. This is a friend of mine, not my boyfriend. Not that it's any business of yours.' She dropped her voice. 'And you're embarrassing me.'

Tom looked up, snapping closed his phone and stood up.

'I have to go. I'll leave you with... your friend, if that's okay.' Sophie looked at Tom, aghast. Was he annoyed or embarrassed that Kyle had turned up? Certainly, he looked uncomfortable and distracted. As though he couldn't wait to get away.

'Well, we were just leaving anyway, weren't we?'

'Sorry, Sophie. I need to go. I'll give you a call.'

With that, Tom was halfway out of the door, leaving Sophie deflated and confused, and worst of all, having to face Kyle, who had an unbecoming smirk on his face.

'Clearly not your boyfriend then. Still, not a very gentlemanly way to treat you, if you want my honest opinion. Mind you, his loss is my gain. What you having to drink, Sophs?'

It was the casual use of the name that he had always used for her, so intimate and personal, which had once made her beam with pleasure, but now only caused her skin to grow cold.

'Just leave it, Kyle. Besides, I'm going home.'

'One drink. It won't hurt.' He held up his pint glass. 'I'm on the lime and soda, I promise you. Come on, Sophs, we need to talk. Don't you think?'

'No, I really don't!'

She scooped up her handbag and turned to leave, bumping straight into Tom, who had just come rushing in back through the front door.

'Sorry! I forgot something.' He placed his hands on her arms, looking into her eyes. 'Are you all right?' he asked, his tone full of concern as his gaze drifted across to Kyle.

'Yes, I'm fine,' she said, hoping he hadn't heard the quiver in her voice. 'I was just leaving.'

'I know, you're coming with me.' He took her by the hand and led her outside to his car, away, hopefully, from Kyle's prying eyes.

'Look, I am so sorry about that,' Tom said, when they were outside. 'I didn't realise. That was your ex, right? It only occurred to me as I climbed into the car. I had a text from Pia and my mind was somewhere else entirely. Apparently Jackson's been involved in an accident and she's rushed down to the hospital to be with him. I need to get down there too.'

Sophie gasped, her concerns about Kyle immediately forgotten.

'Is he okay?'

Tom grimaced.

'Not sure. Sounds as though he could be in a pretty bad way to be honest with you.' Tom pulled his lips tight, shaking his head. 'Look, are you sure you're okay?' he said, gesturing to the pub. 'I should never have left you in the lurch like that. He wasn't giving you a hard time, was he?'

'Oh, my God, don't worry. Kyle just wanted to talk. I understand perfectly.' Well, she did now. It explained why Tom had been in such a hurry to leave. 'Do you want me to come with you?'

'No, I'm not sure how long I'll be down there for, or what to expect, but I'll let you know how Jackson is once I've found out a few more details. Let me drop you off at home first,' he offered. 'I'll be driving past your place.'

Sophie looked over her shoulder. There was no sign of Kyle, but she really didn't want him knowing where she was living.

'If you're sure it's not a problem?'

'Absolutely not. It would make me feel better too.' He leant forward and kissed her gently on the cheek, wrapping his arms around her, a gesture from one friend to another, but to Sophie it felt wholly intimate and made her body react in a way she could never have expected. Most of all, she felt a surge of sympathy and concern for Tom, knowing how worried he would be about his brother.

'Send my love to Pia and Jackson, won't you?' she said, climbing out of the car a few minutes later. 'I'll be keeping everything crossed for them both.'

15

Pia held her breath walking into the hospital bay in the emergency department, knowing that she had to hold herself together, more for Jackson's benefit than her own. Still, nothing could have prepared her for the sight waiting for her as the curtain around Jackson's bed was pulled back by a nurse. Pia visibly gasped, barely recognising the man she loved beneath the plethora of tubes and machines he was attached to. He was flat on his back with a neck brace on, a bandage around his head, and what could be seen of his hair beneath was caked with blood. The remnants of blood could be seen around his eyes and face too.

'Oh, Jackson!' Her hand flew to her chest as she felt an overwhelming surge of love, seeing him lying there all battered and bruised. She leant down tentatively, hardly daring to touch him in case she caused any more damage. She kissed him gently on his forehead. 'Hey, Jackson? Are you all right?'

It was a stupid question, she knew. He looked broken, shattered, but she was hugely relieved when one of his eyes opened to look at her, his face contorting in pain as he forced a smile.

'I'm dandy,' he said, through a grimace. 'Alive, that's the main thing.'

'Yes! And thank God for that,' she said, her gaze running the length of his body, taking in what was left of his black leathers, which had been cut from his body to reveal his messed-up legs. An image of him from earlier that day popped into her head. He'd been on his way out of the hall, heading for the back door of the kitchen. He turned to look at her with one hand on the door handle, his dark hair curling on his collar and a big grin on his face. She thought how handsome he looked in his motorcycle gear. 'Be careful!' she'd called after him, the reminder now making her stomach churn.

'Look,' she urged him now. 'All of this can be sorted. Please don't worry, Jackson, you're in absolutely the right place and you're going to be fine, I know it.'

Jackson sucked on his lips and gave a nod of his head. Of course, Pia knew no such thing, and she suspected neither did Jackson. She was almost too frightened to know the extent of his injuries. Her imagination had already provided the worst-case scenarios.

'What have the doctors said?' she ventured.

'Not a lot. I've had some scans and X-rays so we're just waiting on the results of those.'

Pia took hold of Jackson's hand and very gently ran a finger along his jawline with her other hand.

'Are you in a lot of pain?'

'Yep. Although they've pumped me full of painkillers so I'm hoping they might kick in soon.'

Pia's heart squeezed at seeing how uncomfortable he was. He was putting on a brave face for her, but she suspected she was failing miserably at keeping up a positive front from her end. She had to keep turning away, on the pretext of checking something, anything, so that he wouldn't be able to see the tears collecting in her eyes.

'What on earth happened?'

She didn't want to bombard him with questions, but she was struggling to understand how he could have left the hall earlier that day, full of his usual confidence and assurance, and then be reduced to this pitiful state within a few hours.

'I was riding through the back lanes, over on the opposite side of the valley, when this car came from the other direction on the wrong side of the road.' He spoke slowly, struggling to articulate what had happened, his words punctuated by flinches of pain.

'Don't worry.' She held up a hand to stop him. 'We don't need to do this now.' What had possessed her to ask? He'd gone through enough already today. The last thing he needed was to revisit those awful moments of his accident. There'd be plenty of time for those kinds of conversations later, but Jackson shook his head, determined to go on.

'The guy was speeding, I reckon he must have been doing at least 60 mph, far too fast for that stretch of road. I tried to steer the bike out of his way, but...' He snapped his eyes closed, reliving the moment of impact. 'I didn't have time. He clipped the front of the bike and I came flying off straight over the handlebars. I think I must have rolled over a couple of times because I ended up in a ditch a long way from the bike.'

He closed his eyes again and Pia felt helpless, unable as she was to take away the pain and horror of what he'd been through.

'Christ, the bike... Do you know what kind of state it's in?'

She looked at him, aghast. Was that all he was worried about? She shook her head. It was the least of her concerns.

'Did the guy stop?' Pia asked.

'Yeah. He called the emergency services. He walked away without a scratch, but I think he was pretty shook up.'

Just then the doctor came and joined them at Jackson's bedside, clutching a folder.

'Jackson? Well, the results of the scans are in and fortunately there's no damage to your spinal column so we can probably remove this now, which should hopefully make you feel a bit more comfortable.' The doctor leant over and carefully took off Jackson's neck support. The relief across his features as he stretched out his shoulders was evident and matched Pia's relief at knowing that he'd done no serious damage to his spine. 'You have got some broken ribs and a fractured pelvis, which will need fixing. The orthopaedic surgeon will be along to speak to you shortly, but I think you'll be going down to theatre first thing tomorrow for your operation.'

'Shit! Really? I was hoping I'd be going home tonight.'

'Sadly not. You won't be going anywhere for a while. Your surgeon will probably be able to give you a better idea, but I would say you're going to be with us for a couple of weeks at least.'

'Oh!' Pia's exclamation met Jackson's more emphatic and forthright expletive, and Pia gave an apologetic look towards the doctor, who shrugged it away.

'You'll be in good hands with the orthopaedic team, who will have you back up on your feet just as soon as they can. In the meantime, I'll get some more painkillers organised for you.'

Once the doctor had left, Jackson and Pia fell quiet for a few moments as they both digested the news in their own way.

'This is a bloody disaster,' Jackson uttered. Pia took hold of his hand, intertwining her fingers through his.

'I know it must seem that way, but you heard what the doctor said. They'll be able to fix you up. It might just take a little bit of time, that's all.'

'We've got the car show next weekend. I need to be out of here for then.'

'Oh, Jackson!' Her stomach twisted, knowing how much he'd been looking forward to it, seeing all the exhibits and catching up with his friends. With the best will in the world, there was no way he was going to be able to attend the event this year. It was bound to be a huge disappointment to him. 'The show doesn't matter. What's most important is that you get better. There'll be other years when we can host the show and I'm sure people will understand when they hear what's happened.'

'What are you talking about, Pia?' Jackson shifted his position, the effort making his face contort in pain. She saw the anger and frustration cross his features too. 'The weekend's show will go on regardless of whether or not I'll be there. We can't cancel at this late stage. There are too many people depending on us, people who have been looking forward to the day since last year's show.'

'Okay, I didn't mean...' Her words trailed away. The last thing she wanted was to go ahead with the show without Jackson at her side. It was his passion. He was on first-name terms with most of the exhibitors and stallholders and would know where he wanted all the different classes of vehicles to be displayed within the grounds. To be honest, she hadn't familiarised herself with the details, knowing Jackson had it all methodically organised in his head. On this particular project, she had just acted as his wingman, performing the admin and any ad-hoc tasks, as Jackson had required. Would she really be able to pull off such a big event on her own, greeting and managing all the petrol heads who would be descending on the hall next weekend, when she didn't have the first clue about any of it? She couldn't think about that now, all she could concentrate on was Jackson and getting him better, but she realised, judging by his expression, that he needed to know he had no reason to be concerned about the upcoming event at the weekend.

'Don't worry. We'll manage, of course we will. Mateo and Frank will be on board and we'll do everything we can to make the day the success it deserves to be.'

'Have you told Tom what's happened?'

'Not yet. I was going to text everyone once you are settled up on the ward.'

'Right. Well, whatever you do, don't tell Ronnie and my dad what's happened. I don't want them panicking. There's absolutely nothing for them to worry about.'

'But, Jackson, we can't keep something like this from them. They have a right to know. They're your parents, after all. And obviously I would play it down, tell them that you're fine and you're in good hands.'

Jackson shook his head firmly, even that small movement making him wince in pain.

'Pia, please. Just do as I say.'

She didn't want to argue with him, not when he was clearly in such a distressed state, but how could she possibly keep something of this magnitude from his parents? God forbid, what if something even more serious happened to Jackson and Rex and Ronnie hadn't been given the opportunity to know what was going on? She could imagine how she might feel in the same circumstances. Angry, disappointed and let down. She was sure Ronnie and Rex would never forgive her if she kept something so important from them. She took a deep breath, biting back the protestations ready to fall off her tongue. Perhaps once Jackson had a good night's sleep and had got through his operation, he might be more open to the idea of telling his parents the news.

It wasn't long before the surgeon who would be operating on Jackson arrived and talked through with them both the procedure for the following day. Jackson would be monitored closely overnight to make sure his condition didn't change at all, in which case he might need to be taken to theatre urgently, but all being well he would be first on the operating list tomorrow. Pia felt sick just thinking about what Jackson would have to go through, and what sounded like the weeks of recovery ahead, but Jackson was more pragmatic. There was no alternative. If he wanted the best chance of regaining full mobility then this was his only option. All Jackson seemed concerned about was the state of his bike and the upcoming classic car show.

When the porter arrived to take Jackson up to the ward, Pia took the opportunity to get some fresh air. There were some calls she needed to make.

'Get Tom to come in and see me,' Jackson called in a croaky voice as she went to leave. 'Tonight, if he can. I need to talk to him.'

'Can't it wait until after your operation? You must be completely shattered. You should rest up. You've got a big day ahead of you tomorrow. Nothing is more important than that.'

'Please, get him to come down now. I need to talk to him. I want to see if he can help us out at the hall in my absence.'

Even when he was incapacitated, wrestling with pain and facing a serious operation, Jackson couldn't sit back and simply accept his fate. His body might be broken, but his mind was still working as usual, planning and organising his business interests. Really, did she expect anything less from him?

Standing outside the hospital, taking a few deep calming breaths, which did nothing to soothe the tsunami of emotions rushing around her body, Pia was reminded of just a few hours ago when she was standing in almost the same spot. Then her feelings had been at the other end of the spectrum – full of wonder and joyfulness. Now, something snagged at her heart as she realised how fragile life could be. How everything and everyone that she loved, and imagined would be hers for the foreseeable future, could be snatched away from her in an instant. She couldn't take anything for granted, but the idea of her life without Jackson in it was too terrible to contemplate. She bit on her lip, her gaze stretching out over the uninspiring vista of the car park, her view blurred by the tears welling in her eyes. She needed to be strong. If Jackson was putting on a brave face then so should she. Her tears would have to wait until later.

She took a walk around the hospital grounds, glad to be away from the claustrophobic and intense confines of the emergency department. As she passed other people, she couldn't help wondering what they were doing there. If they worked at the hospital or if they were visiting friends or relatives. Had their worlds been upended in the same way as hers had today?

Jackson might not be in one piece, but he was alive and she needed to keep that at the forefront of her mind. If things had turned out even slightly differently then Pia could have been facing a much worse scenario. She took a deep breath, shaking away that thought. She needed to remain positive, despite the obstacles ahead. *One day at a time.* Wasn't that always the advice? She headed back to the hospital, stopping at the small shop in the lobby to pick up some biscuits, chocolates and crisps. If Jackson didn't want them, they would always come in handy for visitors.

Back upstairs on the ward, Pia was relieved to find Jackson looking much more comfortable. He'd been cleaned up and the blood had been wiped away from his face and shoulders. He was sitting up sipping on a mug of tea. When he spotted her, his eyebrow lifted in a quirk and she was reminded of the man she loved and admired, the real Jackson that she could easily imagine might leap out of that hospital bed and greet her in a hug. If only.

'You're looking better already,' she said, bending down to greet him again, leaving a kiss on his cheek.

'I'm feeling better, although that probably has something to do with the amount of painkillers I have flooding my bloodstream at the moment. You all right?' he asked, squeezing her hand, his gaze sweeping her face.

'Me? I'm fine. Just worried about you, obviously. I'll be happier when your operation's out of the way.'

'Don't worry about me. This is just a bloody inconvenience. I'll be back at the hall before you know it.'

Pia smiled as though sharing in Jackson's confidence, but she couldn't help being beset by doubts. What if the operation wasn't a success, what if Jackson's injuries turned out to be life-changing, after all? How would it impact on their future together? Not that she wouldn't love him just the same, they would face whatever was in store for them, but she was more concerned about Jackson's state of mind, how it would affect him emotionally. He'd suffered depression in the past and she didn't want him to visit those dark depths again.

Her musings were interrupted by the arrival of Tom, which brightened her mood immeasurably and, judging by Jackson's face, which lit up in a wide smile, it had done the same for him as well. Mainly, Pia experienced a surge of relief that she would be able to talk to Tom, to share the worry and responsibility of being there for Jackson.

'Well, mate, you don't half do things in style. Was this your elaborate way of getting out of cooking Sunday dinner?' Tom leant down to give his brother a squeeze on his upper arm.

Jackson raised a smile.

'It's good to see you,' he said, and in that moment of openness with his brother, Pia could see his vulnerability so close to the surface.

'Well, nothing was going to keep me away. As soon as I heard from Pia what had happened, I knew I had to get down here. To see for myself how you were. You had us all worried.' Tom shared a conspiratorial glance with Pia. 'Looks and sounds as though you've done yourself some damage?'

Jackson grimaced.

'A few scratches, some broken ribs and a fractured pelvis. Nothing that can't be fixed.'

He was playing it down, making light of his injuries, but Pia knew that it wasn't a foregone conclusion that the operation would be a success. And far from only having some minor scratches, he had several open wounds over his legs and arms where his body had scraped along the tarmac road. The nurses had done a good job at cleaning out the dirt and gravel beneath his skin, but the deep cuts would need further cleaning and monitoring over the coming weeks.

'I'm guessing this might slow you down, for a little while at least. If there's anything I can do to help then you know you only need ask?' It was as if Tom could read his brother's mind.

'Ha! Well, as much as I'm really pleased to see you, bro, I may have had an ulterior motive in getting you down here.'

'Sure, anything,' said Tom without hesitation.

'Well, you know it's the classic car show next weekend and we're expecting thousands of visitors to turn up so nothing...' he paused and gestured towards his indisposed body, '...can stand in the way of that. Pia's going to need help overseeing the running of the show. She simply won't be able to do it on her own. It's the biggest event on our calendar and it's a lot of work. Having said that, everything is pretty much organised. Some of it is even written down.' He pulled an apologetic face at Pia. 'And what isn't, is all up here.' He tapped the side of his head with a finger.

'That's what worries me,' said Pia with a rueful smile.

He waved away her concerns with his hand. 'All the stalls are booked and the vehicles' classes and entries set up. A mate of mine, Stu Rogers, was going to be helping with the awards of the rosettes so he'll be more than happy to take that role on by himself. I'll speak to him later. He'll be a good contact on the day because he's run classic car shows in the past, so any problems, speak to him. We have a coachload of stewards turning up, a lot of who were at the event last year, so they'll just need shepherding on the day. Catering is all organised – I think Pia will have all the details on that. There's some other stuff that I can run through with you, but does that sound like something you'd be able to help out with?'

'Absolutely.' Tom nodded his head emphatically. 'Pia and I can sit down together, finalise the details and draw up a master plan.'

'Are you sure?' she asked him. 'What about your other work commitments this week?'

'That's one of the great things about being freelance. I can pick and choose when I work and while I don't like to let anyone down, this is definitely more important than anything else. Family comes first.'

Pia's emotions were all over the place today as she felt the tears prick at her eyes again. It was hard to believe that less than a year ago Jackson hadn't even known about the existence of his brother and, when he did find out, he was distinctly underwhelmed by the prospect. Their relationship hadn't got off to the best start, but slowly over the following months they'd come to tolerate each other and Pia could definitely now see the bond strengthening in front of her eyes.

'Of course, this is just a worst-case scenario,' Jackson said. 'I'm hoping I'll get this op out of the way and there'll be every chance of me making it to the show at the weekend.'

Pia gasped, her gaze snagging on Tom's, who gave an imperceptible shake of his head, both of them knowing that, with the best will in the world, the best surgeon operating and even with the wind blowing in the right direction, there was absolutely no chance of that actually happening, despite what Jackson might hope and desire.

16

No sooner had Sophie slipped off her jacket and turned the lights on in the cottage, there was a knock at the front door. She didn't think twice about turning to answer it, assuming it must be Tom. Perhaps he'd had a change of mind and wanted her to go with him to the hospital after all. She would be more than happy to provide a bit of moral support. Only disappointment washed over her when she opened the door and realised it wasn't Tom standing there.

'Kyle!'

'Sorry, Sophs. Please don't be angry with me. I was leaving the pub and saw you down here. I didn't intentionally follow you.' He held up the palms of his hands to her in a gesture of peace. 'I really don't want to upset you, but I just want to talk. We had eight years together. Don't you think that counts for something? Please. If not now, then some other time? We could meet in town for a coffee.'

She glanced at her watch and Kyle jumped on that gesture.

'Just ten or twenty minutes of your time, that's all I want, and then I'll leave you alone. I promise.'

She wasn't sure if it was the beseeching look on his face or the fact that she knew she wouldn't be able to settle to anything else that made her relent and open the door wider to invite him in.

'Thanks, Sophs,' he said, looking relieved and grateful as he wandered inside, looking all around him.

It wasn't that she was afraid of Kyle. He'd never been physically violent towards her, even if she'd been wary of his temper in those last few months they'd shared together. It was more that she was scared to face the past and everything that had happened between them. There was a part of her that knew she had run away from that relationship without really confronting Kyle, and maybe a conversation was long overdue. It might give the closure that was needed, certainly to Kyle at least.

'This is a nice place,' he said, sitting down on the sofa where Sophie had indicated.

'Yes, it's ideal for me.'

'And you're happy here?'

Sophie nodded and she recognised the pained but accepting expression that flittered across his features.

'I'm sorry, Sophs. I really messed up, didn't I? If I could turn back the clock then I would. I'd do so many things differently.' He shook his head sadly. 'Then maybe we wouldn't be in this situation now?'

Sophie caught a scent of aftershave, woody with tones of citrus, but she knew instinctively it didn't belong to Kyle. She took a surreptitious sniff of her jumper and realised the enticing smell was lingering on the fabric from where Tom had hugged her earlier.

'Hindsight's a great thing, but we can't change the past. It didn't work out for us and I'm sorry about that, but we have to learn from it and move on. We both deserve to find some happiness.'

Kyle let out a heartfelt sigh, running a hand through his close-cut fair hair.

'And there's no chance you would consider giving us another go? I know you probably won't believe me, but I've changed. I've been sober now for over one hundred days, the longest I've ever managed. I'm determined not to fall back into my old ways. I can be better, Sophs. Like it was in the early days.'

Looking into his eyes, and seeing how his skin had lost its dull and grey appearance, replaced with a healthier glow, she actually believed him, but whatever Kyle might say to her, she knew that there could be no turning back.

'That's great, Kyle. You are looking really well and I'm pleased that you've taken this decision, I can't tell you how pleased I am, but...' It didn't get any easier, however many times she told him. '...it's over for us.'

She couldn't pinpoint when exactly she'd fallen out of love with him. Whether it was one particular moment in time or if it was a certain incident that had changed things irrevocably, or if, as she suspected, it had happened over a number of months in a catalogue of harsh words, and let-downs, and drunken bad-temperedness. It didn't matter now. All that mattered was that Kyle realised exactly where she stood.

* * *

The next day at work, Sophie mooned about the office, distracted by the events of the previous day. Thankfully she made it her main task to clear out an old cupboard, a job she'd been putting off for weeks, scanning the paperwork inside and then putting it through a shredder, which needed very little brainpower. It was just as well because her thoughts kept drifting off in all sorts of directions.

She felt pleased to have cleared the air with Kyle. Once she'd told him there was no possibility of them getting back together again, he had been sad and regretful over the way he'd treated her, but ultimately, he was accepting of her decision. He'd been right. They had needed that conversation because Kyle could no longer be in any doubt as to her real feelings and desires. Now if they were to bump into each other in the pub or supermarket, she would be able to at least chat to him normally without feeling the need to run in the opposite direction.

Sophie had also been preoccupied thinking about Jackson's operation, knowing that Pia would be beside herself with worry. She'd sent a good luck text early that morning, but her words had felt empty and she only wished there was something more she could have done to support her friend. It came as a huge relief when she heard from Pia in the early afternoon to say that Jackson was out of surgery and in the recovery ward.

The operation had been successful as far as they could tell, but it would be a couple of weeks before they would know for certain if he would need any further surgery. Everyone was keeping their fingers crossed that it wouldn't be necessary and he would be able to concentrate on getting better, regaining his mobility and getting back to Primrose Hall.

Mainly, Sophie had been worried and concerned about Tom. How must he be coping? She'd got the impression that he'd been missing his dad, Rex, who was off on his road trip with Ronnie, putting a temporary halt to the relationship they'd been building on since last year. Now his brother was seriously injured in hospital.

Tom had texted her late last night after he'd seen Jackson at the hospital, updating her on his condition. Sophie had winced reading the catalogue of injuries in the text and her heart had gone out to them all at Primrose Hall, knowing how concerned they must be as they waited for Jackson to get through his operation. Tom had also mentioned that Jackson had asked him to help out at the hall, most pressingly with the car show next weekend, so he would obviously be preoccupied with everything that needed doing while Jackson was out of action.

Now, home from work, the mind-numbing task of shuffling papers all day forgotten, she rolled her shoulders to ease out the tension and picked up her phone, checking her messages. On impulse she dashed off a quick text to Tom.

Hey! I heard from Pia that Jackson came through his operation okay – good news! I hope you're doing okay too…? Pia said what a relief it was to have you helping out at the hall, especially with the car show coming up. Take care, and will look forward to seeing you at the weekend! x

Sophie's finger hovered over the arrow that would send the message on its way, unsure why she felt so hesitant, checking that she hadn't been over familiar or needy, before quickly stabbing at the button before she had chance to change her mind. She supposed her reluctance was due to the fact that until now their interactions had been based solely around the open days at the stables and this seemed so much more personal. Still, she'd really had a desire to reach out to him, to check that he was okay. It wasn't as if she expected a reply, she only wanted him to know that she was thinking about him. She threw down her handset on the sofa and headed to the kitchen to make her customary home-from-work mug of tea, but no sooner had she switched on the kettle than she was diverted by the buzzing of her phone from the other room.

She dashed across to pick it up, not bothering to look who it was before uttering a curious hello.

'Sophie! It's Tom.'

The sound of his familiar deep voice at the other end of the line was a delightful surprise, and even more surprisingly made her heart flutter. What was that all about?

'Hey, how are things?' she asked.

'Yep, okay. I've just dropped Pia back at the hall. We've been over at the hospital most of the afternoon. Jackson was pretty much out of it following his operation so we've left him to sleep it off. Fingers crossed, it's looking as though they might have put him back together again. We shall have to see, but I know Pia was hugely relieved tonight. I've told her she needs to catch up on her sleep too. She's been running on adrenaline these last twenty-four hours.'

'I bet. I still can't really believe that it's happened. He was so lucky that it wasn't any worse. It doesn't bear thinking about.' Sophie heard the sharp intake of breath at the other end of the line. 'You must be pretty shattered too,' she added.

'Yes.' There was a moment's hesitation. 'It was good to get your message.'

She nodded, not that he'd be able to see, of course, but she understood the emotion and fatigue she heard in his voice.

'I'm going to head home now, pick up some food on the way and then unwind for a couple of hours. Then I'll give some thought to what needs to be done in preparation for the weekend. Pia has enough on her plate, I don't want her stressing about the car show as well.'

'Yes, well, if there's anything I can do to help, then let me know.' She knew it was a futile offer. What could she possibly do to help, other than provide some emotional support, of course?

'Thanks, Sophie, that's kind of you. I know I'll appreciate seeing a friendly face, that's for sure.'

'Look,' she said on impulse, 'I was just about to pop some fishcakes in the oven. I haven't eaten yet either. You're more than welcome to join me if you'd like to. I'm sure the last thing you want to think about right now is food.'

There was a noticeable pause at the other end of the line. Tom was probably thinking how to let her down gently.

'I'd hate to put you to any trouble.'

'No trouble whatsoever. It's not fine dining, but it will fill a hole if you're hungry. Only if you want to, of course. If I was you, I'd probably want to get home and collapse into bed.' She said it lightly so that he had an easy get-out clause if he wanted one.

'Well, to be honest with you, there was a part of me dreading going back to the flat and fishcakes round at yours sounds like a much more exciting proposition.'

She laughed.

'Well, I can't promise excitement, but I'll look forward to seeing you round here whenever you're ready.'

'Give me twenty minutes,' he said.

Perfect, she thought. Just the right amount of time to put some new potatoes on to boil, to put the fishcakes in the oven and to prepare some green beans which she would cook once Tom had arrived. A beat of anticipation fluttered in her chest, as she quickly ran around the cottage tidying things away, lighting a candle and plumping up cushions. She dashed upstairs and cleaned her teeth, applied some mascara and some bronzer over her cheeks, before brushing out her hair and giving herself one last glance in the mirror. She even gave a quick squirt of her expensive perfume on her wrists and behind her ears, all the time wondering why she was going to so much trouble. If it had been Pia coming round then she knew she wouldn't be going to the same effort, so why had welcoming Tom into her home brought about such a sense of anticipation? Probably something to do with the way her heart in her chest was acting out of sorts too. Thankfully she didn't have long to consider that predicament because soon Tom was standing on her doorstep.

'Come in,' she said, greeting him with a hug. If she'd hoped that seeing Tom in person might put paid to the unexpected emotions she'd been experiencing then she was mistaken. He looked incredibly hand-some tonight in black jeans and a half-zipped cream jumper, and again the wispy scent of oranges taunted her nostrils. He clearly hadn't tried hard in the same way as she had, but he might as well have done for the effect it had on her. His dark brown hair curled at his collar and weari-ness was etched around his eyes, which only served to accentuate his vulnerability.

If anything, seeing him again heightened the realisation that she'd grown attached to Tom in a way that she could never have expected.

'Let me get you a drink,' she offered.

While Sophie pottered in the kitchen, Tom rested against the worktop and she listened attentively as he told her about Jackson and everything that had happened over the last twenty-four hours.

'It couldn't have come at a worse time, what with the show coming up this weekend, but then I suppose that's a valuable life lesson. What is it they say about best-laid plans? It's a reminder that we can't take any of this for granted.' He opened up his palms to the sky. 'None of us know what's waiting for us around the corner.'

'It's true.' Sophie sighed and poured out two glasses of white wine, handing one to Tom. 'It makes you realise how quickly everything can change in an instant.'

'It's shaken Pia up obviously but with Jackson it's hard to tell what's going on beneath the surface. I think to him it's more of an inconvenience than anything else, but that might be because he's not faced up to the emotional consequences of it yet. He likes to take charge of everything in his life, but this is something entirely out of his control. This will cramp his style for a while, that's for sure, but you know, I'm sure he'll come out the other side, as determined as ever, raring to forge on with all his big ideas and plans.' Tom gave a wry smile and Sophie couldn't help but notice the admiration in his voice.

'He must be so relieved that he's got you to rely on while he's out of action.'

'Well, I certainly didn't need to think twice when he asked me. He's my brother and I'll do anything I can to help. I just hope I don't let him down, that's all.'

'Why would you say that?' Sophie looked up from where she was scrabbling about in a drawer, finding her best cutlery. Her gaze snagged on his. 'You're two of a kind and Jackson appreciates that. I guess it must be strange for both of you, finding your way as brothers when you've only known each other for... what is it, less than a year?'

Tom nodded.

'Mind you, you would never know that to look at you both. To me, it's as though you've known each other for ever.'

'Well, I like to think we're making up for lost time. You know, it's kind of strange. I had this overriding desire to find out where I'd come from, who my real father was and in doing so I discovered I had a brother as well. That was a real bonus to me, the icing on the cake, although I'm not sure Jackson saw it in the same way.' Tom chuckled to himself. 'To him, I was just some interloper whose intentions he couldn't quite work out. It was only thanks to Pia and Ronnie, who welcomed me up at the hall and made sure I was included in the family get-togethers, that we managed to find a connection. You know, I think Jackson might actually be getting to like me now, despite his best intentions.'

Sophie could see through the self-deprecating humour and could tell how important it was to Tom that Jackson respected him and valued his presence in his life.

'I think it's such a great thing that you've all found each other, and can provide that support that you want and need from your family.'

'It's definitely a two-way thing. I feel very fortunate to have Dad and Jackson in my life now.'

Sophie served the dinner up onto plates, handing one to Tom.

'Shall we go and sit down? I'm afraid I haven't got a dining table so we'll have to eat it off our laps.'

'Just how I like it,' said Tom with a smile. 'This looks delicious, by the way.'

They wandered through to the living room and sat beside each other on the sofa. Sophie loved coming back to the cottage after work, especially now it felt more like home after she'd added some personal touches, like the fresh flowers in the fireplace and her fairy lights across the mantelpiece. She had bought some new cosy throws that she'd draped over the chairs and sofa, and added some cushions in a bright orange colour which gave the room a contemporary feel. On the shelves either side of the fireplace were photos of her mum, and her brother and his young family, in pretty frames. Having guests, and she really didn't have many of them, well, apart from an unexpected visit from Kyle last night, made her see and appreciate her home in a new light. Tom held the honour, though, of being her first supper guest and she couldn't think of anyone else she would rather have sitting beside her right now.

'I'm guessing your dad must have been upset when he heard the news about the accident.'

'Ah, well, there's a thing.' Tom rolled his eyes. 'We're all under strict instructions not to tell Rex or Ronnie what's happened, which I think is ridiculous, but one thing I have learnt in the short space of time that I've come to know Jackson is that he can be really bloody minded when he wants to be.'

'Oh!' Sophie stopped, knife and fork in mid-air. 'Why doesn't he want to tell them? They're going to find out eventually.'

'Exactly. He doesn't want them worrying and cutting short their holiday and returning home, but I think they've got a right to know. And so does Pia. It's put her in a very awkward position. I think she's in almost daily contact with Ronnie and it will be difficult for her to keep it a secret. She wants to tell his parents, to reassure them that he's okay.' Tom shrugged as though unable to make sense of Jackson's motivation. 'We're both working on Jackson to persuade him otherwise. I probably won't speak to Dad again until next weekend, but I'm not sure if I'll be able to deliberately keep it from him.'

'Let's hope Jackson may have had a change of heart by then,' said Sophie.

'That,' said Tom, putting his knife and fork down on his empty plate, 'was just what I needed and hit the spot perfectly. Thanks, Sophie. I really appreciate you inviting me round. I wasn't looking forward to going home and this was a much more enjoyable proposition.' She caught his glance, the light in his eyes and the warmth of his smile. A smile shared between two friends. Nothing more, surely? 'In fact, let me do the washing up as a thank you for dinner.'

Despite her protestations, Tom insisted and she followed him out to the galley kitchen where he started to fill the sink, squirted some washing-up liquid into the water and found the dishcloth as though he'd done the task here several times before. Sophie picked up the tea towel and started drying as Tom washed.

'You know, I keep thinking about last night in the pub when I abandoned you to your ex. I feel really bad about that. I didn't work out what was going on until I was sitting in my car.' He scrunched up his face, looking sidewards at her in apology.

'Honestly, don't worry. I'd have done exactly the same thing if I'd received a call like that.'

She thought it was lovely that he had remembered, even if it had been at the last minute, and had come back to rescue her. It showed what a thoughtful person he was.

'You've not heard from him again, I hope?'

'Actually, he turned up here shortly after I got home. I thought it was you knocking at the door!' Sophie noticed Tom's stricken expression. 'No, it was fine, actually. We had a chance to talk and in a way it was good to clear the air. I suppose I was guilty of completely ghosting Kyle when we split up. I stopped taking his calls, then I changed my number and I blocked him on all social media channels. It was my way of coping. I'd finally got round to making that huge decision to leave him and I didn't want to be open to him trying to persuade me to stay, which I knew he would. It felt mean having to take such drastic action, but at the time I could see no other way.' She took a breath, glancing across at Tom as she felt his attentive gaze upon her.

'It sounds as though that took a lot of bravery on your part.'

She nodded.

'I have no regrets, but I was pleased to explain to Kyle my feelings. Hopefully he can now move on in the same way as I have.'

She'd reached a point, after far too many false starts, where she'd needed to think about herself and the only way of doing that had been to draw a final line, move forward and not look back. And that had been absolutely the right decision. Now, she was very happy where she was in her lovely cosy cottage, having made some charming new friends. She turned to smile at Tom. Somehow, she knew this was only the beginning of a new and exciting chapter in her life.

17

'Are you okay? You'll rub a hole in that plate if you carry on at that rate.'

Thinking about her conversation with Kyle had sent Sophie into a daydream and she'd been drying the same dinner plate for several moments now. She looked up into Tom's face, his questioning expression, with one eyebrow quirked, making her smile.

'Ooh, sorry, I was miles away there, wasn't I?'

'Well, I'll help you put these last few pieces away in the cupboard and then I'll be on my way. I've taken up far too much of your time as it is.'

'You don't have to go,' she said, before she'd had the thought to temper her plea so that she didn't sound quite as desperate as she might now seem. 'I mean, obviously, I understand that you need to get home, but...' She giggled, not really knowing what she was trying to say. 'I've so enjoyed tonight. You are my first ever dinner guest here and it's been really special. Thank you. It's another step in making this place feel like my proper home.'

'Well, I am indeed very honoured then.'

'Are you sure you won't stay for a coffee?' she said as she flicked the kettle on. 'I'm going to make myself one.'

'Well, as long as I'm not stopping you from getting on, then great, I'd love to.'

With the coffees made, Sophie found a box of unopened chocolates in the cupboard, a moving-in present from one of her friends, and they wandered back into the living room, where she kicked off her slippers and tucked her legs up to one side of her on the sofa. Tom joined her and for a few minutes their attentions were solely focused on the selection of sweet treats inside the box.

'Which are you favourites?' Sophie asked him.

'Definitely the dark ones, and the nut ones. Oh, and the toffees. Although I am partial to a salted caramel too.' He gave a low warm chuckle. 'Perhaps it might have been easier if I'd mentioned the ones I'm not so keen on. The soft centres I would leave to last, but you know I'm not going to refuse one if you absolutely insist.'

'You see, I knew that was why we were destined to be great friends because my favourites are the soft centres so we can happily share this box of chocolates without fighting over the strawberry creme or the hazelnut whirl. You go right ahead.'

They sat in companionable silence, slowly savouring the chocolates and simply enjoying each other's company. Sophie suspected Tom was thinking about his family and everything he had to do in the coming days, while she was happy enough to let her thoughts relish this moment of unexpected happiness. Spending quality time with a new friend. She was a different person to the woman she was twelve months ago and she was grateful for the people who had come into her life during that period. Greta would be a friend for life now after effectively rescuing her from a situation that she might still be in today if she hadn't come to her aid. Pia was a supportive and encouraging ally, who always took an interest in Sophie's life and her fledgling jewellery business, and the two women, of similar ages, had hit it off from the start. They'd discovered a natural and immediate bond so that now, whenever they met, they would immediately pick up their conversation from where they'd last left off, chatting animatedly and laughing over the same things. *Tom?* Sophie wasn't sure how she would define her friendship with the man who was currently running an eye over the remaining chocolates in the box.

'Just one more,' he said.

'Famous last words,' Sophie added, laughing.

All that she knew was that, disregarding his obvious good looks, she was attracted to his humility, his kindness and his vulnerability that he wasn't afraid to show. He was so easy to be around. She didn't have to pretend to be someone she wasn't, he seemed to like her just as she was, and wasn't that the way real friendships should be?

'I don't want to pry,' said Tom, 'and tell me to mind my own business if you don't want to talk about it, but it sounds as though your ex caused you a fair few problems? You seemed quite...' Tom searched for the right words. '...not frightened exactly, but agitated maybe, seeing him the other night?'

She nodded. Tom was much more perceptive than she'd given him credit for.

'It was unexpected, that was all. I'd been having such a lovely evening up until that point.'

She soon found herself opening up to Tom about the years she spent with Kyle, when it had started to go wrong and how his drinking had impacted on their relationship.

'The trouble is it happened slowly over a long period of time, years in fact, so that one day you wake up and find yourself in a situation that no longer makes you happy and you're left wondering when and how it had all gone so wrong. That the person you're with isn't the person you fell in love with. Does that make sense?'

Tom nodded, hanging on to her every word.

'There's a part of me that feels bad that I walked away, that I didn't realise sooner the extent of his problems. Who knows, maybe I could have nipped it in the bud or done something to help, but it was as though the problem crept up on us and then it was too big for us to navigate our way through. He changed and I guess I changed too.'

'From what I know of these things, and I must admit that's not a lot, I don't think it's a problem you can solve for anyone else. It has to be some-thing they want to change for themselves and if Kyle wasn't ready to do that, then you were never going to be able to help him to stop drinking.'

'Yeah, that was the thing, he didn't see it as a problem. He was great at deflecting the situation onto everyone else, making it their problem and not his. Occasionally he would pay lip service and say he would cut down, and I so wanted to believe him and could imagine how things would be better, but of course it never came to anything.'

'It must have been so hard for you.'

Sophie nodded. It felt cathartic to talk about it with Tom. Generally, she hadn't confided in many people as it had been an intensely private matter and she'd felt embarrassed and ashamed, that somehow it reflected badly on her, but now she had a bit of distance from the situation she could see it in a different light.

'Kyle's sober now and I'm so proud that he's done that. I know it can't have been easy. I suppose some people might think that I should have stayed and supported him through what is effectively an illness, but too much had happened between us. There was too much bad feeling, from my side certainly, and I tried to imagine how I would feel if he did give up the booze. If I would suddenly feel all those emotions that I had in the beginning, but I realised that we'd lost what we had and there was no way of getting it back again. I no longer had feelings for him.'

Just talking about that time made her skin prickle and relief washed over her, knowing that it wasn't her reality any more.

'I understand that. I think it takes a lot of strength and courage to walk away from a long-term relationship even if there are strong and valid reasons for doing so.'

She liked that Tom understood, that he got where she was coming from, but then again, he had been through a similar situation.

'You've been through it too?'

'Yep. And I probably didn't handle it in the best way, but I can't change that now. Anna's a great girl and we got on well, there was no big falling out, but we'd been coasting along for years. Finding out about Dad made me question everything and everyone around me, and sadly that included Anna. She deserved so much more than I was able to give her. Besides,' his voice brightened, and there was a half-smile on his lips, 'I've heard she's met someone else now and is really happy, so I like to think I did her a massive favour.'

'That's good, and I guess you learn a lot about yourself when you go through something like that. I know I did. It gives you a clearer perspective on what you do and don't want from your life.'

Sophie shifted in her seat, snuggling up further into the corner of the sofa. Tom turned to look at her, a smile lingering on his lips as though he was about to say something else, but then thought better of it. Suddenly, he jumped up.

'I must go! It's been great tonight. Thanks again, Sophie.'

She stood up too, surprised by his sudden urgency to leave, but then she supposed it was getting late. He placed his hands on her upper arms and kissed her lightly on the cheek, which she took as an invitation and walked into his arms, wrapping her own around his chest, revelling in his natural masculine scent. She closed her eyes, savouring the brief moment. A hug between friends, that's all it was. Although something resonated deep within her. For the first time since breaking up with Kyle, when she vowed that she would never get involved with another man again, she could envision a future for herself where that might possibly happen. There were some good men out there, men like Tom, and she was grateful to him for making her realise that.

18

Pia barely knew what day it was. Since Jackson had been taken into hospital, the days had merged into one and were busier than ever, filled with visits to the orthopaedic ward, fielding calls from well-wishers asking after Jackson's progress and taking deliveries of gifts and home-cooked meals from friendly neighbours. If there was one thing that Jackson's accident had taught her, it was that they were surrounded by a bunch of lovely people, all too willing to help out with emotional and practical support. This morning, before she nipped off on the first of her daily visits to the hospital, she had organised a meeting around the kitchen table with Tom, Frank, Mateo and Stu Rogers who had stepped in, as Jackson had suggested he might, to help with the organisation for Saturday. Ivy, the housekeeper, was in today and was on hand to make hot drinks and prepare cooked breakfasts for those who wanted them, which turned out to be every single person sitting around the table.

'First of all, I want to say a big thank you from me and Jackson for rallying round to help us put on what promises to be a really exciting show at the weekend. I must admit I didn't relish the idea of doing this by myself when I realised Jackson would be out of action, but now, with such a great team on board, I know we're going to really smash it.'

'It's such a shame that Jackson will miss it, though,' said Ivy, serving up plates of bacon and sausage rolls, which elicited appreciative groans from around the table. 'I know how much he was looking forward to it.'

'I'm going to make sure he doesn't feel left out,' Pia piped up. 'I've promised that we'll film some of the proceedings so that he can see everything that's going on, the stalls, the visitors and the cars and bikes. It will almost be as though he's here.'

Tom gave a wry smile.

'He's certainly still very hands-on, even from his hospital bed. I'm getting hourly texts from him with reminders of things that need to be done. I wish he would just lie back and concentrate on getting better. The show is in very safe hands, especially with Stu here as our chief adviser.'

'It will be absolutely fine.' Stu was in his late fifties, with closely cut white hair, a full moustache and piercing blue eyes that gave him the appearance of a film star from a bygone age. He'd arrived for today's meeting on a 1969 Norton Commando bike, which had brought much admiration from the guys around the table, who had all wandered outside to take a closer look. Stu's visits were always keenly anticipated because he would turn up in a different classic car or motorbike from his vast collection on each occasion. Pia knew if Jackson was here they probably wouldn't have even started the meeting yet as he would have snagged the bike for himself and would be riding it around the grounds of the hall.

'I think we're in pretty good shape for the weekend,' said Stu. 'All the hard work and preparation has been done already by Jackson, Pia and now Tom, so it's just a case of bringing everything together on the day. I'll be on site early on Saturday morning with Tom and we will make sure the stewards know where everything is and what they should be doing and we can deal with any queries as they arise.'

'I've printed out a copy of the schedule of events, the site map and the timetable for the day, and I'll keep a copy here in this folder.' Pia picked up the blue lever-arch file from the table. 'So if anyone needs to refer to it on the day then it will be easily accessible.'

'Might be worth having a walk round the grounds after we're finished here,' said Tom, 'so we can get a better idea of where the different displays will be and where we need to put up the signage for parking, etc.'

'Good idea,' said Stu.

Pia felt a huge sense of relief now that everything was coming together and she had utter faith in Stu and Tom to oversee the smooth running of the day. There was a small part of her that was even looking forward to welcoming all the visitors to the hall and being part of the hubbub, soaking up the atmosphere, but she knew it wouldn't be the same without Jackson at her side. Regardless, she and the rest of the team were all determined to make it a success for Jackson's sake more than their own. After Pia finished her breakfast, she pushed back her chair and stood up.

'Look, I have some calls and emails to see to before I head down to the hospital so do you mind if I sit the tour out? If there's anything important then just call me or come and find me. Thanks for everything, guys,' she called, as they walked out the kitchen door. 'I can't tell you how much I appreciate all your help.'

'Send Jackson our love when you see him, won't you?'

With Ivy clearing the crockery from the table and loading the dishwasher, Pia pulled out her phone from her back pocket. She felt surgically attached to it at the moment, desperate as she was not to miss any calls from the hospital or Jackson, but this time it was a new email that made her heart stop momentarily in her chest. *Ronnie!* Seeing Jackson's mum's name light up on her phone made Pia feel nauseous. Ordinarily, she loved to hear their latest news, how she and Rex were spending their days in the sunny south of France, the people they'd met, the food they'd been eating. Ronnie was always so expansive in her descriptions that it was easy for Pia to imagine being there with the pair of them, enjoying a glass of wine as they took in a beautiful sunset, but now the joy of living vicariously through Ronnie's texts and photos was tainted, knowing that she wasn't being entirely honest with her soon to be mother-in-law. What if Ronnie had heard the news about Jackson's accident from someone else? She would be furious and demanding to know why Pia had kept something so important from them both. With a sense of trepidation, Pia opened up the email to see a long and chatty message filled with emojis and exclamation marks. At least Ronnie was still talking to her, for the moment at least.

We were going to head off to Cannes to do a bit of hobnobbing, but we've decided to stay here for a few more days. It's such a beautiful spot and besides Rex has picked up some bug and is feeling a little under the weather. We'll wait until he's feeling better and then we'll pick up our travels again. That's the wonderful thing about this trip, we're under no pressure to be anywhere at any specific time, we can just take it at our leisure. Gives me the perfect excuse to sit out in my sun chair and read the rest of my book – as if I needed any excuse!

I wonder how you're all doing at Primrose Hall? We miss you all terribly of course. We were thinking how you would all be so busy getting ready for the big show this weekend. I know Rex is very disappointed that he won't be there and he even suggested we jump on a plane back so that we could be part of the celebrations – I think he was only half joking! So you must take lots of photographs for us, especially of all the cars, I know Rex is desperate to see them all.

Pia could imagine Rex feeling left out at not being able to attend the show with his sons. Last year, along with Jackson, he'd been in his element, taking his time to view all the displays, getting down onto his haunches to see the cars from every possible angle. Father and son had spent the day in conversation with all the other motor heads, the pair of them never happier. They could never have known then that neither of them would be able to attend this year's show. Pia scrolled through the photos of Ronnie and Rex, which brought a smile to her face. Hopefully, next year, all three of the Moody men could be together at the show.

Of course, I have been texting Jackson, but he never replies to me, but what's new? Good job I have you there to keep me up to date with the comings and goings at Primrose Hall or else we'd be completely in the dark!

Pia flinched and actually recoiled from the phone as though it might self-combust in her hands. Jackson had been through a dreadful experience and was still suffering a lot of pain from his injuries, but it wasn't fair that he expected her to lie on his behalf. She felt torn between her loyalty to Jackson and to his parents. Jackson was always so persuasive, but she knew in their shoes, she would definitely want to know what was going on and would be deeply hurt to be deceived in that way when they finally discovered the truth. The show was uppermost in everyone's mind at the moment, but as soon as it was over, she would sit down with Jackson and insist that he tell his parents. If he wasn't prepared to do that then she would be compelled to tell them instead.

I'll stay in touch, obviously *tongue out emoji*

Pia smiled at that. She didn't want to think of a time when Ronnie wouldn't be dashing off her frequent bulletins as she always looked forward to receiving her funny and informative updates.

Can we pencil in a Zoom call for Sunday morning over breakfast so that you can tell us all the news from the show? It will be lovely to see you – I miss your gorgeous faces! – and we'll be able to imagine that we're actually there with you in the kitchen.

Pia placed the phone back in her pocket. Well, she would hardly be able to refuse Ronnie's request. They'd had a video call a couple of weeks ago so it was probably about time for another one. Although there would be one glaring problem with this particular upcoming call. There would be no Jackson around and there would be no hiding that fact either. It would be the first thing Ronnie would ask and Pia had no intention of lying. Omitting to mention the small detail of Jackson's accident was one thing, but to lie outright to Rex and Ronnie's faces was something she wasn't prepared to do.

She would reply to Ronnie later, she decided, heading for the office. She tried to take her mind off the conundrum by opening up her laptop and seeing to the long list of other emails waiting in her inbox. With everything that had happened this week, she'd got behind with all the admin, as her days were punctuated with visits to the hospital and replying to all the well-wishers asking after Jackson's condition. Of course, her sole focus had been on Jackson, and secondly the car show, checking and double checking all the arrangements to make sure she hadn't overlooked anything. Once the weekend was over, she would be able to pick up all those other items that she had been neglecting, like the arrangements for the literary festival, which was the next big event on the social calendar, and then the bonfire night extravaganza, before the Christmas carols in December. Would they really have time to fit in a wedding as well?

'Eugh!' Pia exclaimed, more in frustration than anything else, and Bertie and Teddy both looked up at her to see if it was anything they could help with.

She couldn't settle to anything as her mind was filled with thoughts of Jackson, of Rex and Ronnie, the car show and everything else that needed organising. If Jackson was likely to be out of action for several months then something might have to give and the obvious candidate for that was the wedding, which could easily be postponed until the following year. She sat back in her twirly office chair, a finger to her chin, her gaze drinking in the amazing view of the tall and imposing trees of Primrose Woods, and was grateful for the interruption from Ivy.

'You have a visitor. Katy's here with the children. She said she's not stopping, but just wanted to check that you're okay.'

'How lovely!' Pia jumped out of her seat. 'I'm just coming.'

There was an enthusiastic greeting from little Rosie in the kitchen and Pip, who was still strapped into his buggy, but who was clearly delighted to see the dogs, his legs lifting up and down in excitement. The dogs dashed in past Pia and scooted across to say hello, wagging their tails furiously as they made circles around Pip.

'Bertie! Teddy! Come away, Pip doesn't want you goofy pair in his face.'

'I do, I do,' said Rosie, who giggled as the dogs' tails swished past her, and she tried to catch them as they scampered past. The children were very familiar with the dogs and Pia knew that Bertie and Teddy were big softies and would never deliberately hurt anyone, but she was always vigilant when they all came together, just to ensure the dogs didn't knock the children over in their exuberance.

'Oh, Pia,' said Katy, greeting her friend in a hug. 'How are things? You must have had such a worrying few days. We've all been thinking about you.'

'Thanks. It's been difficult, but you know Jackson, he's taking it all in his stride. It was a relief to get his operation out of the way and now we're just waiting to see what happens, if he needs any more surgery. It's a bit of a waiting game now. You'll stay for a cuppa?'

'Could I have a juice, please?' Rosie asked, very politely.

'No! We're not staying. Pia's very busy, and I just wanted to drop these off.' She produced a beautiful bunch of flowers from beneath the buggy and handed them over to her friend along with a Tupperware box. 'They're lemon bars from Mum. She knows how much you love them.'

'That's so kind of you both, thank Lizzie for these, won't you? I'll take some in for Jackson when I go. Please stay for coffee. I'm going to have one, another one! I'm running off coffee at the moment, and it's so lovely to see you all.'

'Is Mr Jackson going to get better? I did a picture. Where's my picture, Mummy?'

'Ah, of course,' said Katy. 'That's the main reason we came. We can't forget that!' She chuckled and delved again around the bottom of the buggy, from where she pulled out an A4 folded piece of paper. Rosie was so proud to show off her handiwork. She pointed to the coloured figures on the front of the home-made card.

'That is me and Pip, and that is Little Star and Twinkle and that is Bertie and Teddy. And we all say, get well soon, Mr Jackson!'

'Aw, well, isn't that super? I can see how much work you've put into your drawing. I know Jackson is going to love it, Rosie. Thank you very much. He is definitely getting better and I know this will really make him smile. I will take it into the hospital with me.'

Jackson and Rosie had a bit of a mutual appreciation society going on ever since the Christmas fair the other year when Jackson had asked the little girl if she could help with naming the Shetland pony and donkey, which he'd recently adopted. It had taken her less than a nanosecond to come up with the names of Little Star and Twinkle, which had been a perfect fit for the animals, and ever since, when Rosie came to the hall, she would always want to see the animals and chat to Jackson too.

With the children settled at the window seat with drinks and choco-late chip cookies, another gift from one of the villagers, Pia fetched the wicker basket from beneath the stairs, which was filled with some chunky building blocks and other toys that she kept for any visiting chil-dren. With Rosie and Pip happily occupied, Pia and Katy were able to snatch a moment to themselves to catch up on the news.

'I still can't believe that it's happened,' said Katy, 'when you think it was only last Sunday that we were at the stables and we were all in such a good mood, so excited for the arrival of Abbey's baby. I remember you dashing off. None of us could have known then what would happen by the end of the day.'

'Honestly, Katy, it was so surreal. One minute I was at the hospital welcoming little Willow into the world, which was the most joyful and magical experience ever, and then later that same day I was back at the same place...' Pia lowered her voice so that little ears wouldn't hear. '...in a state of panic and disbelief, not knowing if Jackson would even survive. It was awful.'

'Oh, Pia!' Katy reached across the table and took hold of Pia's hand, squeezing it tight. 'You must have been terrified. I can't imagine how you must have felt.' Katy shook her head looking grave. 'You must have been so relieved once you knew he was going to be all right. I mean, he is going to be all right, isn't he?'

'Yes, although he might need further surgery yet. The doctors will be monitoring him over the next week or so to see how the repair on his pelvis has taken, then we'll have a better idea of the next steps.'

'Well, that sounds positive. I know he still has a long way to go, but the main thing is that he's still here and it sounds as though they can fix him up.'

'Hopefully.' It brought Pia out in goosebumps whenever she spoke about the accident, the thought that she could quite so easily have lost him was never far from her mind. 'As you can imagine, Jackson's not the best patient in the world. He's fed up and frustrated and wants to get home, but I've told him he needs to take it slowly and do exactly as the doctors tell him.'

Katy gave a knowing smile.

'I wouldn't expect anything less from Jackson. What about the show this weekend? Have you got everything sorted?'

'It's coming together. Tom has stepped in to help. Honestly, I'm not sure what I would have done without him. It's such a relief knowing that he'll be around to rely on.'

'He's a great guy, isn't he? We all love him at the stables. I'm really looking forward to Saturday and showcasing some new products I've been working on. Mum and Bill will be coming along, and Brad will be bringing the children. They're all really looking forward to it. It should be a good day out, if last year is anything to go by.'

Pia's enthusiasm for the car show was growing as she spoke to so many people about it, their own excitement infectious. Of course, this year wouldn't be the same without Jackson at the helm, but she was determined that all their visitors would be in for a treat as soon as they stepped inside the grounds of the hall. There would be something for everyone, with all the cars and motorbikes on display, the stalls selling a variety of goods outside including leatherwear, motor parts, gifts, books and toys, and then the artisan craftspeople selling their wares in the stables. There would also be food and drinks stalls to cover everyone's taste. The only thing that Pia hadn't organised was the weather, but she was keeping everything crossed that the rain would stay away.

'Anyway, tell me, how are you? Are things okay with Brad?' Pia ventured.

'Yes.' Katy exhaled a big sigh, a smile spreading across her face. 'Honestly, I know I moan about him, but I do love him and he is very patient with me. He is very placid, when my moods are all over the place. Sometimes I wonder why he puts up with me.' Her giggle rang out around the kitchen. 'Things are better now, although he is still working all the hours, but now I've got an outlet at the stables and I get more help with the children from Mum and Bill, everything seems much more manageable. Do you know, it stopped me in my tracks hearing about Jackson's accident. You go through life taking everybody and everything around you for granted, all those people that you love, your day-to-day life, grumbling about things that really aren't that important, and then when something like this happens, what's happened to Jackson, you realise how your entire life could change in the blink of an eye.'

'I know, it really makes you think. So many people have said the same thing to me and it brings home what's important to you, how you have to hug your loved ones close and tell them exactly how much they mean to you because...' They shared a glance. There was no need for Pia to go on because they both knew and understood the ending to that sentence.

'Anyway, it's not all doom and gloom. Little Willow has come into the world and she is an absolute poppet. Have you met her yet?'

'Yes! I popped round to Abbey and Sam's yesterday to drop off a card and present. Oh, my goodness, she's so tiny, you forget how little they are at that stage, but she's just adorable, and it's wonderful to see Abbey and Sam looking so happy. Those first days with a newborn are so special, you exist in a hazy fug of wonder, dirty nappies and disbelief that you're actually responsible for this little person. Honestly, it made me quite broody. Well, for half an hour at least! You must be a very proud godmother!'

'I really am.' Pia couldn't help grinning every time she thought of Willow. She was a definite ray of sunshine in what had been a terrible time. 'I was so thrilled that I could be there to witness her arrival in the world. It is something that will stay with me forever. It's just a shame that the day then took on such a dark and unexpected turn. Once I know Jackson is okay and properly on the mend, I'm looking forward to spending lots more time with Willow, and watching her grow up. It's such a privilege.'

'It will be good practice,' said Katy, with a sidelong glance and a wry smile, although Pia didn't take the bait. 'For when you have children of your own!' she said, exasperatedly.

'Ah... well, you never know. Maybe one day,' said Pia, distractedly. She would be lying if she said her mind hadn't drifted towards having her own family with Jackson, sharing that same wonderful experience that her friends had just been through, but she took nothing for granted, especially not now. All that mattered was that Jackson recovered and returned to Primrose Hall. Anything else would be a bonus. 'It will be Ruby's turn next. Their baby is due in a couple of months, and I can't wait to be an auntie. I keep thinking about Mum and Dad, and how excited they would be. I know Connor will make a great dad and it's really lovely to see our family growing.'

'Peeea?' Rosie's sing-song voice called out from the other side of the kitchen. 'Mummy says that you're going to marry Mr Jackson.'

'Rosie!' Katy gently chided her daughter and shook her head as an apology at Pia, who could only laugh.

'Yes, that's right. Aren't I lucky?' she said, giggling, knowing that Rosie was probably Jackson's second biggest fan in the world.

'When, when, when?' The little girl was now overcome with excitement at the idea and had jumped down from the window seat and was bouncing around on the floor.

'Once Jackson is back home and fully recovered then we'll start to make plans. I think it will be a winter wedding so we'll all have to wrap up warm.' What Pia didn't mention was which winter they had in mind. This year, next year? Who knew when? They'd pencilled in a date on the calendar, but they hadn't factored in Jackson being out of action for several months. She would need to have a conversation with him about that.

'I can just imagine how wonderful that will be.' Katy swooned. 'Primrose Hall is magnificent at any time of year, but in December, with all the Christmas decorations and lights, and with the backdrop of the trees from the woods, it's simply magical.'

'Will Father Christmas be there?' Rosie piped up. Both Pia and Katy exchanged a glance and smiled. It was because of Rosie that Jackson had arranged a Santa's grotto as part of the Christmas celebrations last year. 'He will be definitely be at the Christmas fair, but not at our wedding. We've invited him, but it's his busiest time of the year, making and packing the toys that he'll be delivering to all the children around the world, so we don't want to interfere with that, do we?'

'No!' Rosie was aghast at the very idea and Pia smiled to herself.

Everything was so straightforward when you were five, but Rosie had given Pia an idea. One that she would keep to herself for the time being as she didn't want Rosie to be overcome with excitement. Katy wouldn't thank her for that. Still, it had made her attention turn to the wedding plans, and Pia couldn't help but notice the swirl of excitement that built in her stomach.

19

'Hello, you!'

Pia's heart lifted, as it always did, seeing Jackson, now reclining on his hospital bed. His eyes had been closed, but he assured her that he hadn't been sleeping, just thinking, and she couldn't begin to imagine what he might be plotting this time. 'How's things?'

Jackson opened one eye and grimaced.

'It's sending me crazy being stuck here. The staff are great, but honestly, I'm sure I'd get on much better at home. I could take it easy and...'

'Jackson, no! We have to trust in the doctors and what they're telling us. Until they've given you the all-clear then you're just going to have to put up with it.' She sat down in the armchair beside his bed and took hold of his hand. It hurt her heart to see him so down and despondent, especially when there was nothing she could do to make him feel better. 'This is the best place for you at the moment. You're still in so much pain, Jackson, I see it in your features when you're shifting in your bed. That's much better managed here. I don't think you would cope at home. The doctors will want to discharge you as soon as they can, but that's not going to happen until they feel you're ready. I know how frustrated you are, but it's just going to take a little time.'

She leant forward and kissed him on his cheek, wishing she could wave a magic wand and make everything better. 'There's no one who wants you home more than I do. I miss you so much, the house just isn't the same without you in it. Every time the dogs hear a noise outside, their ears prick up and they rush to the door, expecting it to be you.' She pushed out her bottom lip. 'I explain to them that Daddy will be back soon, but I'm not sure they quite understand. You're going to get the biggest welcome when you do come home.'

Pia wasn't sure if they were tears of emotion glistening in Jackson's eyes or if it was the pain that was making his eyes water.

'I'm no good to anyone here. I should be back at the hall making sure everything's in place for the weekend.'

'I've told you, there's no need to worry. We had a meeting this morning with Tom, Stu, Mateo and Frank, and went through the schedule of events. I have to say, Tom has really stepped up and taken charge. Everyone knows what they should be doing now... well, fingers crossed, and it's great to have Stu on board because he clearly knows his stuff. Really, it's going to be absolutely fine, although I know so many people are going to be disappointed that you're not there.' She sighed and squeezed his hand tight. 'It really won't be the same without you, but we're all determined to put on the show you would want it to be. I'll be taking lots of photos and filming as much of the event as I can, so you won't miss out entirely.'

Jackson raised his eyebrows, the despondence held within those dark brown eyes impossible to ignore.

'I know it's disappointing, Jackson, but there'll be next year. And the year after that. You've said yourself that this is only the beginning. We'll look back in years to come and this upset, the inconvenience of this year will just be a faded memory.'

'You reckon?'

She could tell by his demeanour, the set of his jaw, that there would be no getting through to him. He was fed up, frustrated and truculent, but she supposed it was understandable. Jackson was used to doing exactly what he wanted when he wanted, and he didn't like to be thwarted in his plans at all.

'Oh, we had visitors this morning.' She was keen to move the subject on to something cheerier. 'Katy popped in with the children and Rosie wanted me to give you this.' She pulled out the card from her rucksack and handed it over. Jackson took the piece of paper and held it up in one direction before turning it round the other way, but he was none the wiser. He shrugged and raised a smile.

'Is this supposed to be me?' he asked, his brow furrowing as he examined the paper more closely.

'No,' Pia laughed, glad of the opportunity to lighten the mood. 'I think that's Pip and Rosie, and they're the animals. Twinkle, Little Star, Bertie and Teddy,' she said, pointing them out individually.

'Of course they are. Silly me.'

'And Lizzie has sent some of your favourite lemon bars.' Pia peeled off the lid of the box and offered one to Jackson, who took one resignedly, biting into it.

'I shall be twice the size when I leave this place, the amount of cakes and biscuits I'm eating. That's all there is to do here.'

'Oh, stop it, Jackson,' Pia scolded him. She suspected he reserved all his complaints for her especially. 'You're lucky. Lucky to be alive. Do you realise that?'

'You don't understand, Pia. I really need to be at the show. There are some bikes being displayed that I wanted to have a closer look at. This would have been the perfect opportunity to compare a couple of them that I've had my eye on. I know you can look at sales listings online, but there's nothing like seeing them for yourself, in the flesh, to check out the tyres, to listen to the thrum of the engine, to know...'

'Hang on a minute.' She paused to glare at him, putting down her half-eaten cake on her lap. 'You're not telling me you're actually considering buying another bike? Not after what just happened? You have to be kidding me.'

'What?' He scrunched up his nose, as though he couldn't make sense of what she was saying, and ordinarily she might have found it endearing. Only now she found it infuriating. 'You know I've been on the lookout for another bike to add to the collection for some time now.'

'Yes, but that was before the accident. You can't really be considering ever getting back on a bike again?'

'Err, yeah, of course I will. Why wouldn't I?'

'Oh, Jackson, don't you realise how close we came to losing you forever?' Jackson's expression was impassive. 'Look what happened to Ryan. The same thing could so easily have happened to you.'

She didn't like to bring up the subject of his friend who died in a motorbike accident when he was still a teenager. Jackson carried a lot of guilt over that, he'd been with Ryan on the night when he died. The two young guys, close friends, had been racing around the village and over the fields on their mopeds before making their separate ways home. Only Ryan had never made it home and Jackson only discovered the next day that his friend had lost control of his bike and careered off the road. It had been the catalyst for Jackson leaving the village, and his teenage love at the time, Pia, and not returning for several years.

'That was entirely different.'

Was it? It was the first thing Pia had thought of when she heard about Jackson's accident. It must have surely brought back some terrible memories for him too.

'Look, Pia, I appreciate your concern, but you cannot expect me to give up my bikes. They're my passion, what I love to do. You know that.' He looked at her imploringly. 'I could just as easily have an accident falling off a kerb or going out in the car. There are no guarantees in life, none of us know what's around the corner, but I'm not going to give up on something that I love just because I might have an accident one day.'

She looked into his dark brown eyes, tears gathering in her own. Did he have no idea how it was for her? How she felt every time he left the grounds of the hall on that bike, worrying the entire time about his safety and whether or not he would come home in one piece. Now the worst had happened and it took all her self-control not to tell him, 'I told you so.'

'Besides, I think it's much better to go out in a blaze of glory, rather than die sitting in my armchair with a mug of cocoa by my side looking back wistfully with regrets over the things I didn't do.'

'Don't say that! I don't want you going out in a blaze of glory.' She lowered her voice, only just remembering that she was in a busy hospital ward. 'Have you given any thought to how that would make me feel? Or your parents?'

Jackson blew his cheeks out, his dark eyes snagging on hers.

'Well, I didn't say that was my plan. All I'm saying is that I'm not going to stop doing the things I love on the off chance that something might go wrong one day. I'm an experienced rider, Pia. I'm not reckless, I don't take chances. This accident wasn't my fault. I always try to be vigilant and in light of what's happened, I'll probably be even more vigilant, but sorry, I'm not going to stop riding. If I had to do that, then you might as well shoot me now.'

She took a deep breath. She knew he was only trying to lighten his words with humour but she was finding none of this funny in the slightest.

'Hey, don't look like that.' He pulled on her hand and she moved closer so that he could embrace her in a one-armed hug. Even that gentle manoeuvre had him grimacing in pain. 'You know I love you and I would do anything for you. Just not this.' He left a kiss on her cheek and she felt a tidal wave of emotion swell inside her body. 'Don't cry,' he said, spotting the tears which she could do nothing to contain. She hadn't cried once since she heard about Jackson's accident. Her body had been held tight with pent-up emotion, as she ran on adrenaline these last few days, and it was only now in the safety of Jackson's arms that she could let go, hugging him as tightly to her chest as his injuries would allow. She reached for the box of tissues on the side cabinet and blew her nose noisily. There would no point in protesting, in trying to change Jackson's mind, because she knew on some matters he was entirely non-negotiable and this was clearly one of them. *Would she want him any other way?*

He cradled her head and she drank in the scent of him. Entirely Jackson, but with overtones of disinfectant and antiseptic cream. Not that it mattered, she was just happy to be held in his arms. They stayed like that for a good few minutes and if Pia closed her eyes, she could almost imagine that they were at home, curled up on the sofa, with the dogs around them, instead of on a sterile hospital ward. That was until their moment of peace was interrupted by a blonde-eyed, blue-eyed nurse who

Pia hadn't seen before, although it was clear that Jackson had, as she seemed very cheery with him and very familiar too.

'I've just come on shift and you are my first port of call. How are you today?' She beamed at Jackson. 'You're looking a lot brighter than yesterday. I expect that's due to your visitor.'

The nurse went on chatting gaily and Pia reluctantly extracted herself from Jackson's hold. She supposed she was only doing her job, but she wished she would go and do it somewhere else. Was it unreasonable to be resentful of the nurse, who was probably getting to see much more of Jackson than she was right now? She'd been enjoying that moment snuggled up with him, it had helped to dry her tears, but the nurse clearly had other ideas. She busied herself around his bed, looking at charts, refilling his water jug, asking if he'd like a sandwich, and generally making a fuss over him, which seemed to amuse Jackson no end.

'I can't complain about the care I'm receiving here, they're all so lovely and attentive,' Jackson said, once the nurse had left with a promise that she would be back later with his medications. 'Everyone, without exception, has been really kind and helpful, especially when I'm not sure I'm the most accommodating patient.'

'Isn't that the truth?' said Pia with an indulgent smile. It had been hugely reassuring for Pia to know that Jackson was receiving the best treatment from the most dedicated surgeons with the aftercare from the nurses and healthcare assistants second to none, but she would be so much happier when he was at home so that she could look after him for herself, even if she appreciated that might be no easy task.

'Your mum wants to do a Zoom call on Sunday over breakfast so they can hear all about the show. She joked that Rex was considering hopping on a plane to come over for the day. I think he's so disappointed to be missing it.'

'That makes two of us,' said Jackson glumly.

'They're going to notice that you're not there, Jackson! I really think you need to speak to your mum and tell her so that it doesn't come as a huge shock to them when they do find out about the accident. They're bound to at some point. The trouble is it only takes one of the villagers to drop a text to your mum or your dad for them to find out the news from someone else. Can you imagine how that would make them feel?'

'I guess,' he sighed as he rolled back his shoulders, closing his eyes briefly. 'Look, let's get the show out of the way and then I'll give them a call. Everything will be fine, well, just as soon as I get out of this place it will be. You worry too much, do you know that?'

Maybe she did, but then someone had to. This was her family and Pia hated keeping secrets from them. And that wasn't the only thing she had to worry about. As well as the car show, they had a whole calendar of events lined up at the hall, Jackson had a diary packed full of speaking engagements and charity events that would need rearranging and then there was the small matter of a wedding to be organised. Something would have to give and Pia suspected she knew exactly what that might be.

20

The day of the car show dawned and Pia was awake far too early, but there was absolutely no chance of her getting back to sleep, not with all that adrenaline racing around her veins. She threw on some jeans and a sweatshirt and went down to the kitchen to be greeted, as she was every day, by Bertie and Teddy scampering over to see her, their tails wagging excitedly. Honestly, she wasn't sure how she would have got through this last week without them. They offered so much emotional support, simply by being there and bringing a routine to the day which gave her some sense of normality.

She made herself a mug of coffee and plucked a banana from the fruit bowl, before sitting at the kitchen table savouring the peace and quiet, knowing it wouldn't last for long. It would be such a busy day, and she knew she probably wouldn't sit down from the time the first visitor came through the gates until the last visitor had left at the end of the day. She took some time to get her thoughts in order, running through her mental checklist of everything she needed to do, although really all the preparation work had been done and there would be nothing more to do until Tom and Stu arrived in a couple of hours' time for a final briefing meeting. Ivy would be coming in too and would be serving breakfast for anyone on the Primrose Hall team who wanted it. Pia picked up her phone and dashed off a text to Jackson.

Morning! Hope you had a good night's sleep? Today's the day! We'll miss you and I'll be thinking about you, but we're all determined to do you proud! Will send over lots of photos and I've lined someone up to do some filming. I'll keep you posted. The dogs send their love and so do I! Speak to you later xxx

She'd felt a pang of sadness pressing on the green arrow to send. Hopefully Jackson would still be asleep, although she knew that the days started early in hospital and it might be a very long day for him, stuck in bed, thinking about all that he was missing out on. Still, as she kept reminding herself, and him, it was only for one year, and there'd be so many other car shows in their future.

She jumped up from the table, determined not to let the negative thoughts overwhelm her. In the boot room she pulled on her coat and trainers and, with the dogs taking their cue, they rushed to the door to join her.

'Come on then, boys,' she called, and all three of them were relieved to step outside. Pia took a deep breath, relishing the sensation of the cool air on her skin, her heart lifting as she watched the dogs lolloping across the grass. At least she'd done something right already, the weather forecast promised warm and sunny spells, with no prospect of rain, and she didn't care what anyone might say, she was definitely going to take full credit for that.

With a sense of expectation wafting in the air, the grounds of Primrose Hall looked stunning, which was primarily down to Mateo's passion for horticulture and all his hard work. The lawns were newly mown and the beds in front of her were filled with summer blooms of lupins in purples and pinks, puffy sweet-smelling peonies and swathes of blue delphiniums. Over near the stables was the rose garden, filled with old-fashioned varieties, and on the brink of the hill that swept down towards the valley was a bank of wildflowers that always reminded Pia of long-ago summers with long white socks and glasses of lemonade. All the visitors today

couldn't fail to be impressed with the beauty of their surroundings, especially with the tall and imposing redwood trees providing a protective
embrace all around them into the distance. Even for those long-suffering
partners who weren't petrol heads themselves, they would hopefully find
something of interest to amuse them in the grounds of the hall. There
were several pathways to be explored around the gardens with so many
different shrubs and flowers to admire, and old stone benches positioned
in secluded spots where you could sit for a moment to appreciate the best
views of the countryside. There was even a gateway through to Primrose
Woods country park if anyone wanted to venture further afield.

Pia walked around the boundary of the property, which abutted the
woods, allowing the dogs to mooch around at their leisure, accompanied
by the glorious dawn chorus. She was amused at how much racket they
made. It was a noise she would often wake up to, but it was a sound she
would never grow tired of. Occasionally on their walks the dogs would
spot a squirrel and they would be off in hot pursuit, but both Bertie and
Teddy were never quite fast enough to reach those scurrying nimble creatures before they hot-footed it up the nearest tree. She came across one of
those stone benches and took the opportunity to sit and watch the dogs
as they romped around the grounds, their antics making her laugh, as she
was happy to simply soak up the atmosphere.

In a few hours, this place would be abuzz with visitors and activity
and Pia was looking forward to welcoming them all. It was what she and
Jackson had worked so hard for. It had always been Jackson's intention,
ever since he had bought the hall when it was a crumbling ruin standing
neglected amongst overgrown vegetation, to share it with the local
community once it had been restored to its former glory. He often told
Pia how he considered himself to be only the custodian of the hall, with a
duty to preserve it for future generations.

Every day, Pia was struck by how lucky she was to call the magnificent
Primrose Hall, set in the beautiful verdant countryside, her home. She
tried to imagine what her mum and dad would say if they were still
around to see all this for themselves, and she could just picture their
wide-eyed amazement. They would be so proud that she had stepped
right out of her comfort zone and taken on a busy and demanding role,

achieving so much in a relatively short space of time. More than that, they'd be thrilled that she'd found some security and contentment of her own after caring for her parents for so long.

'We should get back!' she said, more to herself than the dogs, who were currently investigating a mole hill over by the meadow. Mateo would not be pleased! The local wildlife was the bane of his existence, especially the moles who were determined to leave their mounds of earth all over his pristine lawns, the squirrels who buried their nuts in the grass and flowerbeds, and the foxes who deposited something much less savoury in all sorts of places. Pia would always listen sympathetically to Mateo as he grumbled about the visiting fauna, but secretly it delighted her to think of all the animals converging in the grounds, having their very own party.

Back at the hall, and after a quick shower and change of clothes, Pia was pleased to find Frank and Mateo in the kitchen, and Ivy had the coffee on and had laid out some pastries and fresh fruit on the oak table.

Soon Tom and Stu arrived too, along with another couple of guys who would be marshalling the stewards hired for the day. Pia had arranged walkie-talkies so that they could all keep in touch and alert each other to any issues that might arise. Hopefully, she had thought of everything, but you could never tell with these events, and usually something cropped up. After the sausage and bacon rolls had been served, everyone made moves to get outside and do some last-minute checks.

'Honestly, Tom, I can't thank you enough for coming. It just gives me so much confidence knowing that I can call on you and Stu in case of any problems. It's a shame Jackson's not here, but it can't be helped. I can imagine his mood this morning, knowing he'll be missing out.'

'Well, I'm very pleased to be here. The forecast is looking good, so I think we'll be in for a great day. Don't worry about Jackson. I've already had several texts from him reminding me about certain things that need doing, an inventory of where things are kept and a list of people I need to talk to. You know, it's almost as though he's here.' Tom slipped an arm round Pia's waist and gave her a sidelong grin.

'Well, aren't you the lucky one? He's not even replied to my text. I'm going into the hospital tonight to give him a blow-by-blow account of the day, so I need to remember to take lots of photos.'

She'd signed up one of the young stewards to film as much of the day's events as was possible and it was a little later, as she stood with him outside the front portico of the hall to watch as the classic cars started to arrive, that she felt a ripple of goosebumps travel along her arms. The cars, in all different shapes, sizes and colours, made a stately procession as they drove along the wide driveway and Pia thought how splendid they looked as they made their approach to the grounds. She bit on her lip, overcome by an unexpected swirl of emotion. She might not know the first thing about vehicles from a bygone age but the sight of them all together, pootling along the drive, stirred a reaction deep down inside of her.

Stu was ready and waiting with his clipboard to direct the participating cars and motorbikes into their display positions and she could see him in the distance, leaning down to talk to the drivers in turn through their car windows, before directing them to the main arena. She spotted Tom too walking around the grounds, chatting to each of the stallholders. From that point on, the day took on a momentum of its own and soon the visitors were arriving, bringing with them a palpable excitement in the air. Pia was pleased to see so many familiar faces and everyone was eager to know how Jackson was doing.

'He's much better than he was, thank you. He's a bit fed up being confined to his hospital bed, but he's going in the right direction.'

'Well, send him our love and best wishes, won't you?'

It was the same message from everyone she bumped into, the air of goodwill radiating around the show lifting her spirits even further. She took a leisurely amble around the grounds, making sure she stopped at every stall, and admired each and every vehicle, which had all been polished to such an extent that they gleamed beneath the summer sun. She pulled out her phone and took some more photos and fired them off to Jackson.

Don't they all look fab! If there's anything in particular you want to see then let me know and I will go and track it down. There's such a brilliant turnout and everyone's having a great time. All your hard work has definitely paid off. Everyone's asking about you, and we're all missing you dreadfully! Hope you're feeling okay today?

She added, as an afterthought:

Lots of love xxx

Perhaps he was having a bad day managing his pain levels. That might be why she hadn't heard from him. She knew that he put on a brave front for her, didn't tell her the extent of his discomfort, but he didn't have to. She could tell, by the way he bit on his lips and how his face creased in agony, how much he was going through. He probably had his head under a pillow trying to get some relief from his suffering and an escape from the realisation that his precious car show would be going ahead without him.

'Stu!' Pia spotted him as he just finished a conversation with a couple of leather-clad motorcyclists. 'How's it going?'

'Great. Just look around you,' he said, gesturing to the crowds milling around. 'Look at those smiling faces. Everyone I've spoken to has said what a great event it is, so I think you've definitely achieved what you set out to do. Bringing all these people together with all these amazing old vehicles in such a beautiful setting, it's the perfect combination. Some people were expecting to see Jackson, of course, so they were pretty shocked to hear about his accident. I expect he'll receive a flurry of "get well" texts.'

'Well, as long as they won't be expecting a reply, because he's certainly not replying to my messages or his mother's!' Pia was joking, but being here today, amongst all their visitors who were so enjoying themselves, brought home to her just how much Jackson was missing out on. She kept looking to her side, expecting him to be there, but instead experienced a pang of loss, feeling his absence keenly. She took a glance at her watch. It was after two o'clock and she hadn't had anything to eat or drink since breakfast. No wonder she was feeling wobbly. Obviously her blood sugar was low.

'Look, I'm going to take a break to have a drink and grab something to eat. Do you fancy coming back for a cuppa or a beer if you prefer? A glass of wine?' There were plenty of food and drink stalls around them, but Pia wanted to get back to the house to check on the dogs.

'A beer would go down a treat,' said Stu, who walked with her in the direction of the hall. Not that their progress was straightforward. They had to keep stopping to talk to people, which was no hardship whatsoever, but it did mean it was another twenty minutes before they reached the hall. They were just about to walk through the side door into the kitchen when something caught Pia's eye.

'What's that?' she asked, Stu's gaze following hers as it drifted down the driveway, where an old lorry had turned into the hall grounds and was making a slow approach towards the hall. 'It looks like we have a late arrival.'

'I'll tell you exactly what that is. It's a Dodge WC-54 ambulance from World War II, although I know we didn't have anything like that on our entry list. Not that it matters, all vehicles are welcome. I've just got to think where I'm going to put them. There's no space in the main display area so I might have to send them across to the car park.' Stu was thinking out loud. 'Let me go and have a chat with the driver and I'll get something sorted. Then I'll be back for that cold beer. Hang on a minute.' Stu placed his hands on his hips. Instead of following the marked signs for exhibitors, the old ambulance had turned off the driveway and was making its approach up to the hall, close to where Stu and Pia were standing.

'What's the silly sod doing?' Stu muttered. 'Can't he read?'

The driver brought the ambulance to a halt just in front of them, turned off the ignition and climbed out of the cab.

'Sorry, you can't park up here, you're going to have to take it around to the car park at the other end of the driveway. I'm afraid we don't have any space left in the arena, but you're welcome to leave it over there.' Stu pointed in the right direction, but the driver just grinned at him.

'I've got a special delivery for you,' he explained, walking round to the back of the ambulance, and Stu and Pia followed him round, looking at each other curiously. Looking inordinately pleased with himself, the driver opened up the doors with a flourish.

'Ta da!'

'What on earth... No, I don't believe it,' said Stu, breaking into laughter.

'Oh, my God,' said Pia, not believing her eyes. 'Jackson! What on earth are you doing here?'

21

'It's so beautiful out there now,' said Katy, who came in through the doors of the stables, her cheeks glowing a healthy pink, after spending some time outside with her family. 'Thanks for minding my stall,' she said to Sophie. 'Did we have a rush on in my absence?' she joked.

'Well, I did sell some of your birthday card packs. I've written it down in your notebook and put the money through.'

'Brilliant, I shall have to go out more often, in that case.'

'Is it busy out there?' Sophie asked.

'Really busy, but it's such a lovely atmosphere, and all the cars look amazing. Rosie is having the best time, and she's dragging her dad in every direction, she's determined to see everything. We went over to see Little Star and Twinkle in the paddock. She just loves them. Every time we come to the hall, she has to go and say hello to "her" animals.'

'That's adorable,' said Sophie, who had met Katy's children on a couple of occasions now and thought how cute they were.

'Rosie was disappointed not to see Jackson, but she understands that he's in hospital. She made a special card for him. Anyway, Brad's taken her to have her face painted now so she's very excited about that. Apparently, she wants to be a Dalmatian puppy, just like Bertie.'

'Oh, I can just imagine how she'll look.'

They were still laughing when Tom wandered in. For the briefest moment, Sophie's mind played tricks on her, seeing the tall and handsome guy through the glazed door of the stables, and thinking it was Jackson, but when he came onto the threshold, his gaze searching out hers, their eyes meeting, she realised instantly her mistake. Tom was dressed in navy chinos and a pale pink polo shirt and looked very handsome in a way that spoke directly to the base of her stomach.

She'd not had a chance to talk to him yet today. She'd given him a wave first thing this morning when he'd popped into the stables, but then he'd dashed off again to see to his duties outside.

'Have you had a look round the show yet?' he asked, when he came across to her.

'Not yet,' she said, noticing the butterflies in her stomach, which were making a habit of appearing every time Tom was on the scene.

'Do you fancy coming for a wander now then?' he offered.

'You were just saying you wanted to go and have a look, weren't you?' Katy butted in. 'You get off and I'll look after your stall. Take your time, there's no hurry.'

Sophie was grateful to Katy, although she wondered if she was perhaps overdoing it in her rallying for her to go off with Tom. She got the message loud and clear. Hopefully Tom wouldn't have noticed Katy's comical insistent nodding and wide-eyed encouragement, she thought with a smile.

* * *

Although Tom had been busy ever since he'd arrived at the hall this morning, he hadn't been that preoccupied that thoughts of Sophie didn't keep sliding into his mind. He spotted her first thing over at the stables as she was setting up her stall, the morning sun catching the red lights in her glossy brown hair, and he'd so wanted to go across and say hello, to give her a hug, to feel the sensations he'd experienced when he'd last held her in his arms, but he was conscious that he needed to hold back on his emotions. Sophie had recently come out of a long-term relationship which he knew had been toxic and had left her emotionally vulnerable, and she'd admitted to him that she was relishing her newfound freedom and single status. Tom thought he might have said something similar himself. They'd established the rules, they were friends, at similar stages in their lives and they were there to support each other as they both navigated their way through the process of picking up the pieces and starting all over again. What would Sophie think if she knew that Tom's feelings had shifted to something deeper?

The other night at her cottage, after the dinner they'd shared together, there was a moment where he'd become overwhelmed with a desire to kiss her and he'd realised then he had to get out of there quick, or else he might have ended up doing something he would come to regret. It was clear that Sophie enjoyed his company as a friend, but he didn't want to jeopardise their new friendship by making an impulsive and spontaneous move that might not be reciprocated by her.

'It's lovely to get out,' Sophie said now, when they stepped outside into the afternoon sun. She lifted her face to the sky and held her arms out in front of her, soaking up the warmth of the day. When she turned to him with those sparkling hazel eyes, any lingering doubt he might have had that the feelings he'd struggled with the other night were down to the food and wine, and the cosy atmosphere, were quashed in that moment. The feelings he felt for her were very real and seemed to grow in intensity with every moment he spent with her.

'How have you been? I'm guessing very busy?' she asked.

'Yes, it's been full-on getting ready for today, so it's been a little stressful, only because Jackson's not here and we all felt that we wanted to get it right for him. Looking around, though, I think we've probably managed it.'

'Too right you have.' Sophie grabbed hold of Tom's arm and shook it gently in a gesture of support. 'Well done.' They locked eyes for a moment before Sophie dropped her gaze and her touch on his arm, as though she only just realised what she'd done. 'Do you mind if we take the far path around the grounds? I've always wanted to go along there, it looks so inviting.'

'Let's do it,' said Tom with a smile.

The path that Sophie referred to abutted Primrose Woods and was laid with bark and lined with wildflowers, painting a pretty pink palette. It was narrow and winding, but offered gorgeous glimpses into the woods. The tall redwoods, monkey puzzles and scattered oak trees rose above them and Sophie craned her head, looking all around her.

'Isn't it beautiful?' she whispered. 'To think that just around the corner there are all those hundreds of people milling about the car show and you can wander a short distance away and find all this peace and solitude. I think Jackson and Pia are so lucky to have this oasis in their back garden. Can you imagine what it must be like to live here?'

'Pretty amazing, I'm guessing.'

A little while later, after following the path all the way around and ending up on the main terrace behind the hall, they found a bench where Sophie plonked herself down.

'I could probably sit here all day and just admire the view. I'm sure I wouldn't get any work done if I worked here like Pia. There're far too many distractions.'

'Yep. Sitting here makes me realise I probably need to move on from my flat.' Tom laughed. 'I mean, it's done me well these last few months, but it's pretty cramped and there's no outdoor space. Even a small patch of lawn would be welcome, especially when you see something like this.'

'Yeah, do you think you'll start looking round?'

'I will, and of course it helps working at the estate agents because I get to see new properties as soon as they go up on the market so there's definitely some perks.'

'You won't move away from this area, though, will you?'

Tom turned to meet Sophie's enquiring expression. She'd asked the question casually enough, but he wondered if it would matter to her if he did decide to move away to another part of the country. Not that he had any intention of doing so. Where would he go? Besides, now that he'd reconnected with his dad and Jackson, he didn't want to do anything that might impact on those relationships. He'd spent all his life looking for that sense of family and belonging and now that he'd found it, there was no way he would allow it to slip through his fingers.

'No, I'd like to stay round here. I've got my family here now.' He felt a swell of pride as he said the words aloud. 'And some lovely friends too,' he said, his eyes snagging on hers.

'Good,' said Sophie, with a smile. 'I'm relieved to hear it. Do you fancy an ice cream? I think I spotted a van over there?'

'Ah, you're a bad influence, Sophie Wright, do you know that? First you tempted me with drinks down at the pub along with a roast dinner and pud, then fishcakes and chocolates round at yours, and now ice creams.' He patted his stomach with the flat of his hand, blowing out his cheeks. He wouldn't admit that she tempted him in so many other ways too. Just being with Sophie made him feel good, a feeling that excited and disturbed him in equal measure. He realised he was falling for her in a way that there was no coming back from. He suppressed a sigh. How had he even allowed it to happen when he'd vowed to himself he would be happy to stay single? Much better for his state of mind, he'd decided, but that was before Sophie had turned up unexpectedly in his life.

'Ha, well, it seems to me you didn't need much persuading. Come on,' she said, laughing, and he realised, in that moment, that her smile fed a hunger that couldn't be sated by ice cream alone.

They mooched around the show in companionable silence, their attentions distracted by the delicious cones they'd purchased. Sophie had opted for a stracciatelli while Tom had chosen strawberries and cream, and they looked every bit as enticing as they'd promised to be.

'Oh, no,' Sophie exclaimed, staring at her ice cream intently.

'What's the matter?' Tom asked, immediately concerned.

'I don't know if this is off or something. There's a very funny smell.' Her nose crinkled up in distaste as she offered the cone up to Tom so that he could take a whiff. He leant forward and no sooner had he done so than she lifted the ice cream into his face so that he had the creamy concoction plastered all over his nose. She hadn't been able to stop herself and quickly dissolved into laughter.

It took a second or two for Tom to realise what had happened, his face showing first confusion and then comprehension of what had just occurred.

'Okay, right. I see how it is,' he said, chasing after Sophie, brandishing his ice cream cone as a weapon, as she hot-footed it away.

'No, don't! Stop!' she said, still laughing. 'I'm sorry, that was mean of me, but I really couldn't resist.' She grinned at him and in that moment he thought he would probably forgive her anything. 'Here, let me clean you up.'

She reached into her pocket and pulled out a tissue and stood in front of Tom, wiping away the vanilla and chocolate from his face. He cast his gaze to the side, plastering on an unimpressed expression. He couldn't look her in the eye, not when she was standing so close, when he could catch the light fragrant scent of her, when it would be all too easy to reach out and place his hands on her waist, and lean across to kiss her. Honestly, what was this woman doing to him? Thankfully, something else caught her attention, and she spun round to look in the direction of the hall.

'What's going on over there? Who is that? It's not...?'

Tom turned round to look and saw one of the old classic vehicles parked up outside the hall. What was it doing up there? On closer inspection, it looked like a vintage ambulance and if he wasn't mistaken they'd gone the whole hog and someone had dressed up as an invalid in a wheelchair. It made him smile as he knew how some exhibitors liked to throw themselves wholeheartedly into these events, dressing up as characters from World War II or as if they'd just walked out of an American diner in the 1950s. Only, as Tom peered more closely, he saw Pia and Stu were there too, and that's when he realised that it wasn't someone in fancy dress after all, but someone else entirely.

'It is...' he said, shaking his head. 'It's Jackson. They can't have let him out of hospital already, surely? Last time I saw him, he couldn't even get out of bed on his own. Come on,' he said, taking Sophie by the hand. 'Let's go and see what's going on.'

22

'Oh, my God!' Pia repeated herself. She knew what she was seeing, but her brain couldn't quite make sense of it. 'They've let you home already, but I thought... No, that can't be right. In fact, that's totally irresponsible. What on earth's going on?'

It took her a few moments before she realised something wasn't quite adding up here. He was in a wheelchair, his legs out in front of him, his pyjamas still visible beneath an unfamiliar black hoody, and he'd turned up in an old ambulance. She knew the NHS was under-funded, but this was ridiculous. Surely they weren't sending home patients in old World War II vehicles now. And why hadn't Jackson told her he was coming home? She would have made arrangements for him and sorted out the ground-floor guest suite. That had been her intended job for the coming week, but it didn't matter. She and Ivy could have a quick whizz around the room to make sure he had a clear route to the en suite and put in place everything he would need to make him comfortable.

'Trust you to make that sort of entrance,' said Stu, still chuckling. 'You always did know how to arrive in style. It's great to see you here, Jackson.' He helped the driver with manoeuvring the wheelchair out of the ambulance.

Pia looked at Stu askance. Did he know something she didn't? And if not, why didn't he have a hundred and one questions like her?

'Don't I get a hug then?' Jackson asked her, with that familiar tempting smile on his face.

'Yes, I suppose. I'm so shocked, that's all.' She looked around, hoping someone might fill in the blank spaces for her. She leant down and wrapped her arms around his chest, but she couldn't enjoy the moment because her head was full of all sorts of unanswered questions. She pulled back, to look into his eyes. 'Where's all your medications and your belongings? You must be so uncomfortable in that old chair. Let's get you indoors, I can make us a pot of tea and you can fill us in on what's happened.'

'I'm not staying, Pia,' Jackson said with a sheepish grin. 'And I haven't come for afternoon tea. It's a flying visit so that I can have a quick whizz around the show and then I'll need to get back to the ward.'

'What?' That's when the alarm bells began to clang for Pia, and a thud of realisation hit her in the chest, as she looked from Jackson to Stu, and then to Tom, who had just joined them, with Sophie at his side.

'Please tell me the doctors know you're here, Jackson. That you actually have permission to leave the hospital?'

She looked at the driver, who had wrapped his arms around his chest and was slowly edging away so that he disappeared out of sight around the other side of the ambulance.

'Not exactly, but don't worry, Pia. It's the weekend and the doctors are never around at this time of day. They won't even know I'm gone. If anyone asks, they'll be told that I've been taken out into the hospital gardens for some much-needed fresh air. They encourage it, Pia. It's healing to be outside, so I can't see that I'm doing anything wrong.'

'What? I can't believe you would do something like that.' Pia looked around at the others for some moral support. What was he thinking? 'This is totally reckless. The whole reason that you're in that hospital bed is so that you can make a full recovery, that you don't take unnecessary risks that might impact on the stability of your pelvis. Nothing is worth jeopardising that for. Not even this stupid show.'

'It might be stupid to you, Pia, but it's not to me,' Jackson bit back at her. 'And if you really feel that way, then are you really the right person to be running the event today?'

'She didn't mean it like that, Jackson.' Tom stepped in and laid a hand on Jackson's shoulder, a calming presence between the two warring factions. 'Pia's worked her backside off to make this day a success. She's just worried about you. We all are.'

'Well, there's no need. I've gone to a lot of trouble to get here so let me go and see what I've come for.' This was directed at Stu, but he turned and reached out a hand to Pia. 'Don't be like this, Pia. I'm really happy to see you, to be home again. Honestly, there were moments when I was lying in that ditch after the accident where I thought I might not make it. I had to come today. I simply had to. I hope you can understand. Are you coming with me?'

She nodded, hardly trusting herself to say anything. Inside she was still simmering with tension, but she had no choice. She could hardly storm off into the house for a cup of tea as she'd planned, although that was precisely what she wanted to do. What would the hospital say if they found out that one of their patients had done a bunk? She couldn't believe the arrogance of the man she was planning to marry, who thought that his desires and needs came above everyone else's and he could do exactly as he pleased like he always did. The hospital would be perfectly within their rights to refuse to treat him any more if he was going to so blatantly ignore their advice.

The driver, who she wanted to interrogate for his role in this charade, avoided eye contact with her and instead concentrated on steering the wheelchair over to the main arena. Stu walked alongside and chatted animatedly to Jackson, giving him a rundown of all the different vehicles on display while Pia walked on the other side, still holding Jackson's hand, still wrestling with so many conflicting thoughts and feelings.

She looked around her at all the smiling faces. Everyone was so pleased to see Jackson, which made her feel even more miserable and truculent when she couldn't share in their enthusiasm. She hadn't meant it when she called the show stupid, it had been her frustration getting the better of her. It was obvious to see and hear in Jackson's voice how buoyed he was by being amongst his pals, but that wasn't the point.

Couldn't he appreciate that he could be putting back his recovery by coming here? Even the journey from the hospital to the hall in that old jalopy presented a risk, rattling his bones in a way she was sure no doctor would advise. She exhaled a sigh, and Jackson looked up, giving her a subtle and conspiratorial wink, and despite herself she felt her body responding in the way it always did, which annoyed her no end, when her mind was still entertaining the idea that she might actually murder him when she got him away from all these people.

The short trip across to the cars took an age because everyone wanted to stop and say hello to Jackson and to hear how he was getting on, and all Pia could do was plaster on a smile, and confirm, through gritted teeth, that yes, it really was lovely to have him home again.

'Are you okay?' Tom came across and put a reassuring arm around Pia's shoulder while Stu took Jackson along the rows of cars and bikes, where they stopped to view each one in turn and chat to the owners.

'I'm not sure.' She shook her head and looked into Tom's kindly expression, grateful to him for being there and for sticking up for her earlier. 'Jackson never ceases to amaze me, and not always in a good way.'

'Yep, but you know what he's like. I guess he's waited all year for this event and he clearly decided that the accident wasn't going to stop him from being here. You have to admire his passion and determination.'

'I suppose,' said Pia, curling up her lip doubtfully. They were qualities she had admired in Jackson, along with so many others, but sometimes his bloody-mindedness drove her to distraction. Once he'd set his mind to something then there could be no turning him. She only hoped that this particular escapade wouldn't backfire.

'There's never a dull moment living with Jackson, I bet,' said Sophie with a sympathetic smile.

'Isn't that the truth,' said Pia. She suspected that she would never be able to change him even if she wanted to and would have to accept that their life together would be a series of adventures, and misadventures. That wasn't to say she would so easily forgive him for today's antics. His actions were a blatant disregard and disrespect for the medical staff who had gone out of their way to give him the best possible care, and he'd thrown that back in their face. He needed to be made aware that it wasn't acceptable behaviour, but probably now wasn't the time to have that conversation. Not when he was being treated like a returning hero by everyone else.

She turned to her friend and slipped an arm through hers, as they watched Jackson, who had gathered a small crowd of well-wishers around him. It was almost as though he was a visiting celebrity. Still, no one could deny that the day had turned out to be the success it deserved to be and the glorious summer sunshine only added to the festival atmosphere.

Now Pia observed Sophie more closely and noticed how happy she seemed. There was a beatific smile on her face, as though she was hugging a big secret to herself. Her freckles across her face and shoulders had been brought out by the sun, along with the natural red highlights in her shoulder-length hair. It occurred to Pia that on the last few occasions she'd seen Sophie, Tom had been with her, and she briefly wondered if there was anything romantic brewing between the pair of them. They would certainly make a lovely couple, but then perhaps Pia's imagination was running away with her and they were just close friends.

One thing she had noticed was that they were both changed people since she'd first met them last year. Then Tom had been guarded and unsure about coming into the family, not knowing if Jackson would be interested in getting to know him better or would even want him in his life. To be fair, Jackson hadn't known that at the time either, as he had been ambivalent about the fact that he had a brother out there. It was only because of an expectation from his dad, and some gentle prodding from Ronnie and Pia, that Jackson had been persuaded to at least meet Tom and see where the relationship might take them. It was a relief to everyone, even if it had taken the two brothers a few months to discover how to be with each other, that they had found some kind of connection, which they were still continuing to build on today. Now, looking at Tom, Pia felt a swell of gratitude that he had come into their lives and enhanced it with his presence. Tom was just like his little brother in many respects, but perhaps he was more measured, and less reckless and impulsive than Jackson. Pia certainly couldn't imagine Tom pulling a stunt like Jackson had done today.

As for Sophie, when Pia had first come across her at the stables she'd seemed scared and emotional, and much smaller than she appeared now, as if she had folded in on herself, swamped as she was in an oversized hoody. Since then, Pia had watched Sophie blossom. It was as though she'd discovered the person she was really meant to be, and that was apparent in every aspect of her personality now. She stood taller, with her shoulders no longer hunched, her hair sometimes worn loose like it was today, a light covering of make-up bringing out her natural features. She laughed all the time now too, which was a lovely sound to hear. Pia didn't know what was going on with Tom and Sophie and if the changes she'd noticed in them had anything to do with them spending more time with each other, but she had to wonder if the magic of Primrose Hall was casting its spell over them as well. It certainly wouldn't be the worst thing in the world as far as Pia was concerned.

'Hey, you see, that wasn't so bad.' Stu and Jackson returned to where Pia was standing with Tom and Sophie. 'I have to say you guys have done a great job. Thanks for bringing all this together, Pia, and sorry for what I said earlier. I didn't mean it.' He held out his arms for a hug and Pia bent down to embrace him.

'I'm sorry too,' she said. How could she stay cross with Jackson for long when her overriding feeling was one of relief that he was still with them? 'I was wrong to call this a stupid show, it's a bloody brilliant event.' She kissed him on the cheek.

Jackson's wide grin told her that she was already forgiven, as he turned to look at his brother.

'Tom, a big thanks to you too for stepping in to help out. Someone over there said how they thought they'd been talking to me earlier in the day when of course they'd confused me with you. Which just goes to show how dispensable I really am.' He glanced between Pia and Tom, looking contrite. 'Anyway, thanks to you all. I really appreciate it. I've seen what I came here to see, have had some interesting conversations with some of my old mates and I might even have lined up a new bike in the process.' Pia's stricken expression gave away what she thought to that idea. 'Which will obviously go straight into the garage and will be admired from a distance,' Jackson quickly added to appease her. 'For the time being, at least.'

She shook her head at him indulgently.

'So no harm done, heh?' he said to Pia. 'I'll be back at the hospital in time for a no doubt delicious and inspiring tea.' He rolled his eyes and grimaced. 'No one will ever know I was away. Although I could just quickly say hello to the dogs before I leave. It seems like years since I last saw them.'

It was funny to think that it was only a week since the accident because in many ways it seemed much longer. The normality of their usual life seemed like a faded memory now.

'Come on,' Pia said, taking charge of the wheelchair and breaking into a trot, shaking off the remainder of her bad mood with Jackson. 'We'll have a quick cuppa and I'm sure we can find you something delicious to eat if you want it. There's some leek and potato soup on the Aga and there's a great selection of cakes to choose from too.'

At least Jackson's appetite hadn't been affected and he managed a bowlful of soup, followed by a slice of moist carrot cake. Seeing him at the kitchen table, she could almost imagine that it was just a normal afternoon and the accident had never happened, but only for the briefest moment.

The dogs went mad seeing Jackson again and Pia had to herd them carefully around the wheelchair so that they didn't launch themselves into his lap, but judging by the look on Jackson's face, it was more than worth it for the way it lifted his spirits. He exhaled a big sigh.

'God, it's good to be home. Do you think I could stay and not go back? I'm sure that hospital bed would be better utilised by someone else.'

'Absolutely not, Jackson. Do you really...' Her words trailed away as she saw the half-smile on his lips, his dark brown eyes twinkling with mischief. He was kidding her, but after everything else he'd done, she wouldn't put it past him to do something like that. She shook her head, wondering if his absence had been noted yet at the hospital.

'You really ought to get back, Jackson, before they send out the search parties for you.' As lovely as it was to have Jackson at home, she was getting very twitchy and annoyed again that he'd ever thought this was a good idea in the first place.

'Okay, I get the hint.' He reached out a hand for her, squeezing it tight. 'I miss you. Us. All this,' he said, sweeping his head around the room.

'I know, me too, but it won't be long before you're home again properly.' At least she hoped that was the case. Neither of them could know for certain, but she was keeping everything crossed that he might be discharged soon. She'd made the mistake of googling his type of injury and discovered all sorts of horror stories about patients undergoing weeks and sometimes months of treatment in hospital and rehabilitation centres. She really couldn't bear the thought of that, and as for Jackson, she was certain in those circumstances he would definitely be contemplating another escape party, and that needed to be avoided at all costs.

23

'Oh, my goodness, you missed all the excitement outside.' Sophie breezed through the double doors to the stables to relieve Katy from minding her stall. Tom had gone into the hall with Jackson and Stu for some refreshments.

'Why? What happened?' Katy was all ears.

'Well, you'll never guess who turned up in a wheelchair in an old vintage ambulance?'

Katy shook her head.

'Who?'

'Jackson Moody. Honestly, it was like something from a movie set. I don't think Pia was too happy about it because apparently she didn't have a clue that he was coming. He played hooky from hospital and had managed to persuade someone to bring him here, in an old World War II ambulance, no less!'

'Isn't that typical of Jackson? I can just imagine him doing something like that. I think he's fond of a grand gesture. I remember, I think it was only the second time I met Jackson, we were in the Three Feathers and he sent over bottles of champagne, as a thank you for us supporting the first Christmas carols event here at the hall. As if we needed thanking! But it was very lovely of him.'

'Yes, I think Jackson's a law unto himself and Pia was a bit shocked at him turning up like that, but hopefully it's all sorted now. I can imagine how Pia felt, though. She just wants him to get better, but I think Jackson likes to do things his own way.' Sophie chuckled.

'I get that impression too. Mind you,' said Katy breezily, 'I could quite happily put up with all his mercurial champagne-drinking ways if it meant living in the lap of luxury in that beautiful house. And you have to admit he's pretty hot too,' she fanned her hand in front of her, 'although don't tell Brad I said that. No, it would be no hardship whatsoever being holed up with Jackson.' Katy clasped her hands to her chest and went all dreamy, obviously conjuring up all sorts of scenarios with Jackson.

Sophie shook her head indulgently at Katy.

'I know you don't mean that. You're absolutely besotted with Brad and your lovely family.'

'Hmm, I suppose, but a girl's allowed to fantasise, isn't she?'

Sophie nodded in agreement, but it wasn't Jackson who filled her fantasies, but rather his older brother Tom who, to her eyes, was a much more attractive and charismatic proposition. She wasn't sure at what point her feelings for him had changed from being simply platonic to something more meaningful, but it had certainly come as a big surprise. She had told herself for weeks that she didn't have the time or the inclination for a relationship. She'd fought long and hard for her freedom and independence, revelling in her newfound single status, and she certainly had no intention of giving all that up for the sake of a man, especially when she knew how easily it could all go so wrong.

Why then was she so suddenly enamoured with Tom, whose natural and easy charm so attracted her? She supposed they had opened up to each other and shared details about their respective pasts, which had created an intimacy between them. She'd seen Tom's gentle, caring side and it made her feel safe and warm inside. He really listened to her, instead of being simply eager to get the conversation back onto him, which she'd found a lot of men did. Tom was genuinely interested in what she had to say, listening intently as though he was consigning it all to his memory, his dark eyes shining with attentiveness as she spoke. Although maybe it was just her hormones playing tricks on her, stirring sensations within that she hadn't felt in a long while.

'Sophie!'

'What?'

'You were miles away there.' Katy shook her head, laughing. 'I was just saying that you and Tom seem to be getting on pretty well these days.' There was an implied question in Katy's wide-eyed expression which Sophie chose to ignore.

'Yeah, he's really nice, isn't he? We were chatting about the workshops that he's organising for later in the year. I think they're a really good idea, but I know I'll be nervous when it comes to it. I've never really shown anyone else how I work and I'm afraid that I'll be found out, that someone will tell me I'm not doing it properly. Do you ever feel like that with your work?' Sophie asked.

Now it was Katy's turn to ignore a question and instead focus on something else she had on her mind.

'Do you think that there might be anything else on the cards for you and Tom, though? You seem so good together and there's nothing stopping you. You're both free and single.'

Sophie smiled, wondering if it was possible that Katy was a mind-reader. She gave a nonchalant shrug of her shoulders, a smile playing on her lips, which told Katy everything she needed to know.

'I thought so! Do you want me to have a quiet word with Tom, hurry things along a little? You know, I'd be ever so discreet.'

'Absolutely not,' Sophie said emphatically. The last thing she wanted was Katy's well-intentioned meddling. Besides, she was a grown woman, not a love-sick teenager. She was more than capable of sorting out her own love life, if she needed to. 'Honestly, we do get on well, but we're just good friends. I don't think either of us is looking for anything more at the moment.' And as she said it, she could hear how convincing it sounded, even if Katy's disappointment was all too apparent.

The rest of the afternoon passed quickly. There was a steady flow of visitors and Sophie enjoyed chatting to those who stopped to look around her stall, hearing where they'd come from and why they were here today. If they were true motor car enthusiasts or whether they'd simply come for a day out in the beautiful English countryside. She handed out a lot of her business cards and sold plenty of items too. It was interesting to see which of her pieces of jewellery were popular with her customers as it gave a good indication of where she should concentrate her efforts on replenishing her stocks. It gave her a sense of pride to hear people talk so positively about her work and it also gave her the confidence to consider her next moves in growing her small business.

'Are we going to the pub?' Katy asked later, as the traders were packing up their wares at the end of the day.

'Silly question,' piped up Mike. 'Of course we're going to the pub after all our hard graft here. I think we deserve a celebratory drink, don't you?'

Katy and Sophie laughed, because although they had been manning their stalls since early this morning, it really didn't feel like work to be here, in such a beautiful setting, amongst their fellow crafters, enjoying the chatter and ambience of such a special day.

'Ah, your ears must have been burning,' said Mike, as the doors to the stables opened and Tom strolled in. 'We were just talking about going to the pub.'

'That is good timing then. Count me in.' He glanced across at Sophie and she smiled before returning to the job in hand, aware of Katy's eagle eyes upon them both.

Everyone was in high spirits as they sat in the garden at the Three Feathers, revelling in the success of the day and enjoying the company of their friends, who understood the sense of satisfaction at sharing their creations with people who were willing to spend money on them. Laughter rang out and Sophie chatted with Josh and Cecily, who sat on either side of her. Occasionally she would look up and catch Tom's eye from across the table and she would give a shy smile, feeling suddenly self-conscious after her earlier conversation with Katy. Perhaps she'd built up her connection with Tom into something it really wasn't.

Sophie went up to the bar with Cecily to order another round of drinks and while they were waiting, Tom sidled up next to her.

'How are you?' he asked, with what was becoming a familiar smile that spoke directly to her insides.

'Really good, thank you. Wasn't it such a brilliant day? I hope Pia has forgiven Jackson. She was in a state of shock when he turned up like that.'

'Yep, what I've learned about my brother in the short amount of time that I've come to know him is that he is full of surprises, but I think it's all smoothed over now,' he said, with a low chuckle.

'That's a relief and oh, I'm sorry about the ice cream. I hope you've forgiven me.'

'Absolutely nothing to forgive, although... if you were to ever try that again then, you know, I might not be responsible for my actions.' There was a devilish glint in Tom's eyes and Sophie thought she quite liked the sound of whatever it was he had in mind. 'Look, I'm going to have to shoot off. I want to pop back to the hall to check that everything's been cleared away. I don't want Pia waking up to an almighty mess in the morning, but hopefully we can get together again soon.'

'Yes, that would be lovely.' Sophie plastered on a smile, hoping it would hide her disappointment. She'd entertained the idea of the two of them staying behind at the pub together again to have a proper catch-up after everyone else had left.

'I would offer to cook for you, repay your hospitality from the other night, but I think I've mentioned that my kitchen is the size of a cupboard and I probably don't have the necessary equipment to rustle up much of a dinner, other than a ready meal in the microwave.'

It made Sophie smile.

'Don't worry. You could always come to mine again or we could grab a takeaway?'

'Or we could go out to dinner? If you fancied it? No pressure.'

'That sounds...' It sounded full of possibilities and sent a swirl of excitement around her body. Her mouth twisted involuntarily as she tried to contain her enthusiasm. '...nice,' she said, as casually as she could muster.

'Great. Well, let me just firm up on what I'm doing this week and then I'll drop you a text and we can get something sorted.'

'Sounds like a plan,' she said, cringing as she said it. She blushed and suspected she was sporting a gormless expression too. She only hoped that Tom would overlook just how awkward she was in the face of a simple invitation to dinner.

24

Pia woke late on Sunday morning. She'd slept heavily as the stresses and the strains of the previous week had finally caught up with her and after a couple of well-deserved large glasses of red wine last night she'd collapsed into bed and slept right through. It was a surprise when she pulled off her eye mask, her sight adjusting to the light coming through the bedroom window, and she saw on the bedside clock that it was past nine o'clock. She never slept that late and her immediate thought was for the dogs, who would be champing at the bit to get outdoors. She pushed herself up and gave a glance around the room and found them still happily curled up in their beds. She sank back down beneath the covers, relishing the moment of peace and solitude. It was a relief that she didn't have to worry about the car show any longer, well, not for another year at least. It was all behind them and according to the exhibitors and visitors alike, it had been a huge success. Once she'd got over her anxiety and nerves, she had really enjoyed the day and even Jackson's impromptu visit hadn't entirely spoilt things for her.

Thank goodness Jackson was safely back in his hospital bed. She'd made a flying visit to the ward last night, mainly to check for herself that he had actually returned as he'd promised he would. She wouldn't have put it past him to have gone off on another adventure, having sampled a taste of freedom.

When she'd arrived at the hospital, she'd found him fast asleep and she quietly slipped into the chair at his bedside, not wanting to wake him, but her presence obviously stirred him as he looked across at her through half-opened eyes.

'How are you feeling?' she whispered.

'Don't ask,' he said, with a sheepish grin. His brow furrowed and he sucked on his lips, as she noticed the pain and weariness etched on his features. There was a tiny part of her that wanted to say, 'I told you so,' but what would have been the point? It was done now and they simply had to move forward, and make sure Jackson never pulled another stunt like that again.

'So was your absence noted by the big bosses here?'

'No, I don't think so. See, I told you not to worry. The thing is, in hospital, as it is in business, it's not what you know but who you know,' he said, with a smile that seemed to require a lot of his effort.

'Well, that takes me very nicely onto my next question. Who on earth was it that helped you arrange your escape? It couldn't have been straightforward getting you out of the hospital and it must have been someone who could have covered for you if any awkward questions were asked when your empty bed was noticed.'

'Ah, you see, if I told you that then I would have to kill you. I need to protect my sources.'

Jackson rested his head back on the pillow and closed his eyes, a small smile playing on his lips.

'Hmmm, well, I have my suspicions and I can't say I'm impressed.' In fact, they were more than suspicions. Pia was convinced it was that pretty young blonde nurse who always seemed to be hovering in the background whenever Pia came visiting and she raised her concerns to Jackson. He neither confirmed nor denied her theory, which only proved she was right in her assumption, in her eyes.

'Don't be cross with me,' said Jackson, still with his eyes closed, holding out a hand to her.

'I'm not cross. Well, not very, anyway,' she said indulgently. 'I hope that nurse doesn't have any more good ideas as far as you're concerned, though. I'm annoyed that she went to such great lengths to help you out, she could have lost her job.'

'You're not jealous, are you, Pia?'

Honestly, if he wasn't lying indisposed in that hospital bed then she might have given him a hefty dig in the ribs.

'No, of course I'm not jealous. Why would I be?' she said, bristling with indignation.

'Exactly, no reason at all.' Jackson shook his head, a weary smile on his face.

'Look, I can see how tired you are. I'm going to leave you to sleep off your exertions of the day. I'll come back tomorrow.' She always felt a sense of sadness leaving Jackson behind but especially so today after all the excitement of the day.

'Do you have to?' he asked. 'Look.' He patted the space next to him in the bed. 'There's room for a little one in here. You could hide beneath the covers. No one would ever know.'

It was sorely tempting. It was one of the many things she missed about Jackson not being at home, being able to snuggle up against his warm, hard body in bed. Their French farmhouse super king-size felt cavernous and cold without him.

'I was telling Lucy...'

'Lucy?' Pia interrupted him.

'Yes, the nurse...' Pia nodded, her eyes growing wide. Obviously on first-name terms then. 'I was telling Lucy how we're getting married later in the year and she has to make sure I'm better and out of here very soon as there's lots we need to get organised.'

Pia smiled, appreciating his attempt to make her feel better, but really the wedding was the last thing on her mind.

'We don't need to worry about that. We could always put it off a few months. It might be the easiest solution. You said yourself we have a very busy few months ahead of us and we'll have to shuffle some things around in the diary as it is. It might be better to postpone it until next year.'

She stood up to make moves to go, leaning across to kiss him on the cheek.

'Don't say that, Pia.' He grabbed hold of her hand and pulled her closer again, his face up against hers so that they were touching noses. 'You don't really want to do that, do you?'

'No, but I'm just trying to be...'

He didn't allow her to finish her sentence before he interrupted, but she knew 'sensible' and 'practical' weren't uppermost in his mind right now.

'We've set the date now and nothing's going to stand in the way of our plans. Not even these gammy legs.'

Now, back at home, in the comfort of their bed, missing his presence beside her, she smiled at his insistence that they still go ahead with the wedding at Christmas. She would have been disappointed but quite prepared to postpone it until the following year, but Jackson was determined not to change the date, his certainty making her feel loved and cherished. Although it also meant that tomorrow she would need to start making firm plans for the big day.

Today, though, she was going to do very little. She deserved a rest after the week she'd had so she climbed out of bed, eschewed a shower and instead ran a warm flannel over her body, tied her hair up in a ponytail and then pulled on her jeans and a fresh T-shirt. She padded downstairs, closely followed by the dogs, and let them out into the secure garden to one side of the kitchen. While Bertie and Teddy happily mooched around outside, she put on some coffee and rifled around in the various cake tins to see what was left over from yesterday. She found some cinnamon buns and popped one on a plate to have with her coffee when it was ready. Ordinarily on a Sunday morning Jackson would head out on his bike to collect the papers and when he came back he would get started on cooking a full English breakfast with sausages, eggs, bacon, mushrooms, tomatoes, hash browns, baked beans and plenty of toast. Sometimes it would be just the two of them but more often than not they would have some of the others from the extended Primrose Hall family sitting around the table to enjoy a long and leisurely brunch. Mateo, Rex, Ronnie, Tom and anyone else who might be visiting. Pia had taken those happy occasions for granted. Now she wondered when they might all be gathered around the kitchen table again for a meal.

After finishing off her tasty bun, she jumped up and out of her seat with a sense of purpose. She couldn't sit there all day mooning over what had happened. It already had and she would just have to deal with the new reality. Nothing would seem normal until Jackson was back home again.

Walking in the grounds of Primrose Hall always lifted Pia's mood and the dogs bouncing their way across the grass never failed to make her smile. It was funny to think that yesterday the place was brimming with cars and visitors, and now it was almost restored to its normal sense of peace and calm. Mateo would have a bit of work to do in making good those bits of the lawns that had been churned up by tyres, but she knew that it would soon be back looking its best for the next tranche of visitors.

Today, with plenty of time on her hands, and after doing a sweep of the grounds, she wandered along the boundary path and went through the old gate that led into Primrose Woods. The dogs skipped ahead, knowing the route, and they bounded off with their snouts to the ground, picking up on the latest scents, their tails wagging happily into the distance. Sunday mornings were probably the busiest time in the woods with families and couples making the most of the park, by walking one of the various routes, visiting the sculpture trail or simply going to the cafe for tea and cake. Runners pounded the paths as well and Pia loved to see all aspects of life within the tall embrace of the trees. It reaffirmed to her that life went on as normal, even if her world had been delivered a bit of a blow this week.

At the lake, Pia sat on one of the benches and threw sticks into the shallow edges of the water. The dogs loved running in and out to fetch them, their enthusiasm for the task never waning, often rewarding Pia with the return of the stick and a full-on shake of their bodies, spraying her with water. Her thoughts strayed to Jackson, as they invariably did, and how he might be feeling today. She could understand his frustration. Jackson had never been the sort of person to sit still at home for long. He was always on the move, never happier than when Mateo or Frank needed some physical help in the grounds, seeing to a fallen tree, or a loose roof tile, or anything that required him to get his hands dirty. She only hoped that his injuries would heal properly so that he could get back to doing all those activities he loved doing best.

With the dogs now happily occupied playing with a couple of spaniels who had joined in the fun and games, Pia pulled out her phone and looked through the string of messages. They were mainly from people asking for the latest update on Jackson's progress. There was one from Tom asking if she needed any help today, and another from her brother Connor giving an update on Ruby, who was 'fat and fed up', her words apparently, and who was impatient for their baby to arrive. Then came a whole flurry of photos of her little goddaughter, Willow, sent from Abbey. Scrolling through the pictures made Pia's heart swell. She still couldn't quite believe that this gorgeous little baby would be playing an important part in her life now and Pia felt so grateful that she'd been offered the privilege.

In fact, Pia was reminded in so many different ways how much they had to feel grateful for. They were surrounded by friends and colleagues who really cared about them and who wanted to help out in any way they could. It was a revelation to Pia because in all the years she had acted as a carer to her mum and dad in their final years, her world had been quite insular, mainly confined to the four walls at Meadow Cottages, and occasional trips to the supermarket, the GP surgeries and hospital visits. Coming to Primrose Hall had opened up her circle, bringing her into contact with such a wide range of people, some of whom had become really good friends and enriched her life in a way she could never have imagined.

Now her attention was distracted by a commotion in the water with a lot of galumphing legs, barks and yelps, the pool party looking as though it might be getting out of hand with the arrival of three high-energy Vizlas, who looked determined to take the proceedings to another level entirely. Wanting to avoid that possibility and the inevitable fallout, Pia called, 'Bertie! Teddy! Come on.'

Thankfully they came at the sound of their names and she slipped on their leads so they wouldn't get any ideas about sloping off again. It was only as she was walking back towards the hall, her mind replaying those text messages she'd received, that she suddenly remembered there was someone in particular who she hadn't heard from and the realisation made her come to an abrupt halt there on the shaded path beneath the trees. How strange. Why hadn't she heard from Ronnie? A sense of unease rose in her chest as she pulled out the phone from her pocket and quickly looked to see when she'd last heard from her. That was it! It was yesterday afternoon in the middle of the show.

Greetings from the French Riviera! We're thinking of you all today and we're just sorry that we'll be missing out on the fun. I bet Jackson will be in his element! Will catch up with you tomorrow over breakfast. Sending lots of love. Xx

'Shit!' Pia exclaimed aloud, attracting strange looks from a couple of dog walkers who happened to be passing at that precise moment. She marched on at a faster speed now, furious with herself for forgetting that she was supposed to be having a call this morning with Rex and Ronnie. With everything else that had been going on in the last twenty-four hours, it had completely slipped her mind. The thing was she couldn't see any missed calls from this morning on her phone, so why hadn't Ronnie been in touch? Had she somehow found out about Jackson's accident? It was entirely possible. Any one of the hundreds of visitors to the hall yesterday could have mentioned it, in a text message, without even thinking twice about it. It was probably most likely one of Rex's pals, messaging him about the car show, and then casually mentioning Jackson's star appearance in a wheelchair.

What must they have thought, being hundreds of miles away from home, hearing that their son had been involved in a serious road traffic accident over a week ago? Pia cursed herself for not sorting out the situation sooner. She knew it was a bad idea not to tell his parents about the accident and now it looked as though her worst fears had been realised. Ronnie would be worried, anxious and panicky, and she would have every right to be furious at Pia, but what Pia couldn't understand is why she hadn't heard from Ronnie in person. It wasn't like Ronnie not to get straight on the phone and demand to know what was going on. Perhaps she'd been trying Jackson's phone instead and had already spoken to him. A swirl of conflicting thoughts assaulted Pia's mind. Probably the most likely explanation was that when Ronnie and Rex had heard the news about the accident, from whatever source, they'd jumped straight back into the van, abandoned their trip and were, at this moment, heading back to Primrose Hall to see their injured son.

Pia literally ran home, the dogs looking up at her to see what all the excitement was about. When they reached the kitchen, she took a moment to steady her breathing, and poured herself a glass of water from the tap, all the time preparing herself to have the conversation with Ronnie that she should have had much sooner. She was worried that Rex and Ronnie would be making the long drive home on unfamiliar roads, in a state of tiredness and heightened anxiety, which wasn't ideal. If anything should happen to them then she would never forgive herself. It would definitely be her responsibility. Jackson had told her not to tell his parents that he was in hospital, but on something as important as this, she should have trusted her own instincts. Rex and Ronnie would feel rightly let down by Pia, but she hoped they would understand once she had the chance to explain. The last thing she wanted was to fallout with her future in-laws. That would be the worst possible start to married life.

She couldn't put it off a moment longer. She picked up the phone and called Ronnie, not really expecting her to pick up, imagining she would be driving, her concentration fixed on getting them both home safely as quickly as she could.

'Oh, Pia!' Ronnie answered immediately and, just hearing the breathy exclamation of those two words, Pia could tell she was consumed with emotion. 'I was just going to phone you. It's awful, really awful.' Her voice wobbled as she continued. 'It's been such a shock and I just didn't know what to do.'

Pia needed to stay strong. She'd had a whole week to come to terms with what had happened to Jackson, but poor Ronnie was away from home and had obviously just discovered the news that would shake her world. Despite their difficult relationship in earlier years, Pia knew just how much Ronnie loved and cherished her son.

'It'll be fine, Ronnie. We'll get through this. Tell me where you are. You're not driving, are you?'

'No, no.' Ronnie sound completely flustered. 'We're at the hospital.'

'What, already?' They must have driven through the night to get there so soon. That would have been a rude early-morning awakening for Jackson, finding his worried parents at his bedside.

'Yes, Pia, that's the thing. Rex has had a heart attack and he's in with the doctors now. Look, I have to go, the doctor's calling me through. I'll let you know as soon as I find out any more information.'

25

Tom woke early on Sunday morning, feeling rather pleased with himself that he'd managed to exercise some self-control last night. Watching Sophie from across the other side of the table, seeing her animated as she chatted with Josh, catching a glimpse of her long, slender neck as she threw back her head in laughter, had only confirmed that his feelings for her were growing in a way that he couldn't have anticipated. Had he known what was coming, he might have been able to do something to stop it, but he realised far too late. Those feelings had seeped their way beneath his skin and looked as though they had no intention of moving on.

There was nothing he would have liked more than to stay in the pub, chatting to the traders, ending up as he had on previous occasions, alone with Sophie. Not that it would have been a problem in itself, it was just he didn't want her thinking that he had any expectations of her. Trouble was it had been such a long time, years in fact, since he'd been in this situation, that he had to wonder how to act around a woman he found attractive, one that he would definitely want to know better. When he stopped to think about it, he didn't have the first idea of the best way to navigate their friendship. Was it too soon to be entertaining thoughts of taking his relationship with Sophie in a more personal direction? And what if she didn't want that? Perhaps she only enjoyed his company as a friend and would be mortified if he was to suggest anything more. He would rather not make an ill-thought-out move that would do anything to alter the course of their easy friendship which he so valued. Did that mean he was destined to keep his feelings to himself forever?

Tom sighed, and shook his head at his own ineptitude. Maybe he was overthinking the whole thing.

He tried to imagine Jackson in the same situation and couldn't. Jackson oozed confidence and conviction from his every pore. If there was something he wanted in his life, then he simply went all out for it. He clearly wasn't plagued with doubts. He was one to make a decision and stick to it, regardless of the outcome. A smile crept across Tom's face, wondering if Jackson held any guilt over his antics yesterday. Somehow he doubted it. Life was too short for regrets as far as Jackson was concerned.

Maybe Tom should channel some of his younger brother's drive and ambition, but then Tom had come to realise that despite the physical similarities they shared, their personalities were different in many ways. Was that a result of their contrasting upbringings or just reflective of their inherent personalities? It was hard to know.

He flicked the kettle on, spooned coffee into a mug and poured the water when it was boiled, stirring the spoon around aimlessly. God, this flat depressed him. It was small and cramped with no natural light and lacked any kind of personal touches. He hadn't done a thing to it since the day he moved in about a year ago now with only his laptop, his clothes and some new bedding that he'd hastily picked up at the local supermarket. The flat was only ever meant as a stop-gap solution. He'd initially taken it on a three-month let, renewing the lease a couple of times since, but in recent weeks he'd realised that he couldn't stay there much longer. He needed something bigger, with some outside space, somewhere he could put down roots and make his own mark. He suspected it was Sophie who was behind his desire to make some changes and move on in his life. It would be good to have somewhere he could invite friends round for a relaxed supper or a morning coffee or a glass of wine in the garden. Somewhere he could curl up on the sofa with a girlfriend.

Spending time with Jackson and Pia had shown him how a good relationship worked, the easy conversation and laughter that spilled between them, and the many benefits of living with someone you truly loved, who shared in your life plans. A constant and reassuring presence at your side.

He could definitely imagine something similar for himself now, so maybe he needed to start making plans to find somewhere more permanent to live, even if that might mean taking on a full-time job to fund the new lifestyle.

Being a Tom of all trades and dividing his hours among incidental jobs that came his way offered some advantages. It meant that he could pick and choose his own work hours, he didn't have to spend the best part of his week travelling the length of the country to visit clients and he didn't have the stresses that came with a demanding career, but he would be lying if he said he didn't miss the money and perks that he'd enjoyed with his previous job.

If he wanted a lifestyle to support a partner and family then he was willing to forgo those advantages to get his life back on a more normal pathway.

One thing was for certain, he knew he had to get out of the flat today. He'd peered out of his bedroom window earlier to see that there was the promise of a lovely day in the sky, the sun already peeping through the clouds. He'd already decided he would visit Jackson in the hospital. He hadn't really had the chance to speak to him alone since the accident because whenever he'd been to see him, he'd had other visitors at his bedside. He would pay him a flying visit to check that he was okay and if there was anything he needed doing. He would also let him know that he would be speaking to their dad today. Then he intended to pop by the hall to check in with Pia.

'Hey!' Jackson's face lit up as Tom wandered onto the ward. He leant down to embrace his brother in a hug.

'So... how are you feeling today after the excesses of yesterday?'

'Honestly? Like shit. Like the worst hangover you can imagine, but without the fun of the night before. Everything hurts.' Jackson grimaced and shifted up in his bed. 'Don't tell Pia, though. She'll say it's only what I deserve.'

'She cares about you. She wants you home for good, and I think she was worried they might throw you out of here for disorderly behaviour before you were properly fixed.'

'Who knows, they might do yet,' said Jackson, his eyebrows lifting. 'Look, Tom, I'm not sure I had a chance to thank you properly for stepping in and helping out this last week.'

'No problem. I was pleased to be able to assist and really, I played a very small part in what was a great team effort.'

'Well, it meant a lot to me. Knowing that you were there at Pia's side gave me such peace of mind. She likes and trusts you. She told me she couldn't have done it without you.'

Jackson held out his arm in a fist bump to his brother, who returned the gesture.

'And I don't want you thinking that I turned up yesterday to check up on you. For me, it was all about the cars and bikes. I wanted to see the spectacle for myself and soak up some of the atmosphere. Great job, though.' Jackson sighed, and dropped his head back onto the pillow, closing his eyes. 'Think I'm probably paying for it now, though.'

A healthcare assistant came round, gave Jackson his painkillers and offered hot drinks, which gave a few moments of quiet contemplation for them both. Tom was able to study Jackson more closely. He noticed the myriad cuts and grazes covering his face and arms, or at least those parts of his skin that were visible beneath his pyjamas. Some of them looked really quite angry and sore and Tom could imagine how they must smart.

'You will keep an eye out for Pia and the folks? You know, if anything should happen to me.'

'Hey!' Jackson's question took Tom by surprise. 'Where's this come from? You're going to be absolutely fine, you know that.'

'Yeah, of course, right, but spending hours flat on your back with only your thoughts for company gives you time to reflect on your life and what's important. I need to get everything sorted because none of us know what's round the corner. It might sound dramatic, but Pia has changed my life. Literally. I'm not sure she realises just how much she means to me, but she's given me a real sense of purpose, a reason for getting up in the mornings. Before I was simply going through the motions. We'll be married by the end of the year and she'll be financially secure, that's not a problem, but I need to know that she'll have someone that she can lean on, if she needs to.' Jackson's eyes were open now, his gaze fixed steadily on Tom.

'Sure. You know that. Don't even worry about it.' Tom sucked on his lips, touched by Jackson's display of vulnerability which reached Tom deep down inside. He was overcome with emotion of his own, knowing he would do anything to help his brother out, and felt a huge pang of sympathy for him, stuck in this bed, troubled by all sorts of dark thoughts.

'And Ronnie and Rex too. They're not getting any younger.' Jackson shook his head. 'The pair of them have made some daft decisions in the past. They need saving from themselves so they don't make any more in the future.' And although Jackson was smiling, Tom wasn't one hundred per cent certain that he was really joking.

'On the subject of Ronnie and Rex,' Tom said, 'I'll be giving Dad a call later on today. I normally check in with him on a Sunday. I'll have to tell him what's happened to you.'

Jackson nodded, without even putting up a defence this time. He might have argued with Pia about it earlier in the week, but he knew now that he was fighting a losing battle with Tom. His parents would need to know at some point and it looked as though that moment couldn't be put off any longer.

'Just play it down. I don't want them worrying unnecessarily or thinking they need to cut short their trip to come home.'

'Yeah, I'll speak to Dad and he can break the news to Ronnie. They're going to be upset, whatever way we couch it, but hopefully they'll be reassured knowing that the doctors have fixed you up. When I tell them you still managed to get to the show yesterday, by escaping from your hospital bed, they'll know that it can't have been too serious.'

Jackson exhaled a big puff of breath that caused the hair on his forehead to flutter.

'It just gets me so bloody frustrated being stuck here when there's so much I could be getting on with. I'm letting down Pia and everyone else too.'

'Don't beat yourself up over it. It's happened and nothing's going to change that. And you're not letting down anyone. All everyone wants is for you to get better. You'll be out of here soon enough.'

Jackson shrugged his shoulders, looking despondent.

'Any idea when that might be?' Tom ventured.

'I've got some more scans and X-rays tomorrow and then I'll be seeing the consultant. We'll just have to see what she has to say.'

'I'll keep everything crossed that it's good news. In the meantime, don't worry about anything at the hall. I'm going to pop in on my way back to check on Pia and see if there's anything she needs doing. If you think of anything then just let me know.'

'Cheers, Tom, that means a lot.'

Tom leant forward and squeezed his brother's shoulder in a gesture of support. As he pulled away, he noticed how Jackson had pulled his lips tight, the emotion brimming in his eyes clear to see, and Tom had to look the other way, as though distracted by some activity over on the nurses' station. He felt privileged that Jackson had displayed his vulnerability in front of him, but he would much rather it was him lying in that hospital bed than Jackson, who really had to be the worst and most crabby patient ever.

26

It took a moment for all the pieces to fall into place. Pia had been so certain that Ronnie had been talking about Jackson that she'd been utterly confused hearing that they were at the hospital. It didn't make any sense until she realised, with an overwhelming sensation of dread, what Ronnie actually meant. Ronnie and Rex were at a hospital in France, and from the sounds of it, Rex was clearly in a bad way. Staring at the phone in her hand, Pia paced up and down the kitchen, her heart thumping in her chest as she wondered what she could possibly do to help. She could just imagine how helpless Ronnie must feel, having to navigate the language barrier and having no one there to provide any emotional support.

Pia didn't even know the name of the hospital or any of the details about Rex's condition. *A heart attack?* Pia confronted all the possibilities that those three words conveyed. She couldn't bear the idea and shuddered away a cold fear of dread that rippled over her body. She would need to tell Jackson and Tom, of course, but there would be no point in doing it now when she had so little information from Ronnie. Hopefully she wouldn't have to wait long before Ronnie called back and then she could think about breaking the news to Tom and Jackson. This was something she knew she wouldn't be able to keep to herself –

she only hoped it wouldn't be the worst possible news that she needed to impart.

She made herself a coffee, keeping her phone within easy reach so there was no chance of her missing the call. There was a part of her that had wanted to immediately ring Ronnie back, but she had to be patient. It sounded as though Ronnie had enough on her plate without Pia adding to her worries and stress with her need to know what was going on. Only, the longer it went on, the more Pia's mind kept visiting those worst-case scenarios. First Jackson and now Rex. They couldn't lose him, not when Jackson and Tom were only just getting to know him.

When the phone buzzed into action, Pia almost leapt out of her skin. She snatched up the phone, her voice breathy.

'Ronnie!'

'Pia!' Ronnie's voice was equally filled with emotion, as she struggled to get the words out. 'Rex has got to have an emergency procedure. They're going to put in a stent. It's difficult because of the language barrier, but that's what I've understood of it. They said it should be fairly straightforward, but it sounds serious to me. I'm not ready to lose him, Pia.' Ronnie had clearly been visiting the same dark places as Pia. 'I've only just found him again after all those years we spent apart. It's not fair. I assumed we'd have plenty of years together in front of us.'

'And hopefully you still will, Ronnie.' Pia's heart twisted hearing Ronnie's distress. She wished she could be there to hug her tight and reassure her that everything would work out fine, but how could they possibly know? She'd had the very same concerns about Jackson a week ago, but he was a fit and healthy young man who she was certain would recover from his injuries, even if it might take several months. Rex was much older and although he'd changed his ways in recent years, he had been a heavy drinker and smoker in his younger days. 'What happened? Did it come on suddenly?'

'Honestly, Pia, I just can't believe it. He'd been off-colour for a few days but we put that down to him having some kind of bug. Then this morning he took a turn for the worse. He had these dreadful chest pains and that's when we both knew it was something more serious. The camp-site manager called the emergency services and then everything moved very quickly from there. I can't fault the care we've received, but I just wish we were at home. This is all so strange. Is Jackson there? Should I have a word with him?'

'He's not here at the moment, but I'm going to tell him, and I'll tell Tom too.' She tried to keep her voice level, but she felt flustered, knowing she wasn't being entirely honest. She couldn't add to Ronnie's worries now, though, not when she was in such a heightened emotional state. 'They'll want to speak to you, I know. When is Rex having his procedure?'

'They've taken him down now. I don't know how long it will take or how long he'll have to stay in hospital. Lord knows what we'll do when he comes out. Where we'll go or how we'll be expected to get home? We've been sharing the driving, but he won't be able to do that now.'

That was when the emotion that Ronnie had been holding on to came flooding out in a series of sobs. It broke Pia's heart to hear her so upset and she felt helpless that she couldn't do anything to support her from so far away.

'Oh, Ronnie, I'm so sorry. It sounds as though Rex is in good hands, though, so try not to worry. I know it's hard, but you need to take care of yourself as well. Can you go and grab yourself a coffee while you're waiting? Have something to eat as well. Your blood sugar is probably low. As soon as you have a moment, once he's out and you know what's going on, then let me know. Just send me a message if that's easier. Once we know what the situation is, we can start making plans to get you home.'

When Pia came off the phone, it was her turn to give in to the emotions assaulting her body. She felt a fear and anxiety seep around her veins as she thought of Rex. She loved him dearly and had done from the very first moment she'd met him. Easy-going, forever laughing and inherently kind, she couldn't bear the thought of him not sitting around the table at Primrose Hall again. His presence lifted everyone's spirits, and seeing the three Moody men together was such a joy, but they hadn't spent nearly enough time together yet. Pia only hoped there would be plenty of other happy occasions for the whole family to enjoy in the future.

Pia jumped out of her seat when she heard a car approaching the hall. As it came closer, she recognised it as Tom's and relief flooded through her bones. She quickly dashed over to the sink to splash water over her face. She stretched her face wide and stuck her tongue out, hoping her features wouldn't give away all her worries and concerns, but she should have known that Tom was far too perceptive and empathetic not to notice.

'Hey, what's the matter?' As soon as he walked through the kitchen door, his eyes snagged on hers and he held open his arms so that she could walk straight into them. She would have liked to have stayed there with her head buried in his chest, finding comfort in his solid form, but the sooner she came out with what she had to tell him, the better. He pulled back to take a closer look at her, looking into her eyes. 'It's okay. All this stuff with Jackson, it's been really hard, but you've handled it brilliantly. It's okay to have a wobble every now and then.'

'Oh, Tom. It's not Jackson. I've just had a call from Ronnie. It's your dad. He's had a heart attack.'

'What?' Tom's expression held all the confusion and bewilderment that Pia had experienced earlier hearing the news. He took a step backwards, holding his hands up in front of him.

'Jesus Christ! Is he all right?'

'I think so. Try not to worry,' she added quickly, knowing her words were meaningless. She rubbed her hands along his upper arms, looking into his eyes, trying to reassure him. 'He's in hospital and he's undergoing a procedure, right now. Ronnie's going to call back as soon as she knows any more.'

'When did it happen?'

'This morning. Apparently, he'd been feeling a bit under the weather for a few days, but they didn't really think too much of it. They've just been taking it easy, but then he suffered chest pains earlier today and that's when Ronnie called for help.'

'Damn!' Tom walked away, running a hand through his hair, turning to look at her, concern etched over his features.

'He'll be all right, Tom. We need to stay positive. He's in the right place and he's getting the treatment he needs. They can do marvellous things with hearts these days.' She heard the edge of hysteria to her own words, desperately wanting them to be true.

'I need to get out there.' Tom's anxiety was evident in the way he paced up and down the kitchen. 'I'll see if I can get a flight today. Ronnie shouldn't have to deal with all of this on her own. How did she sound?'

'Scared, and emotional, obviously. I'm not sure she's really taken it in. It's such a shock for everyone.' Tom especially, if his pale grey expression was anything to go by. 'Let me make us a coffee. We can't do anything until we hear back from Ronnie.'

'Do you want me to tell Jackson? That's where I've just come from, the hospital. I wanted to see how he was, if there was anything he wanted me to help out with.'

'It's okay, I was planning on going in later anyway.' She went across and took hold of his hand, squeezing it tight. 'Tom, you've been an absolute star, stepping in to help us out like this. I'm not sure what we would have done without you.'

'It's nothing. It's what you do for family, right?'

He might be playing it down, but it warmed Pia's heart to see how deeply Tom cared for them all, Jackson, Rex, Ronnie and herself, and how he wanted to find solutions to all their problems. She gazed across at him with a thankful smile before turning her attention to the coffees, but there was no disputing the tension in the air. Both of them were on tenterhooks as they waited for what seemed like hours for some news from France.

'How was Jackson this morning?' she asked as they took a seat at the table, clasping their mugs as a form of comfort.

'Good. Well, fed up, actually, but I suppose that's only to be expected. I know he's desperate to get home. He really doesn't like the idea of you having to deal with everything on your own.'

'I know, but he shouldn't worry about me. I can manage everything here. And I have Frank, Mateo and Ivy on hand to help me out. And you, of course. I'd rather he stay at the hospital getting the treatment he needs than coming home early when he's clearly not ready, causing havoc.' She gave a wry smile. 'I'll wait to hear from Ronnie and once we know what's going on, I'll go in and tell him the news.' She sighed, not relishing the idea, but knowing that it had to be done. Her gaze drifted out of the window, struck by the contrast of the beauty of the landscape outside against the dark swirl of emotions she suspected they were both experiencing right at that moment.

'Are you doing all right, Tom?' Pia asked him. She laid a hand on his at the table. 'You're being strong for everyone else. I hope you're remembering to look after yourself in all of this too.'

'I'm all right,' he said, with a sad smile. 'Or at least I will be when I know Dad and Jackson will be okay. I wanted that sense of family for a long time and now I've found it, they're both putting me through the wringer a bit. Is this some kind of weird initiation process, do you reckon?'

Pia laughed.

'Not at all. Hopefully it won't be too long before they're both home and sitting round this table with us, laughing. I'm glad you're here with me now, though.' Tom nodded his agreement. 'How are you enjoying being over at the stables?'

'I love it! I'm not sure I'd call it work, though. It's more like a jolly day's outing with a great group of people.'

'Well, I know the traders all love having you as part of the gang, and also the changes you've implemented, well, mainly the one about meeting up at the pub regularly.' Pia laughed. 'It's great to see you getting on so well with Sophie too...' She let the unasked question hang there, her gaze appraising him.

'Yeah.' He looked up from where he'd been examining his clasped hands. 'She's a great girl. I like her.'

'That's good. You always seem to be having a good time together. Have you told her?'

'What? No...' He shrugged. 'Do you think I should?'

'Well, if you're at all interested in taking things further, it might be an idea.'

Tom sucked on his lips as though that was a very big and difficult consideration.

'I'd hate to offend her or find out that she only sees me as a friend.'

'Well, the thing is you'll never know if you don't talk to her, and I hope I'm not talking out of turn here, but Sophie always seems to be enjoying herself when she's around you.'

Tom nodded, buoyed by Pia's encouragement.

As for Pia, she was just glad of Tom's company and conversation as the time stretched interminably, and her fears grew, as they waited for news. It was getting on for a couple of hours later when the phone finally rang and Pia jumped on it, her gaze snagging with Tom's.

'Ronnie! Thank goodness. What's happening?'

'It's all done. He's out and they've taken him up to a ward. He's sleeping at the moment, but oh, my goodness, I can't tell you what a relief it was to know that he'd come through the operation okay. Honestly, I would have been so cross with him if he'd bailed out on me when we were on our holidays together, I would never have forgiven him.'

Pia laughed, grateful to hear Ronnie sounding so much more upbeat.

'And what have the doctors said? Are they pleased with how it went?'

'I think so. I had a quick conversation with one of the doctors and it all sounded very positive, even if I didn't really understand a word of what she was telling me. I just nodded along.' She chuckled to herself. 'I'm just relieved he's back with us. I don't know much else, to be honest with you, but I'll find out. How long he's likely to be in for, and what his follow-up treatment will be. I'm not sure how we'll ever manage to get home, but I can't worry about that now.'

'No, don't. We can help you get something sorted. Tom's here, do you want to have a word with him, and I'll tell Jackson later? I know he'll want to call you.'

'Well, that will be a first,' said Ronnie, laughing. In that moment, as Pia handed the phone over to Tom, she thought there was no better sound than the tinkle of Ronnie's laughter ringing in her ear. Pia collected the dirty mugs from the table and pottered around the kitchen, tidying things away, while Tom spoke to Ronnie.

'So that sounds positive,' she ventured, when Tom finished the call.

'Yes, it's a relief that the procedure seems to have gone okay, but I'll be happier when we know the full details of what's happened and what the outlook is.'

'So, what's the plan?'

'Ronnie's given me the name of the hospital and the ward Dad is on so I'll give them a call in a while and see if I can find out some more information. I'll need to get out there so I can see Dad for myself and get a better feel for what the situation is. Then we can start making arrangements for getting them home again.'

'You do think Rex will pull through, don't you?' asked Pia, unable to contain her concerns.

'If I have anything to do with it, he will. I've only had Dad in my life for a year and I'm not prepared to say goodbye to him yet. Besides, he's far too young. He's got plenty more years to give. We'll get him home so he can see his own doctor and then we'll know what we're dealing with.'

Pia couldn't help thinking how Jackson would take the news. Even though he'd always known who his father was, it was only in recent months that they'd spent some quality time together, so much so that Jackson had invited Rex to come and live at the hall. With Ronnie living in her motorhome parked at the back of the hall, Pia relished being part of the warm, if dysfunctional family that she was now a part of.

'Well, let me know when you get something sorted. I ought to get off soon to see Jackson and tell him what's happened. I know he's going to be upset, but I just hope that he doesn't think it gives him the perfect excuse to discharge himself from hospital.'

'Don't worry about that. I think he knows he'd be pushing his luck after yesterday. Besides, he's seeing the consultant tomorrow. He won't want to do anything that might jeopardise his discharge. Once I've sorted out the arrangements for getting over to France, I'll go and see Jackson again so I can reassure him that everything is looked after.'

Pia breathed a huge sigh of relief. Not for the first time over the last couple of days, she had to wonder how she would ever have managed without Tom at her side. Knowing he would be with Ronnie and Rex in a matter of a few days gave her a great deal of comfort, but she knew she wouldn't be entirely happy until she could see them with her own eyes and they, along with Jackson, were safely back home under the roof of Primrose Hall.

27

'Shit, no!' Jackson, his brow furrowed, shot up in his bed, immediately regretting that decision. He hadn't got used to the idea that sudden fast movements were a very bad idea. 'How is he? Where is he? When did this happen?'

'This morning. Ronnie called to tell me.'

Pia filled Jackson in on all the details she knew. She had tried to break the news gently but there was no easy way of telling someone that their father had suffered a heart attack, so she'd come out with it in the baldest terms.

He pushed himself up further in his bed, but Pia could tell he was in a lot of pain today.

'I'll need to be there for him.'

'Jackson!' Pia laid her hand on his wrist as though physically stopping him from jumping out of his bed. It was a big shock obviously and she had half expected him to go immediately into problem-solving mode, in fact she wouldn't have expected anything less. 'You can't. The best thing you can do for your mum and dad right now is to stay here and get better. We really don't need any heroics from you right now.'

She flashed him a side glance and his top lip curled in protest at her comment. A whole range of emotions flitted across his features; fear, confusion and pain, as he shook his head, trying to process the news. She understood that he felt powerless, but however much he might want to help, there was nothing he could do, certainly not in his condition.

'Do we know how he is?'

'Okay, I think. They've put the stent in, they did that as an emergency procedure, and he's now back on the ward resting.'

'Christ!' Jackson dropped his head into his hands. 'Well, that's come out of the blue. He looked so fit and happy when they left. He was positively beaming. I could never have imagined something like this would happen.'

'Me neither.' They both fell silent for a moment, lost in their own heads, and Pia wondered if Jackson's thoughts had strayed in the same direction as hers. That the image of Rex, grinning wildly, waving out of the passenger window of the van, as they pootled off on their travels, could very nearly have been the last one they had of him. It didn't bear thinking about.

'I couldn't believe it when Ronnie told me. I haven't really got many more details yet. I didn't like to push Ronnie too hard because she was obviously upset and a bit confused too. She's having to deal with all of this on her own and her French isn't the best, so I don't think it can be easy for her. When I spoke to her the second time, she sounded better, knowing that Rex had got through the procedure okay.'

'Poor Mum.' Pia nodded in understanding as a pang of sympathy twisted in her chest. He rarely referred to Ronnie in that way. 'Can you make some enquiries then and find out the best way of getting them home again? We can always get the van sent back separately.'

'Don't worry about it. Tom is already on the case. He came round this morning just as I'd heard from Ronnie. He's obviously as concerned as we are. He was going to phone the hospital to see if he could find out any more information about your dad's condition. He's going to fly out as soon as he can to be with them. We don't know yet how long Rex is going to be in hospital for and how soon he'll be able to travel home, so we'll have a much better idea when Tom gets out there.'

'Jeez! I should be going out there with him.'

'We all know you'd be straight out there to see them if you were well enough, but you're not, Jackson. You can't do it,' she told him gently. 'And really, Tom will have it covered. He'll let us know exactly what the situation is once he's out there.'

'I guess.' Jackson slumped back on his bed, his frustration and despondency evident to see. 'I need to get out of this place, though. It's driving me mad. I'll talk to the doctors tomorrow and see what they say. There's no point in me blocking a bed that would be better used by someone else.' He ran a hand through his hair. 'Thank God for Tom, eh?'

'Yeah, he's been a star, and I know if the situations were reversed, you'd be doing exactly the same, so don't worry about it.' She knew that her reassurance went no way to make Jackson feel any better. 'Once Tom's firmed up on his travel arrangements then we'll let you know his plans so really you don't need to worry about the practicalities.'

He closed his eyes and shook his head.

'It's fine, Jackson. You don't always have to be in control of absolutely everything. There'll be times, like now, when it's not possible and then you need to know when to let go. Tom and I have got this.' She gave a smile, encouraging him to see the truth of her words, but she could tell how much it frustrated him not to be able to jump on that plane over to France himself.

'And Tom really doesn't mind going out there?'

'Absolutely not. He wants to go. It was the first thing he said when he found out.'

'What about his other commitments? Is he all right for money? Can you check with him? I don't want him being out of pocket at all.'

'I'll speak to him and see if there's anything he needs from us. You know, he reminds me so much of you. If there's a problem, he immediately wants to find a way of fixing it. He is a real sweetheart, he cares about everyone. You're two of a kind, do you know that?'

'Do you think? I'm not so sure about that,' he said, his mouth turning up in a crooked smile. She detected an air of melancholy about him. 'I think he's probably the prototype, the real deal. I'm the knock-off version. I've noticed how people seem to like him, really like him. They're drawn to his genuine personality, his humour, his ability to make people feel at ease.'

It was true and while the brothers were alike in so many ways, there were plenty of ways in which they differed too. Tom was a calming influence as opposed to Jackson's hot-headedness. He was thoughtful and considered while Jackson was spontaneous, and often spoke without thinking first. Their differences complemented each other, though.

'People like you too,' Pia reassured him. Jackson was a successful public speaker, articulate and engaging on his subject of personal development. It was part of his job to make people like him, but that was in front of an audience of hundreds of people. On a one-to-one basis, he could sometimes come across as being awkward and brusque, his inherent shyness and reticence coming to the fore. 'I think sometimes people might find you intimidating, whereas Tom is probably a bit more approachable.'

'Really? So you're my brother's number one fan these days, is that it?'

'No, I'm *your* number one fan, but I do think Tom is lovely. I think we're lucky that he's come into our lives, don't you?'

Jackson grunted, but Pia knew that he felt the same, even if he wasn't about to admit it to her now.

'I should call Mum and see how she's doing. She'll probably have more details about Dad's condition by now.'

'Yes, I said you'd want to talk to her. Remember she doesn't know about your accident yet. I was going to talk to them about it this morning, before I heard about Rex's health scare, obviously. Then, of course, it didn't seem the right moment to tell her. Tom said it's probably worth waiting now until he gets out there. It will be better if it comes from him direct.'

'You two really have thought of everything, haven't you?' he said with a smile.

'Only so that you don't have to,' she replied, kissing him gently on the cheek.

'You're right, though, it's probably a good idea. Honestly, I won't be able to relax until those two are back at the hall so that I can see for myself that they're actually okay.'

'Me too, and I especially want you back home as well. It's getting very lonely in that big bed of ours without you at my side. Look, I should get back and see if Tom's managed to sort his flight out yet. As soon as we have any more information, I'll let you know. I think he wants to pop in and see you before he goes anyway so if there's anything else you can chat it through with him.'

Pia stood up and collected her bag ready to go. Jackson grabbed hold of her hand, threading his fingers through hers.

'You know, when I think about the accident, it makes me realise how lucky I am.'

'Oh, my goodness, I know! It could have been so much worse. You could have died, Jackson. It makes me shudder to think about it.'

'No, I didn't mean that. It's made me appreciate just how lucky I am to have my family around me. You have to remember that Mum and Dad weren't really around much when I was a teenager so to be given a second chance to rebuild that broken family unit feels like a real blessing, even if Ronnie, bless her cotton socks, seems to go out of her way to irritate me.' He chuckled to himself. 'Having Tom turn up, the brother I never really wanted, has been a bonus. He's a great lad, even if it must be tough for him knowing that he'll never be the better-looking brother.' Pia shook her head indulgently. 'But I don't think we would have this tight unit now if it wasn't for you. You're the great homemaker. You bring everyone together and make it work, for which I am very grateful.'

She bit on her lip, deeply touched by this rare show of sentimentality, although she could tell he was growing weary by the strain he carried in his voice.

'Have I told you recently that I love you, Pia?' he said, looking up at her with soulful dark eyes from the depths of his hospital bed.

'Not nearly enough, Jackson. Not nearly enough.'

28

Every other Tuesday night was quickly becoming a highlight in Sophie's social calendar. It was a regular date with Greta, who would come round to the cottage for a glass of wine or two, and they would sit and catch up on each other's news, barely stopping for breath, invariably ending up laughing hysterically over something or other. When Sophie had been living with Greta and her family they would usually get together in the kitchen, just the two of them, around teatime when they would natter about the highlights and lowlights of their respective days. After Sophie moved out, they both quickly realised that they were missing out on those special times when they could share literally anything with each other. Although Greta had rescued Sophie from an awful situation by offering her a place to stay, Sophie had been a huge support to Greta as well. Their relationship went both ways. Sophie provided a listening ear to her friend when she was worried about her children away at university, didn't pass judgement when she grumbled about her caring duties for her husband Bob's elderly father, Edward, and laughed when she recounted her many frustrations with Bob and his hapless DIY skills. That special time spent together gave them both the opportunity to voice their innermost hopes and fears, however silly, in a safe and supportive space.

Tonight, Sophie had prepared some antipasti on her wooden chopping board, some cold cooked meats, along with some cubes of cheese, and olives, something to nibble on as they chatted.

'How did it go at the car show last week? Did you sell lots?' Greta asked, popping a Padron pepper in her mouth.

'It was such a brilliant day.' Sophie's thoughts flittered to that Sunday and not for the first time. Everything about it had been perfect. 'I sold loads of pieces, met lots of new customers who were there for the first time and who promised to come back, and it was such a lovely atmosphere all round.'

'There really was. Bob enjoyed looking at the old cars, but I was happy to wander around and admire the house and the gardens. It's such a beautiful spot. We called in to the stables to see you, but someone said you'd popped out for some lunch. We had to rush off to visit Edward, so we missed you.'

'Oh, that's a shame.' She could only think that she had been out with Tom at the time, walking through the grounds. It had only been an hour at the most, in the middle of a very busy day, but it was a moment in time that Sophie had revisited in her head so many times since. She could conjure up the warmth of the sun on her skin, the sweet smell of the grass and the excitable buzz of anticipation in the air. She'd replayed her conversations with Tom, recalling the way he'd looked at her with those long lingering sidelong glances and how they'd laughed, but more than that, she'd sensed that they'd connected on a level that couldn't be so easily defined. All her instincts, and the tingling sensations that had travelled along her body giving her goosebumps on a sunny day, told her that he must have been feeling it too. Now she had to wonder if she'd been mistaken.

She'd been disappointed that she'd hadn't spent any proper time with him at the pub, but his promise to call her and arrange a dinner date had kept her going through all of last week. By the time she'd got to the weekend without having heard from him again, she had to wonder if Tom was having second thoughts about their friendship. Perhaps he'd thought they were becoming too close and had wanted to put some distance between them. After all, hadn't he told her he was enjoying being on his own and was in no rush to get into another relationship? Funny thing was she'd told him the same thing, only in the matter of a few weeks, her perspective on the subject had completely changed.

'Sophie... Sophie, are you okay?'

'Sorry!' She shook her head and brought herself back to the moment. 'I was miles away there.'

'I could tell. Not thinking about Kyle, I hope. He's not still bothering you?'

'No, thankfully. I'm glad he and I got the chance to clear the air. Now, all of that is very much in the past. It's just...'

Sophie let her words and thoughts trail away, but there was no chance Greta would allow her to get away with that.

'Just what?' Greta shifted her body so that she was facing Sophie, placing an arm along the back of the sofa.

'Well...' She paused, wondering where to start. She'd been hugging her feelings for Tom to herself, unsure whether it was just a passing infatuation, or the beginnings of something more serious. Would voicing her feelings aloud give them an importance that wasn't really warranted? 'I've told you about Tom?'

'Oh, he's Jackson's brother, isn't he? And he's managing the stables now?'

'That's right.' Sophie couldn't help the smile that twisted at her lips which Greta noticed immediately, and the significance of it, eliciting a knowing and wide-eyed stare.

'Ah, I see... So it's another man causing you sleepless nights, but for all the right reasons this time, I'm hoping?'

'Yes, I mean, we've always got on really well ever since we first met up at Primrose Hall on Christmas Day. I honestly never thought I'd run into him again but since getting to know him better at the stables, well, we've really enjoyed hanging out together.'

'Well, that's good, isn't it? Do you think there might be romance on the cards?'

'I don't know.' That's where it got sticky for Sophie. 'You know I always said I wasn't interested in seeing anyone else, not after Kyle.

Honestly, I think I'd resigned myself to being forever single, but then I realised I was beginning to develop some kind of feelings for Tom.'

'And does Tom know about this?'

'That's the thing. I don't really know. He's in a similar situation. It wasn't that long ago that he broke up with his long-term girlfriend and we both kind of bonded over being free and single, and saying how happy we were that way. We've met up a couple of times in the pub and he came round for supper one night, which was really lovely. I suppose it was seeing him here, sharing a meal, chatting and laughing over the same things that made me think how nice it was spending time with him. It felt so natural and easy, as though we were a proper couple and it got me thinking... I mean he is really hot.' There was a smile on Sophie's lips as she brought Tom's handsome face to mind. 'I should imagine it would be very easy to fall for him.'

'So, what's stopping you?'

'The thought that I might have got it all wrong. That he meant what he said. That he is actually happy being single and he just sees me as a friend. Oh, God, Greta, I'm so hopeless at this sort of thing, and now I've got the thought in my head, of where it could go, it's all I'm thinking about.'

'Sounds to me as though you have a bad case of lovesickness.' Greta chuckled, seeing Sophie's stricken expression. 'You know you could just be upfront and tell him how you feel.'

'Are you mad?' Sophie spluttered over her Prosecco. 'I might be a modern and independent woman and all that, but that really is taking things too far. What if he tells me straight that he doesn't see me in that way?'

'Well... at least then you'd know.'

'What if he rips out my heart, tears it into tiny shreds and tosses it in the bin?'

Greta shook her head indulgently.

'That's always a possibility. It's a risk you take when you fall in love with someone. If you're not quite ready then you'll just have to take it slowly and see where it goes.'

Sophie sighed and took another mouthful of the delicious frothy bubbles that tickled her nose. It was definitely helping talking it through with Greta. If she had any doubt about her feelings for Tom, then voicing them aloud had made her realise it was already too late. Despite her best intentions, she'd found herself mooning around like a teenage girl, wondering if and when Tom might call her. She hated herself for it, but she was also secretly enjoying the excruciating swirl of emotions that had last tormented her mind when she'd been one of those teenage girls herself.

'I guess... When he left the pub the last time I saw him, he said he'd call me to arrange a date to go out for something to eat, as a thank you for hosting him for supper the other week.'

'Well, that sounds promising then?'

'I know, I thought so too, but I'm still not sure if he means a platonic dinner between friends or something more intimate, like a date. And of course it's all totally irrelevant because he hasn't rung yet! I'm wondering if he's having second thoughts. Honestly, it shouldn't be this difficult!'

'It's only difficult because you're making it so. Looking for problems where there are none. There could be any number of reasons why he hasn't called yet.'

'Like he's changed his mind!' Sophie said flatly.

'No, he could just be very busy at work. Or perhaps he's poorly?' Greta shrugged her shoulders. 'Well, you know what men are like. It's probably man flu or something, and he's been laid up in bed for days.'

'Oh!' Sophie didn't like the sound of that at all. 'I wonder if I should call him then? I could run him round some honey and lemon.' She quickly thought better of the idea. 'More likely, just after I saw him, he bumped into a gorgeous, lithe, red-haired creature at the garage and they've disappeared off into the sunset together.'

'Why the garage?'

'That's not important,' she chided Greta. 'It could have been anywhere. At the launderette, or the supermarket or the garden centre. What's important is that he's met his soulmate, has completely forgotten about me and is living out his happy-ever-after.'

'Unlikely,' said Greta with disdain.

That was when the evening took a turn, as it often did when the pair of them got together, when they would wander off into the realms of fantasy, this time coming up with increasingly outrageous scenarios as to what had been poor Tom's fate, which included being trampled by a herd of cows, abducted by a UFO and being arrested for criminal damage. It went no way to helping Sophie understand how Tom might be feeling about her, but it made her laugh until her ribs ached and she was so grateful to Greta for helping her see the funny side.

29

Sophie had that Wednesday hump feeling, which probably had something to do with the Tuesday night over-indulgence feeling that was lingering into the following morning. As she quickly got herself ready for work, applying her make-up and running the straighteners through her hair, she kept giggling to herself as she remembered how she and Greta had laughed last night, so much so that it had got to the point where they'd forgotten what they were even laughing about. Still, it had taken her mind off Tom and his reasons for not contacting her about that dinner date. Her heart-to-heart with Greta had clearly done the trick because she'd hardly thought about Tom the whole morning, well, only on a couple of occasions at least instead of the usual dozens of times. Climbing into her black trousers and a bright green short-sleeved jumper, she padded down the stairs to the kitchen, filled up the kettle and flicked it on at the wall, and pulled out a mug from the cupboard, popping a teabag inside.

Last night had given her a clearer perspective on the situation and she realised she had let her imagination run away from her. Tom had done the right thing in putting some distance between them. They had a good relationship, even if it was destined to stay forever platonic, and she would hate to lose that close connection that they'd made. Sophie needed to put her impatience to one side and just allow their friendship to develop organically. You couldn't push these things, they needed to happen at their own pace and time. And it wasn't as though she wouldn't be seeing him again. She would have plenty of time to catch up with him at the upcoming Sunday craft fairs.

She rested her bottom against the worktop, clasping her mug in her hands. The weekend couldn't come soon enough. Most of it would be spent in her little studio at the back of the house, making some new pieces to sell at the stables. The forecast was for fine, sunny weather so she would open the back door into the garden, so that the warmth of the day could seep inside the cottage and she could listen to the birdsong, the best soundtrack to accompany her as she worked. She would spend some time on her website too, which was slowly coming along. She'd done the home page and Greta had taken an atmospheric photo of her the other week, in the studio, sitting on her stool, an Anglepoise lamp to one side of her, as she crouched over a piece of work. It would be the photo she would use on the landing page and she thought it would give exactly the right impression of her small artisan business.

She was also planning on fitting in a visit to Primrose Woods. She loved it over there and she could spend hours wandering off the beaten track to find new spots of interest. Sometimes she would just sit on one of the benches beside the lake and watch the movement of the water, smiling at the activity of the ducks, the moorhens and swans. It brought her a sense of calm and peace and it never failed to lift her mood. On her travels around the woods, she would collect small branches and twigs, pinecones and leaves, and anything else that took her interest, her hands running over their form, assessing their colours and texture, before she would pop them in her rucksack to take home with her. Back in the studio, she would place them on her worktop and they would act as inspiration for the pieces she was working on, trying to incorporate the natural movement within the flora into her jewellery.

Sophie glanced at her watch. She still had plenty of time before she needed to leave for work, so she cut herself a slice of granary bread and placed it into the toaster and reached for the marmalade in the cupboard. She often imagined how it would be waking up every day to go to work in her studio, rather than into an office to do a job that served her perfectly well but didn't inspire her in any way. Her dream of working for herself full-time was still a long way off, but at least she had begun to take tentative steps in that direction.

As she ate her breakfast, she scrolled through her phone, not only to check that she hadn't missed a message from Tom, but also to see if she'd heard from Pia. Sophie had been wondering how they were all getting on up at the hall and if Jackson had been discharged from hospital yet. She'd sent a card and some flowers to Pia last week and had received a lovely thank you message from her, with a promise to be in touch again soon with 'all the news', but she hadn't heard anything since. Poor Pia was probably rushed off her feet with hospital visits and dealing with everything at the hall.

Just as she'd popped the last piece of toast into her mouth, wiping away the crumbs from the corners of her lips, she heard a scrabbling noise coming from outside the front of the house. She wandered through into the living room, expecting a knock to come at the door, but it wasn't forthcoming. She thought she might get some bumpf through the letter box, which would go straight in the bin, but maybe her ears were playing tricks on her. There it was again! This time she went across to the window and peered outside, but she couldn't see anyone. Perhaps it was a visiting fox or a hedgehog, she often had visits from the local wildlife during the early hours and maybe they'd had a late night like her and were only just making their way home. She picked up her handbag from the sofa, checking she had everything she needed for the day ahead, but when she heard the noises from outside again, she couldn't ignore them. It was probably kids messing about. She marched over to the front door and yanked it open.

'Oh!'

On his hands and knees, scrabbling around on her covered porchway was Tom, with a bunch of flowers in his hands, which he was attempting to lean against one of the oak struts of the porch.

'Hi! Sorry,' he said, looking up with a sheepish smile on his face. 'You weren't meant to see me. I just wanted to drop these off. I was supposed to be in and out like a ninja, undetected, but it's clear my ninja skills need some work.' He pushed himself up off the floor to face her and handed her the flowers with a smile.

'Well,' she said, gathering her thoughts and trying to ignore the thumping in her chest. 'These are lovely, but... why? I mean, thank you. Did you want to come in? I need to get off to work soon, but we could have a quick coffee?'

'No, I don't want to keep you, but maybe if I could just wash my hands,' he said, looking down at the soil covering his fingers.

'Of course,' she laughed. 'Come in.'

Inside, while Tom washed his hands, Sophie found a vase for the profusion of blooms, a heady mix of delphiniums, lilies and sweet peas, which brought a welcome burst of colour into the room.

'These are beautiful,' she gasped, holding them to her nose. She couldn't remember the last time a man had bought her flowers and it filled her with happiness.

'I mean, I hope you don't mind. That it's not too much...' he grimaced. 'But I realise I'd said I'd call you and then, well, that's when everything blew up and I had to go away. So these are by way of apology. I didn't want you thinking I'd forgotten... well, completely forgotten.'

'No, not at all, it really didn't occur to me,' she said disingenuously, looking up at him from beneath her long lashes, her mouth pursed in nonchalance. She really hoped her nose wouldn't grow in front of him.

'It's been one hell of a fortnight.'

'Has it?' Now, she felt bad. 'Why?'

'Well, I don't know if you heard, but Dad had a heart attack while he was on holiday in France.'

'No!' Sophie gasped, holding a hand to her chest. 'That's awful. Is he okay?'

'Yeah, he's on the mend. He had a stent put in over there and was given a ton of medication. He'll have to take it easy for a few weeks as he's still very tired, and he'll be followed up at the hospital here, but fingers crossed it looks like he's going to be okay.'

'Oh, my goodness, what a worry for you. On top of Jackson's accident too.'

'I know, right. As soon as I heard about Dad, I jumped on the first plane out there. He had to stay in the hospital for about a week and then when they gave him the all-clear, we made the journey home in the camper van. I wouldn't have wanted Ronnie doing that trip on her own, not when she's acting as chief nursing officer to Rex. She's obviously been so worried about him, so it was a relief to get them home. They're both now safely ensconced back at Primrose Hall.'

'Blimey, you must be exhausted.' Sophie felt a pang of guilt at the way she and Greta had been joking over what had happened to Tom when in fact of all the scenarios they'd imagined, this one hadn't even entered their minds, and it was so much worse than all their most fanciful ideas. She was only grateful that it looked as though there was a happy ending to the story.

'The thing is,' Tom went on, 'while I was away, I kept thinking about you...'

'Ah, okay.' Sophie felt her skin prickle and she wondered if this was the point where he told her that they could only ever be friends.

'Yeah.' His mouth pulled to one side. 'I hope that doesn't sound weird or entirely freak you out?'

She shook her head, still not certain where this was going.

'And I wondered if maybe... you'd been thinking about me too?'

This time, she easily nodded her head, and he seemed to be buoyed by that small gesture. He went on, warming to his theme.

'I've realised that I really quite like you, I mean, if you're okay with that and, well... I just wanted to let you know. If that's okay?'

As far as heartfelt declarations went, it wasn't the most eloquent one she'd ever heard, but to Sophie it sounded like a romantic symphony.

'Yes, that's fine, absolutely fine because I've realised I like you too,' she said, her gaze snagging on his, and that brief moment said so much more than any words could convey. 'I've missed not seeing you,' she admitted.

'Really? Well, that's great then. Perfect. And we'll go out to dinner very soon. Right, well... I'll leave you to go to work, but it's been great seeing you again, Sophie.' He leant forward to kiss her on the cheek, a light fleeting kiss that sent shivers down her spine, and after she saw him out of the front door, she realised a big smile had appeared on her face that she thought might possibly be still there by the time she arrived at work and would probably stay for the entire weekend too.

She was so pleased that they'd got all of that settled. He liked her and she liked him. And that was all that mattered for now, even though she knew it was only the beginning of something really special.

30

What an eventful couple of weeks it had been at Primrose Hall, with some horrible and unsettling lows, but also some special high moments too. Now, Pia could dare to hope that they might get back to some kind of normality, well, a different kind of normality at least.

Last Monday, Jackson had been given the news that he'd been dreading. He was told by his consultant that he required further surgery, which came as a huge blow to them both. Jackson saw it as a backwards step, but the consultant had insisted that it was absolutely essential and would be the quickest route to a full recovery. The operation was performed the following day and it wasn't until the end of the week that he was told the operation had been a success and he could move on with his recovery in the form of intensive physiotherapy. He was discharged the next week with several follow-up appointments made to see the consultants, a physiotherapist and a hydrotherapist. He still faced a long road to recovery, between three and six months, and would need to use crutches in the intervening months, but they both knew that his rehabilitation would be given a boost by being at home.

With wonderful serendipity, Jackson arrived back at the hall a few hours before Ronnie and Rex, who had made the long journey home from France. With Tom at the wheel, they'd taken it slowly, spacing the journey over a couple of days, so as not to tire any of them out.

Pia joked that she had turned the ground floor of the hall into a very upmarket residential home, as she'd made up Rex's room with new bed linen, fresh flowers and had put a water carafe and glass on his bedside table. In the other guest suite, she'd repurposed the room in a similar fashion for Jackson, as she knew he wouldn't be able to make the trip up to the master bedroom anytime soon. Not that it mattered. Pia would be sleeping downstairs with Jackson until he could navigate the stairs and it had been such a joy to fall asleep alongside him again with her arm flung across his broad chest, soaking up his natural scent, the sound of his steady breathing in her ear sending her off to the most satisfying sleep she'd had in ages.

The following morning, Pia was filled with relief and gratitude to see Rex, Ronnie and Jackson sitting around her kitchen table as she pottered about preparing breakfast. There'd been several times recently when she thought that might never happen again.

'Anyway, Jackson, I have a bone to pick with you. What's all this about you not letting Pia tell us about your accident? We're your parents and we need to know about these things.'

'Sorry about that, but I didn't want to worry you.' At least Jackson had the grace to look sheepish. 'It might have spoilt your holiday and I didn't want you thinking you needed to rush back to see me. I know what you're like, Mum. If it had been any more serious then of course Pia would have kept you informed, but we had it all under control, didn't we, Pia?'

She flashed him a doubtful look, but she knew Ronnie understood what Jackson was like when he got a bee in his bonnet and that Pia would have had very little say in the matter.

'Any more serious and you would have been dead, Jackson!' Ronnie chastised him. 'I hope you'll be keeping all those bikes locked up in the garage from now on.'

'He's just bought another one.' Pia sighed resignedly, although she'd given up trying to persuade him otherwise. She'd fallen in love with a man whose passion was for motorcycling, she could hardly expect him to change for her now. And she had to believe him when he told her that he would be especially careful from now on, although she couldn't help feeling pleased that he wouldn't be getting on a bike for several months at least, not until he was fully recovered from his injuries. It gave her a small respite from all that worry.

'I was thinking, though,' continued Pia, as she placed glasses out on the table and put out jugs of orange juice and apple juice, 'it might have been a blessing in disguise that we didn't tell you, otherwise we might have forever thought that the news of Jackson's accident had something to do with your heart attack, Rex.'

'Well, you needn't have worried about that, love. I half expected something like this to happen, especially when you get to my age. I was hardly a health freak in my youth. It's much more likely this was down to all the booze and fags I got through in my younger days.' There was that irrepressible smile again that lit up the kitchen that Pia had been worried she might not see again. 'Not that I have any regrets. You can't live your life like that. Mind you, I'm a paragon of virtue now, and I'm off all those forbidden delights, including chocolates.' He rolled his eyes dramatically.

'And women, hopefully,' said Ronnie dryly.

'Definitely. I'm a one-woman man these days, and it just so happens that you're the woman of my dreams.'

Ronnie shook her head, but it was evident to see how she beamed in the light of Rex's words.

It was lovely to see the to-ing and fro-ing between them. She never believed she would say it, but Pia had missed their bickering, although since returning from France, she'd noticed there'd been a remarkable absence of that and now it was simply much better-natured teasing between them. Ronnie had moved into the guest suite to be with Rex, determined to keep a close eye on him all hours of the day. Whether or not she would move back out again into her cherished motorhome was anyone's guess.

'How are you feeling now, Rex?' Pia asked him.

'I feel good, relieved to still be here. I mean, I rattle with all the pills I'm taking, and I still get tired easily, but the doctors warned me about that. It's probably going to take a bit of time to get back to where I was, but I'll get there. Mentally, it's been a bit of a wake-up call.' He grew reflective for a moment. 'It makes you realise that you're not invincible and you're not going to be around forever. It's a sobering thought.'

'Listen to me, Rex Moody, you're not going anywhere. We haven't had nearly enough time together yet so you can get any ideas of leaving me behind straight out of your head.'

Rex chuckled.

'I'll do my best, love.'

'Honestly, what was he thinking, giving me a shock like that?' Ronnie's face showed the strain she'd been under the last couple of weeks and Pia was determined to make sure Ronnie had the proper chance to recover from their ordeal too. Nothing a little tlc from Pia and the healing properties of Primrose Hall wouldn't put right. Rex and Ronnie were full of energy, vibrant and forward-thinking, with so much life to live, but this episode had been a reminder to them all that the pair of them weren't as young as they once were. 'I'd never want to go through anything like that again,' Ronnie added.

'No, I can understand that, but now we have to put all this behind us and look forward to all the exciting things ahead.' Exciting definitely, but with Jackson still out of action, Pia knew she was going to be incredibly busy preparing and running the upcoming events on the social calendar. There was the writing festival, the bonfire night celebrations, the charity coffee mornings in the kitchen of Primrose Hall as well as the Christmas carol event. They'd also pencilled in dates to run some creator workshops over at the stables. Pia was also looking forward to becoming an auntie in the next few weeks. Oh, and then there was the small matter of becoming a wife to Jackson too. Her head grew dizzy just thinking about it all.

'Did you know we've fixed the date for the wedding?' Pia asked, knowing full well that they wouldn't know, but wanting to spread some good news.

'What? Not something else you haven't told us! Honestly, I'm never going away again!' Ronnie declared, to which Jackson pulled an exaggerated face.

Pia giggled.

'Yes, it's going to be on 21 December, the weekend after the Christmas carols event when the hall will be looking her absolute best.'

Ronnie gasped and threw her hands in the air, her face a picture of delight.

'I can just imagine it now! It's going to be simply amazing. Maybe it will snow? Can you imagine a white wedding?' Ronnie was off, entertaining all sorts of possibilities. 'The best thing, though, is that we'll gain such a wonderful daughter-in-law as you, Pia, in the process.' Now, Ronnie clasped her hands to her chest. 'We're so lucky to have you in our lives. You've made Primrose Hall a proper home and we couldn't be happier to be here, could we, Rex?' Pia turned away on the pretext of getting some fresh coffee, but really it was to hide the tears brewing in her eyes. 'You know, we could even think about renewing our vows at the same time. Wouldn't that be lovely? In the beautiful grounds of Primrose Hall.'

'Don't be daft!' Rex chastised Ronnie. 'You can't renew your vows if you're not married,' he said gruffly.

'Ah...' Ronnie seemed to have overlooked that small matter. 'Never mind. Well, I shall need a new dress and a hat either way. New shoes as well, of course, but we don't know what the weather will be doing so I'll need to have a proper think about that. Oh, but what about your dress, Pia? Have you had a chance to look yet?'

'Not yet,' she said, wondering when she might ever find time to do that.

'Well, we can do that together, can't we? This is so very exciting. We should mark out a day when we can go shopping for dresses. You'll need a new suit too, Rex. And we need to start looking at flowers and cakes, as well. There isn't that much time when you come to think of it.'

'It's months away yet,' said Rex, a look of confusion on his face.

'Exactly. That's no time at all when it comes to weddings. Some people take years to plan their nuptials.'

'Enough time for people to change their minds, I reckon!'

'Rex! Pia and Jackson are not going to change their minds,' said Ronnie, indignantly.

'I know *they're* not. I was just saying. People should take a leaf out of our book and be spontaneous. We just went off to the registry office and then down the pub. It was a great day.'

Ronnie shook her head dispiritedly.

'And look how well that ended. Take no notice of Rex. He doesn't know the first thing about romance or weddings. We'll make a list of everything that needs to be done and go from there. Dresses, flowers, guests, table decorations, menus...'

Pia's head was spinning just thinking about all the things Ronnie was listing, and as for Jackson, he'd hidden himself behind the newspaper, blocking out the chatter, which was probably the best idea as far as he was concerned.

Mind you, Pia had known she needed to make a start on the arrangements for the wedding and Ronnie would be ideal at ensuring she was on top of that, although whether Ronnie would turn out to be a hindrance or a help on the wedding planning front Pia was yet to discover.

31

Sophie wore her hair loose, teasing out her natural waves with her fingers, checking her reflection in the mirror. After much deliberation, and several discarded outfits which were now lying in a heap on the bed, she'd opted for a yellow floral tea dress, not too dressy, but pretty and summery and hopefully just right for her dinner date. She was a bag of nerves and she wasn't entirely sure why. She'd spent enough time now with Tom to know that he was easy and relaxed company and that he would naturally try to put her at her ease, and once they started chatting they wouldn't stop, but still her heart fluttered in her chest and her skin tingled with anticipation. Tonight seemed potent with expectation, much more like an official date than any of the other occasions they'd spent together, and it was only natural that Sophie's mind would drift to where it might take them.

'Hey, you look great,' he beamed when she opened the door to him at her cottage. He leant forward to kiss her on the cheek, his hand gently touching her waist, the lightest of touches yet it still caused a ripple of delight to travel her body. She was pleased to discover that he was wearing his trademark aftershave again too.

'Thank you. So do you!' Her gaze had already checked him out, surreptitiously she hoped, taking in his navy cords and a pale blue open-necked shirt. He wore clothes well as he was tall and lean, but muscular too, as she'd found out previously, when he'd held her in his embrace and her arms had wrapped around his torso.

She smiled into his dark brown eyes, bringing her thoughts back to the moment as she realised she'd probably been staring far too long at the iridescent pearl buttons down the front of Tom's shirt, her mind entertaining all sorts of possibilities. So much for being surreptitious.

In the restaurant, they ordered a glass of Prosecco each as they pored over the menu, which had far too many options to choose from, all of which were equally tempting. It was something they'd immediately bonded over, their love of food, and so tonight they were in their element as they discussed the various choices available before they finally settled on their selections. Tom went for the Mediterranean prawns in garlic butter, followed by the sea bass cooked in a butter and lime sauce, while Sophie opted for the antipasto italiano and the seafood linguine.

'How are things now?' Sophie asked, when their orders were placed. 'How is your dad doing?'

'Yeah, he seems to be doing okay. I think obviously it's shaken him up a bit, but I know he's very relieved to be back at home. I think these heart ops are very successful these days, so we're all hoping that he'll make a full recovery. He's got various follow-up appointments booked with his GP and the hospital so he's in good hands. Ronnie is watching him like a hawk, obviously, and Pia is doing a great job at looking after them both. I think it's lifted their spirits to know that the wedding is going ahead this year, so Ronnie especially is full of excitement and plans.'

'That's so lovely. It will give them all something to focus on and look forward to. I must admit I'm looking forward to the wedding myself. It's been years since I've been to one.'

'Well, knowing those two, it promises to be a great day. Jackson has asked me to take on a few more responsibilities at the hall while he's out of action so I'll be spending a bit more time over there myself.'

'How do you feel about that? I know you mentioned possibly looking for another role.'

'Yeah.' Tom picked up his wine glass and took another mouthful. 'You know it's no hardship being at the hall. I enjoy the variety of the role, and working alongside Jackson too. We work pretty well together, actually, and being outside too brings a freedom and rewards of its own. I've decided to leave it until the new year and then make a decision on what to do next. One thing is for certain. I want to get out of that flat as soon as I can and find something bigger and brighter. I'm ready for that change now.'

'I understand that. I feel so lucky to have found my cottage. Every day when I get home, I close the door behind me and shut out the real world and relish the calm and peace of those four walls. It's my safe haven. Everyone should have one.'

'It is a lovely home.' Although Tom wasn't certain if it was the cottage he was so enamoured by or Sophie's presence within it. Either way, he always found it a warm and welcoming space. 'Anyway, how's your mum doing at the moment?'

Sophie appreciated how Tom always asked after her mum after she'd previously told him how she lived at Rushgrove Lodge, a local care home, and how her health had slowly declined over recent years. It was sad, but a huge relief too when her mum had reluctantly accepted that she needed full-time care and Sophie was reassured that she wouldn't receive the late-night phone calls telling her that her mum had suffered yet another fall. Now she was in a safe environment where she received the best possible care.

'She's not too bad at the moment. I saw her today and she'd had her hair and nails done so she looked really pretty, and they'd had a speaker in this afternoon, who talked about local history, which Mum's always found interesting, so she was on good form.'

'Well, if you ever fancy some company when you go to visit your mum then let me know. I'd be happy to come along with you.'

'Really? That's so kind. I'll definitely take you up on that.'

Kyle had rarely joined Sophie when she'd visited her mum, and Sophie should have taken it as a warning sign that she absolutely preferred it that way. The thought of taking Tom along with her was a much more pleasing proposition and she knew her mum would be delighted to meet a new face.

The food was delicious and they took their time savouring each course, enjoying a glass or two of white wine with their meal. For pudding, they shared a creamy tiramisu and as Tom took a spoonful, popping it in his mouth, his gaze roamed her face.

'Thanks, Sophie, for coming tonight. I hope you've enjoyed it. I know I've had a great time.'

'Oh, it's been lovely, a proper treat.' She couldn't remember the last time she'd shared a romantic dinner with a good-looking guy, but it had been as delightful as she might have expected it to be and she couldn't imagine anyone else she would rather have sitting opposite her than Tom.

'I've been wanting to do this for ages,' he said, 'but I wasn't sure that you'd say yes, so I'm really pleased that you did.'

The taxi dropped them off at Sophie's cottage. The evening had been so wonderful that she hadn't wanted it to end and she invited him inside for a coffee.

'I'd love that, thank you.'

With the candles on the hearth lit, the curtains drawn and some Classic FM playing in the background, the cottage was cosier than ever tonight. Sophie made coffees and they sat together on the sofa, still chatting away as they had done all evening. There'd been no awkward silences and they'd never run out of things to say, until now. Tom's arm, which had been resting along the back of the sofa, now found its way onto Sophie's shoulder and she lifted her legs up to the side of her, nestling into Tom's side.

'So would you like to do this again some time?'

'I would,' said Sophie, turning to look up at him, catching his gaze. There was no point in playing coy. She'd had a lovely evening and she would love to repeat it again soon.

'Great!' said Tom, sounding relieved. 'I know you said once that you were happy being single, so I was conscious of not over-stepping the mark or of offending you at all.'

Sophie laughed, snuggling up further into Tom's side.

'Yes, it's funny how you change, isn't it? Although... I think you may have said the same thing too.'

'Did I?' Tom's brow furrowed. 'I was clearly lying.' Which only made Sophie laugh more.

'Really,' he said, turning to look into her eyes. 'I love spending time with you, Sophie. I think you're a great girl and I hope that this is only the beginning, that we can get to know each other much better.'

Sophie gazed up into those dark brown seductive eyes, willing him to kiss her, and her powers of suggestion were obviously spot on tonight as he leant down to meet her lips with his. It was every bit as magical as she'd imagined it to be as his kisses sent all the delicious sensations to every part of her body.

She was looking forward to getting to know Tom much better too.

32

It had been another successful day at the stables. The sun had shone, they'd had a record number of visitors and Sophie's new range of jewellery based on the natural elements had proven to be a big success with her customers. She'd sold so many more items than she had expected to and she'd had several requests for specific items in her catalogue of products that she would make to order. It would certainly keep her busy over the next couple of weeks.

There had been something of a celebratory atmosphere in the air, not only because it had been Cecily's birthday in the week and Maddie had brought in two tins of cupcakes and a couple of bottles of Prosecco, which had been shared between the traders during the course of the day, but Pia had popped in a few times to chat to everyone and her infectious personality had brought some summer cheer to the day's proceedings.

Sophie was in a celebratory mood too because every time Tom entered the building, her skin erupted in goosebumps responding to his proximity. He would come over and have a chat, and she felt herself lighting up in his presence. They'd already spent more time together after their gorgeous Italian meal with a walk over at Primrose Woods. They were taking their time, getting to know each other better, and Sophie was enjoying every single moment of it.

'See, I knew you two were destined to be together,' said Katy, as they packed away their items at the end of the day.

'We're getting on well, but it's still early days for us. We're just seeing where it takes us. There's no hurry.' She shrugged nonchalantly, as though it was no big deal.

'Well, judging by the way the two of you have been making eyes at each other all day, I would say it's going pretty well.'

Sophie laughed.

'He's a really lovely guy, and we hit it off well... so watch this space.'

'Ah, Tom!' Pia was back again and she spotted Tom at the other end of the stables talking to Aysha. He turned around at the sound of his name.

'Jackson's asked if you'd go over to the hall when you've finished up here. There's something he wants to talk to you about.'

Sophie sidled up to him and whispered in his ear.

'You'll be CEO of the entire hall at this rate,' she joked. Not that Tom minded in the least. He enjoyed working at Primrose Hall and being part of the team, helping out Jackson and Pia where he could.

'You'll come over too, won't you, Sophie? There'll be plenty of tea and biscuits, or something stronger if you prefer?' Pia had a glint in her eye.

'Well, in that case, how could I possibly refuse?' Sophie laughed.

'I like cake. And something stronger,' piped up little Rosie, who had just arrived with her dad and her brother Pip to collect their mum.

'Do you now?' said Pia, laughing. 'Then you must come over for a slice of cake too, if Mummy says that's okay?'

'If you're sure you don't mind,' asked Katy, 'our daughter is very good at inviting herself to all the best places. I can only apologise.'

'Absolutely not. The more the merrier.'

There was even more of a party atmosphere over in the kitchen of Primrose Hall later that afternoon, especially when Abbey and Sam arrived with little Willow.

'Oh, my goodness,' said Pia, looking into Abbey's arms at the little poppet wrapped up in a soft cream blanket. 'She's changed so much since I last saw her. My little goddaughter is so beautiful.'

'She really is. We spend our entire time gazing at her.' Abbey proceeded to give a rundown of Willow's daily routine and she seemed, quite rightly, to have her parents running around to her every whim. 'Here, have a cuddle while I drink my tea,' said Abbey, depositing the baby in Pia's arms, who gasped simply at the wonder of holding her goddaughter, drinking in her lovely baby scent. Cradling Willow, Pia was overcome with emotion, tears pricking at her eyes at the sheer perfection of the little bundle in front of her. She took the baby around the room, showing her off proudly to everyone, all the time noticing the strange stirrings in the base of her stomach. She'd never considered herself broody before, but little Willow was playing havoc with her emotions and her hormones.

'Suits you,' called Jackson from the other side of the room, his eyes shining devilishly.

He was sitting on the window seat, his legs out in front of him, receiving his visitors like the lord of the manor he was. Rex and Ronnie had joined him at the table and were enjoying their tea and biscuits. Katy and Brad were supervising Rosie and Pip, who were playing with the dogs in their beds. Sophie had been handed a glass of Prosecco and was happily chatting away to Pia and Abbey, soaking up the atmosphere.

'Can we have a baby sister, please, Mummy?' asked Rosie, who was looking at Willow with great interest. Katy spluttered on her glass of wine, which elicited giggles from Pia and Abbey.

'No way!' said Katy rather too quickly and vehemently. 'I mean, Willow is lovely, but you have a gorgeous little brother. I think that's quite enough, don't you?'

Rosie's face curled up with disappointment.

'A baby sister is much better, though. Isn't it, Daddy?'

'Might be an idea?' he said, with a teasing smile, which only exasperated Katy even more.

Tom made his way over to Jackson.

'Was there something you wanted to talk to me about, Jackson?'

'Ah, yes, that.' Jackson looked around him, as though considering whether he should come out with it now or leave it until later. He looked across at Pia, who egged him on with a nod of her head. 'Well, fine, now's as good a time as any. As you may or may not have heard, the wedding of the century is taking place here in December and I was hoping you might be able to help me out?'

'Of course, you know that. I'm happy to help out wherever I can.'

'Well, this isn't work as such. This is something much more personal. What I wanted to ask is if you would agree to be my best man?'

'Oh.' The question took Tom totally by surprise and he was momentarily lost for words. He had been entirely prepared for Jackson to ask him to oversee the running of the event. Was it possible that he'd misheard him? 'Sorry, what did you say?'

'I'd like you to be my best man, Tom.'

'Ah... right.' No mistaking that, even if Tom's expression was still one of complete bemusement. 'Are you being serious?'

'Of course I am. Who else would I ask to do such an important job? It would mean the world to me if you would.'

'Great, that's great!' Tom bit on his lip, but not quickly enough for Pia and Sophie not to have noticed the tears welling in his eyes.

'What are they like?' Pia whispered to Sophie, as she gestured towards Rex, who was looking equally as emotional and was dabbing his eyes with a hanky.

Tom pulled back his shoulders and stuck out his chin.

'Jackson, it would be an absolute honour to be your best man. I'm chuffed, really chuffed to be asked. Thank you.'

And with that, there was an awful lot of manly back slapping, congratulations and laughter ringing around the kitchen.

'This calls for a celebratory drink,' said Pia, who handed Willow over to her dad, Sam, and collected the opened bottle of Prosecco from the fridge, pulling out a new one as well. She topped up Sophie's glass and poured fresh ones for the others.

'Obviously,' said Tom, as he took a sip from his drink. 'As long as you won't mind being upstaged in the photos by your better-looking, more charismatic brother.'

'Huh, you reckon?' said Jackson, joining in with the laughter around him. 'There's absolutely no chance of that.'

'Oh, that's reminded me,' said Pia. 'I have a question that I need to ask

someone too. Where's Rosie?' she asked, looking all around her exagger-
atedly, as though she didn't really know where she was.

The little girl popped her head up from where she was giving belly
rubs to both Bertie and Teddy on the floor.

'Yes?'

'Come here!' Pia held out a hand to the little girl to beckon her over.
'Rosie, I have a very important job that will need doing on my wedding
day and I wondered if you would be able to help. Will you be my
bridesmaid?'

Only Pia's question didn't get quite the response she was expecting.
Rosie pushed out her bottom lip, she scrunched up her eyes and her face
crumpled as she burst into noisy sobs, cutting through the previously
happy atmosphere in the room.

'Noooo! Don't cry!'

But there was no stopping Rosie, her sobs came in heavy gulps, big fat
tears running down her cheeks. It took several moments, her mum's
gentle persuasion and a handful of tissues to calm Rosie down, before
she managed to splutter, 'Can I really be your bridesmaid? With a pretty
dress and a crown? And everything?'

'Yes, absolutely!' said Pia. If it was a crown that would swing the deal,
then why not?

Rosie gasped, her little face beamed and the tears in her eyes sparkled
brightly, all thoughts of baby sisters completely forgotten, which was
probably a good thing.

'I think it's going to be the best wedding ever,' the little girl
announced to the assembled crowd.

Pia looked all around her at the happy faces of her friends and family
witnessing the moment, feeling the excitable air of anticipation in the
room. After the year they'd had, they all deserved something special to
look forward to and what could be better than a winter wedding at Primrose Hall? Pia leant down to pick Rosie up and spun her around, her legs
flailing in the air, the little girl's excited squeals filling the room.

'You know something, Rosie?' Pia said, laughing. 'I think so too!'

ACKNOWLEDGEMENTS

It's amazing to think that this is the fifth, and penultimate, book in the Primrose Woods series. I've loved writing these novels and I am so thrilled by the positive reception the characters and their stories have received.

Getting a book 'out there' is very much a team effort and I simply couldn't have done it without the support of my publishers, Boldwood Books. It's truly wonderful to witness their continued success because it really couldn't happen to a nicer and more dedicated bunch of people! Thank you Amanda, Nia, Claire, Jenna, Marcella, Ben, Issy, Niamh and the entire Boldwood crew for everything that you do. I feel very lucky and grateful to be part of the Boldwood stable.

As always, special thanks to my editor, Sarah Ritherdon. Knowing that you are there to make sense of my first drafts and to offer your unerring advice and guidance is always so wonderfully reassuring. Your kindness and patience in the face of my occasional writerly wobbles is also very much appreciated.

A big thank you to Rachel at Rachel's Random Resources for organising the blog tours and to all the amazing bloggers who take part. I am incredibly grateful for the time, effort and thought put into your insightful reviews and for spreading the word across the internet. It really does help – a very big thank you to you all.

To Nick, Tom, Ellie and Amber – thank you, as always, for your love and support. I really couldn't do it without you all.

Finally, a big hug of gratitude to you, my lovely readers, for supporting my writing journey. The best thing in the world is to hear that my stories have provided some much needed escapism, something I think we all need in these current times. The beautiful setting of Primrose Woods and the characters who live there have become like real friends to me, and I hope to you as well.

Thank you so much for picking up this book to read and I really hope to see you again for the final instalment of the Primrose Woods series!

Much love,

Jill xx

ABOUT THE AUTHOR

Jill Steeples is the author of many successful women's fiction titles – most recently the Dog and Duck series - all set in the close communities of picturesque English villages. She lives in Bedfordshire.

Sign up to Jill Steeples' mailing list here for news, competitions and updates on future books.

Visit Jill's website: www.jillsteeples.co.uk

Follow Jill on social media:

facebook.com/jillsteepleswriter
x.com/jillesteeples
instagram.com/jill.steeples

ALSO BY JILL STEEPLES

When We Meet Again

Maybe This Christmas?

Primrose Woods Series

Starting Over at Primrose Woods

Snowflakes Over Primrose Woods

Dreams Come True at Primrose Hall

Starry Skies Over Primrose Hall

Sunny Sundays at Primrose Hall

Dog & Duck Series

Winter at the Dog & Duck

Summer at the Dog & Duck

Wedding Bells at the Dog & Duck

Happily-Ever-After at the Dog & Duck

LOVE NOTES

LOVE IN EVERY CHAPTER

WHERE ALL YOUR ROMANCE
DREAMS COME TRUE!

THE HOME OF BESTSELLING
ROMANCE AND WOMEN'S
FICTION

 WARNING:
MAY CONTAIN SPICE

SIGN UP TO OUR
NEWSLETTER

https://bit.ly/Lovenotesnews

Boldw∞d

Boldwood Books is an award-winning fiction publishing company seeking out the best stories from around the world.

Find out more at www.boldwoodbooks.com

Join our reader community for brilliant books, competitions and offers!

Follow us
@BoldwoodBooks
@TheBoldBookClub

Sign up to our weekly deals newsletter

https://bit.ly/BoldwoodBNewsletter

Milton Keynes UK
Ingram Content Group UK Ltd.
UKHW041825110424
440927UK00002B/15